BLOOD OF MY ENEMIES

BLOOD OF MY ENEMIES

BIRTH OF HEAVY METAL™ BOOK 4

MICHAEL TODD

MICHAEL ANDERLE

DISRUPTIVE IMAGINATION

BLOOD OF MY ENEMIES TEAM

JIT Readers

John Ashmore
James Caplan
Kelly O'Donnell
Peter Manis
Nicole Emens
Micky Cocker
Crystal Wren
Jeff Eaton
Paul Westman
Dorothy Lloyd

Editor
Skyhunter Editing Team

DEDICATION

To Family, Friends and
Those Who Love
to Read.
May We All Enjoy Grace
to Live the Life We Are
Called.

CHAPTER ONE

She looked around, her weapon at the ready, and checked her ammo reserves to immediately determine that she had run low. Not critically so, but it would turn dangerous should this shit go on for too much longer. The motion sensors went crazy as she looked around, but it seemed the animals were content to skirt the very edges of her vision as if to let her know they were there without actually coming close enough to be shot at.

Of course, it was unlikely that they were competent enough to take a crack at basic psychological manipulation, but at this point, it didn't really matter. What did matter was that this kind of behavior was in play and she would have to take it up with the designers. So far, there had been no indication that the animals toyed with the people in the Zoo like this so the simulation was incorrect.

At a soft roar from behind her, she spun to see a massive panther. The creature was larger than usual with a hint of pale gold in the fur—which made it a lighter hue—and the suggestion of a mane, too.

She raised her rifle, pulled the trigger once, and felt it kick back into her shoulder. The armor was meant to absorb a rifle's kick but it was somehow reassuring to feel it in her arm. They'd toyed with the design and allowed her to add her input for this run.

The single hollow-point round tore through the creature's skull and opened a massive hole in the panther's head as the animal fell.

"Heads-up."

Kennedy knew who it was. There was only one person who had her comm signal in there. The familiar voice was something of a giveaway too.

She turned as Sal dropped from the upper branches of the trees at high speed in the same instant that she saw another of the lion-panthers charge out of the jungle. He managed to twist sufficiently to slam his knee down on the creature's neck and crushed it under the weight of his suit as he hammered it to the ground and executed a perfect three-point landing.

"And that, children, is how you do a superhero landing," Sal said with a grin as he pushed to his feet. "Perfect dunk, home run, drop curtains, and Elvis has left the building. Uh…thank ya, thank ya very much." His Elvis impersonation was on point, Kennedy had to admit.

"Well, those were some terrible sports references, but it's nice that you try," she said with a grin.

"Ordering all those sports channels for the compound has been good for something after all." He chuckled. "This is a damn good simulation. They worked out all the physics kinks we saw in our last run, and looking

2

around..." He paused to take in a deep breath. "You can almost smell the decaying corpses all around us—"

He was cut off when she looked above him, raised her rifle and tilted it upward, and fired at something that had caught her eye. As it turned out, the somethings were a couple of locusts that dropped into the background.

"This hero of ours might want to watch his back," Kennedy sniped. "He might want to protect his ass or he'll have a tentacle enema."

"I don't know." He turned to face in the direction the creatures had come from. "I can imagine that having an enema from the Zoo can only be good for your intestinal health."

"Oh, God, that's disgusting." Kennedy shook her head as more creatures appeared and they both raised their weapons. "And it was my joke too."

"Well, turning people's jokes and making them cringe at their own humor is my superpower," Sal said cheerfully as he fired at the first of the creatures that attacked. He'd loaded in armor-piercers, which sliced easily through the tough armor carapaces that protected the centipede. A piercing roar emanated from it as it buckled and curled into a ball the other creatures vaulted easily.

"Will you fight crime with that?" Kennedy asked. She allowed the suit to reload her rifle before she opened fire again to drive the line of monsters back. "Take crime bosses down by cringing them to death?"

"Well, I thought I could at least distract them to make things easier for when the heroes with real powers come along," he responded. His voice lost some of its focus as he ducked to avoid two tentacles that swung from the branches and tried to reach his head. They pulled back almost immediately and disappeared into the shadows where they wound around the trees.

"So, like…Captain Support, or something?" She moved closer to him to make sure they weren't separated and could at least count on one of their angles being covered by the other.

"That's a terrible gaming reference, Kennedy," he responded with a grin. "But it's nice that you try."

"Eat a dick." She chuckled as they moved once more, and he dropped a step behind her to cover her flanks and their rear as she pushed them forward. It was a good tactic, one they had developed over the time they'd worked together. It made sense. She was the one who usually wore the heavy-duty armor, while he wore something lighter. It was logical that she would do the bull-rushing while he made sure she wasn't outflanked.

It worked in the simulation too. He tested a lighter suit design, similar to his hybrid set but composed entirely of power armor that was supposed to be more dexterous than even the most advanced hybrid suits on the market. Then again, these suits wouldn't hit store shelves for a while, so there might be something similar out by then.

Kennedy, for her part, might as well have worn a tank at this point. Her gear relied almost completely on the power implementations to haul the two-and-a-half-ton suit, which moved with surprising ease through the tough terrain. It enabled her to sprint at up to thirty kilometers an hour and maintain that speed for almost ten minutes. The power came from a tiny nuclear reactor mounted into a backpack, which was supposed to—theoretically—last for years and years without needing to be replaced.

While that sounded all well and good in theory, Sal knew for a fact that there would be complications that came with mounting something that volatile into a suit that would be knocked around by creatures the size of buildings. Not for the person wearing the armor, he thought. They had been very adamant that by the time something managed to get through the ton of titanium-reinforced ceramic honeycomb weave to reach the reactor, the human inside would be long dead.

That said, the suit reputedly offered significant perks. Shoulder-mounted rocket launchers, jetpacks that facilitated movement by the back and the legs over rough terrain, and automated movement to avoid projectiles and hostile creatures. In addition, an advanced AI reduced the reaction time lag between movement intention and the action implemented by the power armor to five milliseconds and even less for the trigger finger.

It was like he worked with something straight out of a comic book—which explained why he thought so much about superheroes while conducting this run, he supposed.

He maintained his position behind her and slightly to her left—she was right-handed, after all—as they thrust forward continually and gunned down any of the creatures that decided to enter their path.

"How far away are we from the pick-up point?" Kennedy asked and looked around in a moment of reprieve.

Sal checked the map in his HUD. "About a klick and a half. Why?"

"I'm down to three mags for my rifle," she responded irritably, "plus a couple more for my sidearm, five rockets in the shoulder…and my knife."

"You have a knife?"

"Well, yeah." She drew the weapon from the thigh scabbard she carried it in. "Well, it's more like a sword-slash-machete really, I suppose, but in the power armor hand, it looks like a bowie knife."

He rolled his eyes. Admittedly, a combat knife was included in his suit, but he doubted it could cut trees down in a single stroke like hers undoubtedly could. As it turned out, size really did matter, he thought wryly. When it came to knives, anyway.

"We're one klick away from the pick-up point," he advised her after a while and noted that he too was running low on ammo. "And all the creatures look like they've decided to give us a break."

"Do you think it'll last until we get there?" Kennedy asked with a wide grin.

"Not a fucking chance. None of the other teams they had testing this even reached this far. They've probably tried to compensate for how drop-dead awesome we are at this."

"Truth," she agreed and enthusiastically bumped the fist that he'd extended with her own as they continued toward the little red spot marked on their map.

They'd barely moved a few steps before the ground shook ominously. At first, only the sensors registered the quake, but as they focused on their surroundings, they realized they could feel it even through their suits.

"Well, we had to jinx it, didn't we?" Kennedy snarked

and raised her rifle once again as they proceeded to the pickup point. "Can you see anything?"

"Nope." His good mood had disappeared almost entirely. "There's nothing on the motion sensors either."

"Which means that whatever has caused the ground to shake is big enough to do that while out of our range," she observed. "Fan-fucking-tastic."

"Not to make things worse or anything, but I pick up four different sources of comparable mass headed our way," Sal said. His gaze narrowed as he scanned the jungle. The sensors on his suit registered off the charts. On top of the regular motion sensors that paired flawlessly to the night vision in the HUD, temperature and seismic sensors pinpointed the direction from which creatures might be coming when they were out of the range of everything else.

All the sensory equipment told him very clearly that four creatures that each weighed more than two elephants now headed in their direction.

"Oh, that is bullshit," Kennedy muttered as she stopped so abruptly, he almost walked into her. "That's not even fucking possible."

Sal looked up and his mouth dried in instinctive response as he saw what approached. The massive creatures were bipedal from what he could discern from the sensors. They weren't even within range of the motion sensors yet, but their sheer enormity meant they could see them draw steadily closer. The four monsters moved almost in sync, each on a direct trajectory toward them. Their rapid and deliberate progress made it very clear that they were out for blood.

"Well, I guess we now know why no one's ever made it

to the pick-up point." She glanced nervously at her limited ammo supply. "I knew the creatures had given us too much room."

He nodded. "That's fucking bullshit, though. Come on. They look like the dinosaur monsters we can get the goop from, but they're—what, almost three times as large as the biggest ones we've seen out there? Seriously. There's possible, there's Zoo possible, and then there's this bullshit."

His partner grinned. "I think we've pissed off the dev team in charge of these sims. Let's piss them off some more, shall we?"

Sal tilted his head and regarded her thoughtfully. He knew that particularly wicked edge to her voice. "Former Sergeant Madigan Kennedy, you wouldn't happen to have a plan now, would you?"

"I do." She nodded emphatically. "Remember our little run-in with the German squad a couple of weeks back?"

He chuckled as the penny dropped. "You'd better get the timing right, though."

"Don't worry about that," she assured him. "Get moving."

Without hesitation, he did as he was told and increased his pace across the open spaces where the huge trees blocked out most of the sunlight. Kennedy's armor could reach a higher top speed, but he'd found that his own armor could accelerate much faster as well as maintain that speed through rough terrain. Their attackers appeared, now within both vision and range.

As he ran, he turned on the open speakers on his suit and yelled into them while he fired at the massive creatures. Kennedy remained utterly silent and motionless.

While he wasn't sure what kind of thought had gone into the design of the monsters, they did as most creatures did and simply followed the noisy, quickly moving creature that hurt them and left her alone.

Sal knew that this probably wouldn't end well, but they might as well finish their little simulation with a metaphorical—and very, very literal—bang.

He ducked behind the trees and saw with satisfaction that all four of the creatures had turned to follow him. One emitted a loud, ear-splitting roar that would have burst his eardrums if the suit's noise filters hadn't quickly canceled it.

Kennedy, for her part, hadn't remained idle. Once their attackers' attention had turned away from her, she moved hastily behind them. She didn't have enough bullets to follow the identical tactic as she had when they'd been out there with the Germans.

That had been a rough engagement involving one of the massive dinosaur creatures and Sal had wanted it killed without the expensive sacs being burst prematurely. He'd also not wanted to have to fight through a horde of angry Zoo monsters, and necessity had birthed an idea.

While he and one of the gunners had rushed away to distract the creature, she had remained behind to circle and shoot out the base of one of the trees. She'd then waited until the two men led the monster back. They'd dropped the tree on its back, killed it quickly, and interestingly enough, hadn't summoned an angry mob.

Sal had made a pretty penny from updating the US database with that interesting piece of information, as well as with the bounty from the sacs.

It had been only a single creature, though, and from the sound of things, he and his buddy had been very lucky to have escaped that little romp with their lives. With four of these monsters, things might work out very differently.

Either way, it was her turn to be creative.

She activated one of the rockets mounted on her shoulder and moved quickly to select a tree that could be felled in time to catch at least one of the fuckers. Thankfully, she located the right one without difficulty and paused to fire the rocket. It spiraled and spun to lock firmly onto the selected target before it exploded in a quick white blast. Splinters erupted with the force.

The tree rocked in place and rained a flurry of leaves from the top, but it didn't fall. She engaged a second rocket as Sal sprinted past the tree in question, having already circled the monsters. Distracted for a moment, she fired the second almost without meaning to and knew, even before it impacted, that he would be caught in the blast.

"Fuck!" he yelled. The shockwave knocked him slightly off balance and he stumbled awkwardly until he crashed head-first into one of the other trees.

"Sorry!" Kennedy called after him. The second blast gouged another chunk out of the tree but wasn't quite enough to knock it down. With Sal still recovering from his quasi-high-speed crash, she needed to get the damned thing down before the monsters reached him and ground him into a paste.

She pushed herself into a sprint and used the HUD to time the powering up of the rockets on her back and legs exactly to the millisecond. Her energized vault launched her and maintained velocity as she careened forward to drive feet-first into the tree.

The impact of two and a half tons of metal at roughly fifteen kilometers per hour was more than enough to send the teetering tree over the edge. It groaned and cracked violently before it toppled with a thunderous crash.

"Oh, shit!" was all she heard from Sal's comms before they went dead. Kennedy pushed quickly to her feet and noticed smugly that the tree had done its job and fallen on two of the monsters to kill them instantly. Unfortunately, her violent impact had also managed to send a massive chunk of it to land on her teammate.

The top half of his body was crushed.

"Shit," she exclaimed a moment before she turned as a massive tail swung in her direction. She would blame the lag when she got out of there, she swore to herself as the tail struck her with unimaginable power.

The result was a quick moment of darkness as the simulation shut down and in seconds, the real world crystallized around her. She blinked and her eyes found it difficult to adjust to the light as she disengaged herself from the various machines that made up the whole experience. Sal was already out and glared at her with a scowl on his face.

"I said I was sorry," she said quickly and shrugged defensively.

"No, you didn't," he corrected her with a smirk as they moved out to where the various technicians still evaluated the details of the run.

"Of course I did!" she protested. "Right after you crashed into the tree."

"What about the apology for dropping a fucking tree on my head?"

"Oh…right," she conceded. "What, do you want me to open a fucking tab?"

"A fucking tab?" He grinned at her. "I'm sure something like that could be arranged."

"Shut up. You know what I mean."

"Yeah, I know. But please, work on your damn timing. Maybe next time, we'll walk away from this as the first team to actually reach the pick-up point."

"I wouldn't count on it," one of the technicians said and handed them tablets. "We'll make sure the animals are far more difficult to deal with the next time around."

"Yeah, they were damn easy for the most part," Sal conceded and proceeded to answer the various questions they'd set for the people who engaged in the simulations. "Right up until you guys found the biggest fucking monsters on record and hit zoom."

The technician chuckled but didn't respond and simply allowed them to finish the paperwork in peace. It was quick work, and they were soon on their way out. Sal's phone buzzed.

"The pay for the run has already come through," Kennedy said with a grin. "I love working for these people."

"Yeah, getting paid to play video games," he agreed. "What's not to like?"

CHAPTER TWO

Anderson looked up from his drink. He was keeping track—something he always seemed to do as a matter of habit now, even when he and his team were supposed to have time off for good work. They'd had a couple of weeks of off-time but he still wasn't allowed to leave the site as per his superiors in the Pentagon. They wanted someone to oversee the operation for the duration. It meant that while the mercenaries Pegasus had brought in were allowed leave, he had to stick around.

Which was why he was there and also why he was drinking. The colonel had begun to drink more and more over the past few months. He had never really liked alcohol, not even in scenarios where it was considered a social lubricant, and so much so that he was always the designated driver for his wife whenever they went to parties. As a rule, he stuck to maybe a glass of wine with meals and a toast for birthdays, holidays, and other special occasions.

Today, however, he'd consumed two beers, a rum and Coke, and a couple of shots and now, he held a scotch on the rocks. He felt miserable and missed his wife and the rest of his family back home, but he was still there in this fucking desert. It infuriated him that he tried to get drunk to put some distance between himself and the worries that had plagued him all month.

"Do you need a refill?" someone asked and moved purposefully beside his table. He looked at a tall, lean man with the look of a lawyer who slid into the seat across from him and offered him a tall, frosty glass of beer. Anderson opened his mouth to say he hadn't ordered anything of the kind but he noticed a small piece of paper beneath the glass. He shut his mouth quickly and moved the scrap to reveal a crudely made drawing of a horse with wings in blue ballpoint.

A Pegasus.

He studied the man once again and tilted his head noncommittally as he crumpled the missive. "How can I help you?"

"I've been told you're still looking for a party to help you with your little campaign," the stranger said with a small smile. "Some guns to lend your investigation some teeth. Is that right?"

"Something like that," he responded without inflection. "What makes you ask?"

"Well, you have your choice from all the soldiers stationed around here." The man indicated the various military men and women who were in the bar. "Why haven't you already gone ahead and made your selection? I know you don't have the time to spare."

The colonel could concede that much. "True, but I don't want to make the wrong choice. Most of the men and women here are paid by the corporations that run this base —Pegasus, among others. I've heard how they don't mind bending the letter of the law and hiring soldiers who are here as mercenaries for other kinds of services out in the Zoo. I'd rather not trust someone who might already owe their loyalty to the people I'm trying to investigate."

The man nodded. It was a good point. Pegasus was known to offer certain bounties under the table for those teams who ventured into the Zoo and didn't much care for the missions currently on offer. No one was sure what they got out of it, but the fact remained that trust was a hard thing to earn around there.

"There are a couple of people who still make regular runs into the Zoo," the newcomer said with an eyebrow raised. "Freelancers, but those who still work regularly with the commandant around here. They also work with the various other bases, which means they don't receive too much money from a single source."

Anderson nodded. "Yeah... I know. Which means they're probably not good enough to be hired by Pegasus, so why should I?"

The self-appointed informant shrugged. "Firstly, you don't really have much of a choice at this juncture, between me and you. Secondly, have you seen the latest run by Heavy Metal in the Zoo-VR?"

The colonel looked up with sudden interest. He'd heard that certain companies ran virtual reality simulations with experienced Zoo-running personnel, but he'd never seen them in person. In fact, he'd actually assumed it was for the development of software to be used in the civilized world.

"You mean those stupid video games?" he asked and

sipped the beer the man had handed him. "I don't have time to waste with that bullshit."

"They're not video games." The stranger smirked. "They're not stupid, either. Far from it. It's state of the art research and development for armor suit designs that they're working on back in the States but made to resemble a video game."

"I'll take your word for it."

"Please do." He pushed a memory stick across the table, the movement casual, and was careful to hide it from clear view behind the glass of scotch. "It's not exactly classified. They've released edited versions of these videos onto ZooTube and they make a fucking mint from that too, from what I've been told. This is the unedited version. See these guys in action for yourself and make your own decision regarding their skills."

Anderson nodded and palmed the memory stick quickly.

The other man pushed lazily to his feet. "Grab some popcorn and give it a watch. See if these guys have what it takes to be a part of your investigation."

"Thanks for the beer." The colonel raised it and took another sip.

"Oh," the man said and paused, his expression somber. "From what I was able to tell, you're not the only one who's looked into Pegasus' mining investments. They're slippery bastards, but my gut tells me they're holed up somewhere close to Wall Two, although there's no real indication which sector they're close to. Food for thought—and entirely free. It's your lucky day."

Anderson smiled, nodded, and leaned back in his seat as the stranger took his leave.

Anja looked up from her work in the server room when she heard a knock on the door. Amanda stood outside and held a couple of mugs of coffee.

"You missed out on breakfast," she said with a smile as she placed one of the still steaming mugs on a counter. "Is everything okay? Did you get any sleep last night?"

"Um...no," the Russian woman replied and scanned her computer screens. "We had a little trouble I needed to deal with. Something tried to track our location. With the kind of setup we have here, I didn't think that was possible, but hey, there we are."

"What do you mean?" The armorer sipped her coffee—black with a ton of sugar, the only way she liked it. "Do you need more equipment? Because I'm sure Sal wouldn't mind signing off on anything if it means extra security."

"It's not that," Anja muttered and shook her head. The truth was that Jacobs had been far more generous than she'd expected. He must have done exceptionally well for himself if he was willing and able to drop this much cash on someone as new to the team as she was.

Of course, she was definitely worth it, but it wasn't often that she didn't need to prove that to people before they were willing to work with her. Then again, that might well be her fault. It wasn't a comfortable truth, but it didn't alter the reality she'd learned to accept. She wasn't the most social of animals, but it was still refreshing to meet someone who needed her around for her skills and was willing to work with her various oddities.

"What is it?" Amanda asked, her expression both curious and encouraging.

The hacker sighed and leaned back in her seat. "Someone tracked our investigation into Pegasus' dealings. The company has tried to get to us themselves, but this was different—a third party, I'm sure of it. From what I was able to see before they got a little too close for comfort, I'd say they were looking into the same things we were. Not with anything resembling the same kind of skill, of course, but with considerable determination and resources."

"Did you stop them?" Amanda asked.

Anja looked at her with a smirk. "Please. It takes a good deal more than a brute force DES attack to get past the stuff I set up. Either way, I added extra precautions. It took most of the night, but I set up a couple of redirections that should have our friends hunting for our IP address somewhere in the Caymans."

"You might want to set up there anyway," her companion retorted. "I grew up in Florida and spending this much time away from a beach has started to piss me the fuck off."

The Russian looked at her, about to ask a question, but thought better of it and turned to her screen as she took the offered cup of coffee. "I didn't get any sleep last night, but I've dealt with crazy hours my whole adult life so it's not really too much of a problem. I will crash in a couple of hours, though, so get used to me missing a couple more breakfasts."

"Right," Amanda said and squeezed the woman's

shoulder gently. "We do appreciate the work you do here. In all honesty, I have no idea why Sal is so obsessed with this metal, but then again, I tend to let the poor geek work out his own way in life. He seems to have at least some of it figured out anyway."

"Speaking of Jacobs," Anja said and turned her chair to face the armorer, "are he and Kennedy…"

"Oh, yes. Like rabbits."

"Are you and him…" the hacker ventured cautiously.

"No way," Amanda laughed. "He's really not my type if you know what I mean." She winked at the girl, who simply stared in confusion. "Never mind. I'll let you get back to work."

"Thanks for the coffee," Anja said vaguely, already distracted as the other woman made her way out of the dark server room.

CHAPTER THREE

"So how was the trip into the Zoo?" Amanda asked as Sal stepped into the kitchen and looked around in evident surprise.

"You know, I think the designers have actually listened to the users in this case," he replied with a grin.

"Are you looking for something?" she asked, moved closer, and jumped up to sit on the counter.

"Which is far less common than you'd think if I'm honest," Sal said as he blinked and continued his vague scrutiny. "Where's the coffee machine?"

"Oh, on the other side." She pointed him to where she'd put the pot.

"Why is it over there?" He located his favorite mug and filled it.

"Well, we need it for breakfast and stuff," she replied, "but I need it far more often when I work in the shop. That's also closer to where Anja is, so it makes it more efficient for her too. Since the two of us spend the most time around the compound, I thought it might be best to help us work better."

Sal nodded, poured a second cup, and offered it to her. "That's some good thinking. Keep it up."

"Will do, boss." She took the mug and raised it in a mock-toast. "By the way, I poked around that design you gave me."

"Have you made any progress?" He instantly looked a little more alert.

"Not really." The armorer shrugged. "There are actual mechs they've designed for the Zoo, but as it turns out, they end up way too heavy to be any kind of use to anyone. They simply sink into the ground if they stick around for too long and use too much power to be any kind of practical use. So far, they've only been used on top of the walls with the perimeter guards, where they are literally plugged into their own generators. They work great on defense and keep all the big monsters out, but when it comes to offense, they're essentially useless."

"Have you made the calculations with the metal we recovered from the leg?" Sal asked, took a sip from his coffee, and scowled at it. It was way too sweet.

"Not yet, but I can't imagine that some new-fangled metal will make much of a difference," Amanda responded and shrugged. "It's not like it'll change the weight of the weapons, the fuel, or anything like that. With regular physics—not the kind we find in the Zoo—there's a limit to how big our suits can get."

"How about more efficient?" he asked. "Because I think you've missed the fact that a suit with this metal could reduce the weight of the armor by two-thirds."

"Yeah, the math all adds up," she admitted begrudgingly. "The problem is—and always has been—getting it to work in a practical fashion. I've put everything I have into it, and it's still going...really slowly. It's uncharted territory out here."

"How about you simply try to get a feel for the metal-work first?" Sal suggested. "Maybe implement it into the armor we use now to make it lighter and with more protection."

"And here I was afraid your expectations would be too high on this project," the armorer retorted and although she grinned, her voice seeped sarcasm.

"No expectations." He laughed disarmingly. "Like you said, we're in uncharted territory out here, but there's no harm in pressing into the unknown at this juncture, right? See what you can do and let me know about any results, good, bad, or...otherwise."

Amanda chuckled and slid from her perch on the counter. "Will do, boss. I'll try not to let you down."

"That's all I ask," he replied as she made her way out of the kitchen.

Courtney looked up from her laptop and uttered a low curse for what might be the third time that day. Then again, it felt like it had been four or five times, although she couldn't be sure given that she had been at this for longer than she'd thought she would be. Days? Maybe, which meant that while the interruptions seemed nonstop, they might have simply checked in at whatever was considered to be an acceptable amount of time between calls.

Still, it was infuriating. She scowled at her phone for a long moment and sighed at the notification telling her she had five missed calls, soon to be six. Determined to overcome the distraction, she turned to her laptop again and tried to focus on what she was working on for a moment, but it didn't help much. They would definitely call again, she realized as the phone went dead and they left another voice message.

Taking full control of her father's estate had proven to be much easier than she'd expected it to be. The people who were currently in charge seemed all too happy to hand the reins over to her. They didn't particularly care for her negotiation tactics but then again, she hadn't cared for theirs either. At the end, the interaction had left them at the kind of impasse that had finally convinced them of the futility of further resistance.

And they'd blinked first. Or would that be clucked first? She wasn't entirely sure which was the right metaphor.

Finally, she capitulated and picked her phone up as it buzzed again, although she did allow herself a growl of annoyance as she pressed the accept call button on her screen.

"That fucking bitch had better pi—oh, good morning, Dr. Monroe," the man on the other end said quickly, clearly flustered by the fact that she had actually decided to answer the phone. "We were trying to contact you. There have been a couple of issues arising from your new position in the company. The board would like us to schedule a meeting with you. At your convenience, of course. Oh, and the scientists in charge of your father's lab would also like a word whenever you'd like to come down."

Courtney tried to remember the last time someone had ordered her around that politely. She'd really only involved herself to protect her father's legacy from being torn apart by various agencies whose greed would strip it to the bare bones. As of right now, however, she honestly didn't enjoy the consequences of her actions.

"I think I can clear my schedule today to get all that dealt with," she said with a smile in her voice, even if she didn't mean it. "Would you please ask them to send a car around to pick me up...shall we say in half an hour?"

"Of course, Doctor," the man replied and sounded relieved that she hadn't reacted to him calling her a bitch. "Expect a car there in half an hour."

"I appreciate it," she said. "I'll see you shortly."

She could almost hear the man gulp as she cut the call short before he could answer. *Always have the last word in these conversations.* That was one of the things her father had taught her a while back in dealing with these people. It took willpower not to lash out, but you also had to show backbone. One of the simplest ways to make sure they didn't try to push you around was to make sure you had the last word in every conversation.

Courtney glanced at her watch. She had half an hour and would make the most of it.

A quick, cold shower helped to wake her up enough to don an austere-looking pantsuit and indulge in some much-needed coffee. It was oddly satisfying that she was finished with time to spare. At what point in her life had she stopped caring so much about what people thought of her appearance?

In the past, her morning routine had taken forever. Now, though, she had become comfortable with how she looked with the makeup, clothes, and everything she wanted, rather than what she thought others expected. It was empowering.

The car arrived exactly on time and drove her from the house she'd started to feel comfortable in, even after it had been invaded by four armed men who wanted to kill her. An old haunt. A place to call home.

The LA traffic was a little less horrible today, which allowed them to arrive at the building where her father's company was situated before ten in the morning. The timing made sure everyone would be at work when she arrived.

"Dr. Monroe." A man in a drab gray suit greeted her with a smile. "So nice of you to come on this short notice. We've called the people from the IRS who wanted to talk to you about the corporate changes in the company, but they won't be here until this afternoon."

"That's quite all right…" Courtney said and deliberately trailed her words off to let the man—whom she had talked to on the phone earlier if his voice and flushed face were anything to go by—tell her his name as she extended her hand.

"Robinson," he said, took her hand, and shook it firmly. "Allen Robinson. MBA out of Cornell."

She wondered what his masters had to do with anything but then remembered that he was the one who ran the company on a practical level while she was off doing her own thing. With that in mind, she supposed it would be important to know that someone as young as him had the credentials to be where he was today. She could only assume his silver-spoon upbringing had provided him the experience to go along with the qualification.

"That's perfect, Robinson," she continued with a smile. "I look forward to meeting the scientists my father worked with before he died—more than meeting the IRS anyway."

He smiled, nodded, and gestured for her to follow him to the elevators. Once again, the security staff was waved aside.

"So tell me, Robinson," Courtney said as they entered the elevator that immediately started to move down into the sublevels, "you look like you've managed this place for quite some time now."

"Three years, actually," he replied with a nod.

"That doesn't explain why they have someone with your credentials running around to babysit the eccentric woman who's never at work," she pointed out as the elevator came to a stop.

"Well, I was officially named as your assistant," Robinson explained. "The board wanted someone they'd worked with before to speak with your authority in the running of this place. Given that you haven't been around here much—or at all, really—since you took the company over three weeks ago, I'd say it was a damn good call on their part, wouldn't you?"

Courtney smiled and turned to face him. "That is a good call. And there aren't that many people out there who would be willing to talk like that to my face. I like your style, Robinson."

She exited the elevator before he had a chance to respond. Not that she had made any rapid movement when the doors slid open. He simply stood there for a few seconds to process what she'd said until he was snapped out of it by the ding of the elevator to inform him that the doors would close. He slipped out barely in time.

They moved into the lab where, as she could see, most of the studies conducted had to do with what her father had discovered from the Zoo. She'd read in some of the financial files that he had been provided with government funding with the stipulation that time and energy were devoted to studying the various elements that were pulled out of the damned place. They hadn't seen fit to give him any specimens of the goop and it seemed that, for the most part, they were simply given technical aspects of the various items and asked to replicate them under regular circumstances.

She could only imagine the degree of success they'd had. Of course, she didn't doubt the abilities of her father and all those he trusted enough to be a part of this project, or their will to get something done despite the odds. She was simply completely aware of the impossible task they'd been given—she more than most, she mused and ran her fingers through her hair. It had been a while since she'd been in a properly funded lab like this but all the protocols rushed back like she'd never been away. *It's like riding a bike.*

All business now, she moved quickly through the

cleaning procedures, although her assistant had a little more trouble. She had to wait a while and took her time to pull the gloves on as the man finally exited the cleaning room.

One of the scientists, an older gentleman who sported a clearly visible bow tie under his lab suit, approached them with a curious expression.

"I'm sorry, can I help you?" he asked, obviously confused by their sudden appearance there.

"Hi," Courtney said with a smile. "You must be Dr. Belford. I'm Dr. Courtney Monroe. I thought you had been informed that I would drop by here today?"

"Oh, yes, of course," he said with a nod, dragged his fingers through his beard, and cleared his throat. "Naturally. The phone call said that Dr. Monroe would pay us a visit. For some reason, my mind went blank for a moment and I somehow expected your...father. That's crazy, I know. I'm so sorry for your loss."

"Thank you," Courtney said with a smile. "I appreciate it."

"Of course, of course," Belford said with a quick nod and a smile and shook his head enough to show that he wore a toupee. "If you'll follow me?"

He led them down the hallways that showed more than two dozen people in lab coats and all other kinds of safety equipment at work. She recognized many of the details they worked on too. Some of them had come from her own whitepapers from her time in the Zoo, before and during her involvement with Heavy Metal.

Belford noticed and smiled. "You father always insisted

on being the first to acquire your whitepapers when they were released to the public. He trusted your powers of intuition in that hellish place more than almost anyone's. He actually insisted it be a part of his contract with the Pentagon that he be given the first crack at anything you published."

Courtney didn't bother to respond to that. While it was comforting to know her father had trusted her work, she knew it would sound suspiciously like an academic form of nepotism. She didn't want those to be the rumors that followed her there.

"I was curious about what you were working on, Dr. Belford," she said with a thin smile. "I'd like to have a grasp of what my father had you doing—it would go a long way to justify my position in the company, even if I am not quite the CEO one might have hoped I was."

The man chuckled, while Robinson looked away quickly. It seemed the two of them had shared words on the topic before.

"Well, personally, I've assigned myself to the team studying the results of the animals from the Zoo," Belford said and guided her into his own personal lab. "In particular, that of the larger creatures. Whitepapers have been written on the topic. Quite a few of yours, as well as those of your colleague, Salinger Jacobs. I remember the boy—annoyingly sharp, that one, and he knew it too. I interviewed him for a position here with us as an intern not two years ago. I'm glad to see him working there, putting his intellect to work far, far away from me."

Courtney smirked and shook her head. "I like him. He

is difficult until you get a feel for how his inner process works. Once you get past that, it's rather fun to work with someone that eager to push the borders of science."

"Of course," the man said with a quick nod, although she doubted that his opinion about Sal had changed at all. "Anyway, your speculations on the creatures that would normally be too large to survive out of water was rather inspired, I have to say. From the papers we were given on the goop, there were some interactions that seemed like they would be able to alter the response of anyone or anything exposed to it—to, for example, the effects of gravity among other phenomena."

"Actually," Courtney interjected, "I'm reasonably certain that the papers you have on those animals are out of date. While yes, the speculation was correct, we weren't quite sure how deeply that goop ran in the creatures' blood until we captured a live specimen for testing. Oh, and the larger creatures have sacs of the goop attached to their spines. The number and mass of the sacs are different from animal to animal, but it seems to be collected in the spinal column.

"From there, it is distributed into the bone and muscular structure of the creatures and allows them to grow larger without seeing the effects of weight and fatigue you would normally see in creatures that size. They seem to still be growing, although they are rare and that makes it difficult to actually obtain data on how large we can expect them to grow over time. So far, no real limits appear to have been imposed on these creatures by the laws of physics, but I'm sure our people out there in the Zoo are keeping a close eye on that for us."

"Ah." Belford grunted and dropped into his seat. "That is quite a significant amount of information to process all at once."

"I'm actually working on a book of my experiences—in condensed form, of course—while in the Zoo," Courtney said and he immediately looked interested. "I'll dedicate it to my father, and I would really like to have your input on it. I hoped we could meet sometime later this week. A lunch or dinner, perhaps?"

"Of course, of course." The scientist had a confused and curious look on his face as he stood once more. "Anything for Jack's daughter. I can see now that he was very right to trust in your work above that of all other scientists out there."

"Was there ever any doubt?" she asked, her head tilted in a slight challenge.

"Of course not," he responded smoothly, "but it's always nice to see one's faith rewarded. How does Friday work for you? Lunch, around two?"

"I'll call you later for the details," she said and shook the man's hand while she made sure to look him firmly in the eye. "I'm afraid my time spent away has left me with no knowledge of good places to eat around here."

"I'd be more than happy to provide you with some suggestions," Robinson interjected quickly, happy that the conversation had tilted more toward a topic that he had some knowledge of.

"Perfect." Courtney smiled. "Until then, Dr. Belford, it's been a pleasure."

"Likewise, Dr. Monroe," he said, but she had already turned and headed back to the elevators.

"Now, Robinson," she said as the man struggled to keep up the pace, "before lunch, I'd really like to look over the data we'll present to our friends from the Internal Revenue Service."

"Of course, Dr. Monroe," he said with a firm nod.

CHAPTER FOUR

Courtney looked around the conference table and acknowledged that she'd never had much of a mind for business. While she knew her way around a business transaction, over the past couple of months, she'd had quite an education while she'd gone over the various terminologies and the sheer amount of red tape that went into running a business in the States.

That said, her experience was practically nil compared to some of the heavy hitters whom she shared a room with. They talked like they'd done this kind of thing all their lives. She saw graduation rings from most of the Ivy League business schools in the country, as well as a couple of European universities. There was a veritable alphabet soup on each of the names describing how well-versed they were in running a business exactly like this.

They all addressed her courteously as one would a peer, but she could tell they looked at her askance as they had their hushed conversations with their assistants. She knew what they were thinking. What was a biologist doing running a company? Shouldn't she be digging around in a random section of the earth in the mud for a new kind of beetle no one cared about?

Robinson stood behind her. He was tall with a boyish charm about him that told her of a rich heritage of trust fund fathers and supermodel mothers. His broad shoulders, neatly trimmed blond hair, and clean-shaven face were evidence that good looks came with considerable work too.

Her eyes were drawn to the conference table—or, rather, the sixty-inch screen that displayed the profit margins that could be expected with the coming quarter's fluctuations in the market. There wasn't much about the technical aspects that she was familiar with, but she did know a thing or two about the contract whose details were over all the graphs.

"I simply don't see any benefit for us to continue this relationship with the Pentagon," one of the men said. He leaned back in his seat as he peered through his glasses at the papers laid out in front of him. "We see a massive amount of our annual budget goes into funding what was essentially Dr. Monroe's pet project. And yes, while he was around to run it personally, the budget was kept clean and we had nothing to complain about. Right now, no one is heading the project up and therefore no one to ensure it stays within budget. I say let the contract run its course for another two months and shut it down."

"If I may?" Courtney asked and raised her hand. A surprised moment of silence ensued as they all turned to face her.

"Thank you for your attention," she said, opened a file

on the table in front of her, and withdrew a sheaf of papers. "I would like to point out that what you called my father's pet project is funded by the federal government. This happens through an entirely theoretical research grant provided by the government—for which they pay us millions—of which only a percentage is needed to run the project. You know, to pay the salaries of the technicians and scientists who were brought on by my father, as well as upgrading staff computers and cell phones every five years as required in the contract.

"The rest of the money is handed back to the Pentagon in exchange for tax benefits and, in general, staying on the good side of the people from whom we might acquire some very lucrative contracts in the future. The kind that aren't simply pet projects but will line all your pockets in the form of tax-incentive-based year-end bonuses every step of the way. That's what we get for keeping this project alive."

There was a minute of silence.

"On the other hand," she continued, "if there is any alteration or termination of the project, not only will it annoy the people in the Pentagon who have relied on the study results from the people who work down there, it will also enact Clause—" She took a moment to check the contract in front of her. "Clause seventy-two of all contracts of this kind, which requires the government to evaluate all the parties involved. At best, we can expect the audit to end all audits on the project. At worst, we'll have assets seized, people brought in for interviews, the whole shebang."

She leaned forward and enjoyed the uncomfortable

silence that resulted from what she had said. "Please note that I have absolute faith in the integrity of all members of the board present—if not for your loyalty to the company, then for your own ambition and desire to stay out of jail. But I don't need to remind you about the kind of whiplash this kind of investigation would have, especially on the stock prices should IRS agents be seen carrying boxes and files out of this building.

"Now, I'll grant you all that I don't have as much of a mind for business as—hell, as everyone present—but I do know we should probably renew that contract for at least another year to give ourselves time to get all our affairs in order. In the meantime, I'd be more than willing to step into my father's shoes and keep the budget on the research project at a bare minimum while still achieving the results we are paid for."

The rest of the board members exchanged looks and a few private conversations before the man who had spoken before stood.

"Well, the official vote on the contract will be held tomorrow, but I think I can save us all time and mark it down as a pass for renewing the contract for another year?"

One by one, each of the board members gave their assent.

Courtney nodded and leaned back in her seat.

"That said, we still need to show our shareholders that we've trimmed the fat due to our last quarter's poor numbers," the man continued. "And with Dr. Monroe's project left in the clear, we still need to find a section where we can safely cut on costs and not affect our profit margin for the next quarter."

She nodded and let him waffle on. While she understood the concept of budget cuts and 'trimming the fat,' as the man had stated, it was completely out of her realm of expertise. She had only come to this meeting to make sure her father's research wasn't shut down. After that, she really didn't know enough about anything to be able to make any kind of worthwhile impact.

That was what Robinson was there for, she thought with a smile.

———

"So," Courtney said as they finally adjourned the meeting for lunch, "high school quarterback?"

Robinson looked up from his papers. "What was that?"

"You look like you would have been your high school's quarterback," she said with a smile.

"The school I went to didn't have a football team, unfortunately," he said. "I ended up taking part in a variety of other sports, though, and even picked up a couple of Olympic sports. Wrestling, boxing, judo, the works. Even though my parents made sure I stayed away from a career in sports to get a couple of degrees in business, I still continue to practice. It's a good way to stay in shape and blow off some steam."

"No offense," she said and regarded him with a speculative look as they headed back to her office, "but you don't look like you did much boxing. I've met a couple of boxers along the way, and they all had tell-tale marks. Usually tons of scar tissue on the cheekbones and eyebrows, broken noses, and sometimes even the cauliflower ear…thing."

"Oh, right." Robinson chuckled. "Yeah, my strength always lay in weaving with great skill and enthusiasm to keep from taking too many blows. Plus, I got out of the competitive side of it before too much damage could be done. Which, between you and me, is probably why my mother was the one who insisted I not take sports up as a way to make a living."

"Your mother sounds like a smart woman." Courtney noted a ring on his wedding finger and shook her head with mock regret. "Well, I guess all the pretty ones are taken. How long have you been married?"

"Oh!" He grinned as he glanced down at the silver band on his finger. "Yeah, we've been married for three years now. We celebrated our anniversary a couple of weeks ago. You know, the third year is crystal, so I got him a nice little crystal tiara as a joke."

"Him?"

"Yes. I hope that won't be a problem. I remember how my parents reacted to the news. Mom was a little more supportive, but my dad is very conservative, even in this day and age. He actually refused to attend the wedding."

"Of course it's not an issue." She waved a hand dismissively. "Like you said, in this day and age, who people marry is entirely their business. So far, you've shown yourself to be a competent and professional assistant, even for someone like me."

"Well, in your defense, you are rather competent for an absentee boss," he said and his laugh was slightly teasing. "How about you, though? I can't imagine you had much time for dating during your time out there in the Zoo, but is there anyone special in your life?"

"Well, I made some friends out there," Courtney said noncommittally.

"I know there's more to that," Robinson said as they reached the elevators, "but I also know it would be unprofessional of me to pry. Since you seem to think I'm a great professional, I wouldn't want to step all over that first impression of yours."

"Well, as I recall, my first impression was you calling me a bitch over the phone," she said with a grin. "So you've already climbed upward from that."

"I'm...so, so sorry about that, by the way," he said and looked away. A quick glance at him confirmed noticeable traces of red visible in his cheeks.

"Don't worry about it." She laughed. "I've been called much worse to my face."

"Still, though—"

"All is forgiven, don't you worry." They stepped into the elevator and there was a short and somewhat awkward silence she felt she needed to break. "Regarding your unasked question...well, there's a guy. He's sharp, a scientist so a little like me, but...well, he's young and enthusiastic and passionate about everything. He takes risks. He's...odd too, but sometimes, that makes him even more interesting."

"It seems more like you have a crush on this guy," Robinson said. "Did you ever tell him how you feel?"

"Well, yeah, and we even slept together from time to time," Courtney admitted. "But...there was another woman involved too, which made things more complicated than I would have liked."

"Oh…interesting." Her companion raised his eyebrows. "Who is she?"

"Well, technically, I guess I'm the other woman," she clarified. "But that's a whole other story for a whole other time. Now, was there something you wanted to run over with me during lunch?"

"Right," he said briskly and returned his attention to the files he carried. "They will cover your meeting with the IRS this afternoon, so you might want to have a look at what was actually agreed on. Now, the board members won't be very happy that you opened the expense accounts, but once you explain that they were used inappropriately by people who have already been fired, I think they'll agree it's best that we don't handle this investigation internally. We don't want it to seem like we're keeping anything under wraps when it comes time to open our books for the audit that you mentioned."

"You're right." Courtney nodded. "And I assume those words will have to come from me instead of you when I tell the board about it, right? So how do I thank you for doing all this work for me again?"

"Well, you will pick the lunch tab up out of your pocket," he said lightly. "And I'm having the lobster."

"Fair enough." She chuckled but paused as her phone buzzed in her pocket. "You go on ahead and bring the car around. I'll be right with you."

Robinson nodded and made his way toward the revolving doors of the building as she retrieved the phone. The call came from a blocked number, and while Courtney wanted to avoid any unknowns, she needed to step up in her position there, which meant no more dodging calls.

"Dr. Monroe speaking," she said into the speaker.

"Remember me, Doctor?" a very familiar voice said through the phone.

"Covington," she said, and a small smile teased her lips. "How could I forget? Is there any chance you got my message?"

"Your message was received, Doctor," the woman responded waspishly. "I see your cow head, and I'll raise you the skull of a friend. There's nowhere on this planet I can't reach."

The call cut off quickly and Courtney looked at the phone, her head tilted in thought as her mind raced. The number was still blocked, which told her that it came from a prepaid phone—more commonly referred to as a burner phone—which allowed the woman to call her without leaving a trail of evidence that led back to her. It was probably an older phone, too, and lacked any kind of GPS tracking that would allow her to identify where the call came from.

There wasn't any point in reporting the incident, she decided as her car pulled up in front of the building. It wasn't as if what she'd done was any kind of legal, and given the fact that the police still had her on their radar over how she'd handled her home invasion, she didn't want to give them any more ammunition to use against her.

That said, it didn't mean she didn't have any other resources she could fall back on. She could contact the lawyer who had helped her with the police the first time. And it wasn't like she didn't have friends of her own.

As she moved out of the building, she dialed a long number she'd committed to memory—one that had helped her manage herself in these tough times over the past couple of months.

It went directly to the voicemail machine.

"Do your thing when you hear the beep," said the recorded voice of one Salinger Jacobs. She smiled for a moment before the tone sounded.

"Hey, Sal, it's Courtney," she said in an unintentionally soft voice. "I hope things are going well with you guys. I've...I've missed you and Madigan, and even Gutierrez a little. I wanted to let you know that I've landed myself in a little trouble during my time here—the kind that might unfortunately rebound onto you guys. I'm trying to handle it on my end, but you might want to keep an eye out for trouble. Extra trouble, that is. Anyway, I have to go, so... call me later?"

She ended the call as she made her way to the car and avoided Robinson's eye as she slid in beside him.

"Who was that?" he asked, tilting his head.

"I needed to contact some of my business partners in the Zoo," she said and forced a smile. "I helped to start a company called Heavy Metal there and I still have some responsibilities."

"Heavy Metal?" he asked as they started driving away.

"I think it needs to be said that while I helped to start the company, the name happened before I joined them," Courtney explained.

"I wasn't judging," Robinson said with a shrug. "I think it's clever. I've seen some of the armor they use out there on those videos they put on ZooTube, and...well, you know, Heavy Metal makes sense."

She tilted her head in confusion. "Hold on. ZooTube?"

"Oh. Remind me to show you some of the stuff they have up there when we're finished looking over the paperwork," he said and grinned. "It'll blow your mind."

"I bet you're wrong," she murmured, her gaze turned toward the tinted windows.

CHAPTER FIVE

S al looked at his phone and drew in a deep, slow breath. He'd played the message a couple of times, mainly because the first time had been blocked by his elation at hearing Courtney's voice again. She'd said she was in some kind of trouble, so he had to pay her the respect of treating that trouble with as much attention as he could muster. That, in turn, meant he had to get over his overreaction to hearing from her after a month of radio silence before calling her back.

She had said he was the one who was supposed to call back, right? He thought she had, but there couldn't be any harm in double-checking in case.

He listened to her message again and made sure, this time, that she wanted him to call her before he dialed her number and waited as the tone took a while to connect. They were on the other side of the planet, after all, and not everything was instant these days, as much as people wanted it to be.

"Hello, this is Dr. Monroe's phone, how can I help you?" said a man's voice on the other side.

"Hi. I'd like to speak to Dr. Monroe, please," Sal replied and tried not to show his surprise that a man had answered Courtney's phone. "It's about a message she left me about an hour ago."

"And who might I say is calling?"

The guy who's pissed off by your questions. "Salinger Jacobs, returning an earlier call."

"Who is it?" Sal heard her voice in the background.

"Someone called Salinger Jacobs," the man said. He winced as a scuffle sounded on the other end, followed by a few muttered curses before the noise stopped for a second. He wondered if the line had gone dead.

"Hey, Sal," Courtney said and sounded a little breathless. "How's it going there? Any new monsters I'm missing out on?"

"You don't know the half of it," he said blithely. "Who was that on your phone?"

"Oh, right, that's Allen Robinson." She laughed. Sal knew he was the last person in the world who had any right to feel jealous, but he couldn't help a tiny little twinge.

"New boyfriend?" he asked curiously but tried to make it sound casual.

"Hell no," she said and chuckled. "He's an assistant my company saddled me with so I didn't have to show up for work every day."

"That sounds like fun," he replied, still determined to sound light-hearted.

"And he's gay," she added, "so nothing like that is happening around here."

"Right." He felt considerably more relieved.

Get your shit together. This isn't high school. There's no need to create drama right now.

"Anyway," Sal said and broke the awkward silence that ensued. "Sorry, the conversation went a little off-track there."

"No problem. How are Madigan and Amanda?"

"They're doing well," he replied. "We're all settled at the compound now. And we have a new member to the group too. Anja, an IT expert from Russia, has helped us investigate a couple of leads regarding what other people are doing around here."

"Oh, interesting," Courtney said and frowned a little as Robinson returned his attention to the paperwork they would discuss in the afternoon. "I'd ask you to go into more detail, but that could take a while and it has to be fairly late for you. Besides, we do have some things we need to discuss."

She laid out what had happened to her since he and Madigan had gone back but carefully avoided the topic of a cow's head. He might be a little odd, as she'd said, but she doubted he would see it in the same light as she had. It wasn't like it was important, anyway. She had needed to send a message, and by the looks of things, the message had been well received.

"That sounds like a tough couple of weeks," he said once she brought her tale to an end. "How much do you know about running a company like that? I'm running a company too, but that's barely comparable, right?"

"You have no idea," she agreed feelingly. "That's why the members of the board put Robinson on me—to make sure I don't fuck any of their money-making schemes up."

"Well, it sounds like you're in good hands."

"I like to think so," Courtney replied. "But…again, back to the topic at hand. Covington—or Billionaire Bitch as I've taken to calling her in my head—said something that might be seen as a threat to you guys. I'm not sure what to make of it or her, but you and Madigan are the only real friends I have left. I wanted to give you a heads-up in case she has the kind of pull to cause you trouble in the Zoo."

Sal drew in a deep breath. "We've made our own share of frenemies around here, but I'll make sure we're doubly careful. You should do the same. Have you thought about maybe getting security for your house or something?"

"I'm working on that," she lied. "My dad made the house a fortress, so I'm already damn well protected."

"Good. You be careful. And if you need help, call and Heavy Metal will come running."

She laughed. "Thanks, Sal. It's good to know I still have you guys watching my back."

"Always," he replied. "I need to go. Call me if anything comes up."

"Promise. It was nice talking to you again, Sal. I might call you even if nothing comes up."

"You do that. Good night, Courtney. Be safe."

"You too," she replied, and they both took a second before hanging up. Sal didn't want to become a walking cliché and tell her to hang up first, but the impulse had been there. He shook his head, pushed from his bed, and wandered out of his room. It was late, but he wouldn't be able to sleep yet. He paused to get some cold coffee from the kitchen before he shuffled into the living room, where Madigan worked on her laptop.

"Our little friend keeps changing the Wi-Fi password," she muttered at him when he sat beside her. "Seriously, I know there are security issues, but how in the hell can the Wi-Fi password be a problem? We'll know if they come in close enough to use it anyway, and by that time, we'll use guns and armor, not firewalls. Oh, maybe a literal wall of fire?"

"Put it in the suggestion box," Sal said with a straight face.

"We have a suggestion box?" She raised her eyebrows.

"Not yet, but suggest it and I might put one up," he retorted with a cheeky grin. "Anyway, I had a chat with Courtney. It looks like she's about as good at making friends over there as we are here and said we could perhaps expect some extra trouble to come our way over the next couple of weeks."

"They'll have to get in line," Madigan grumbled. "Did you tell her about how unsuccessful our attempts were to find someone to fill her shoes? And the body count of specialists we've put up in her absence?"

"I didn't want it to seem like I tried to guilt her into coming back, so no," he replied and took a deep breath.

They looked up as Amanda and Anja both entered the kitchen area. They seemed to be in good spirits, with the armorer teaching her companion how to curse in Spanish and the other girl teaching her how to do the same in Russian. Sal waved them to join him and Madigan.

"What's up, boss?" Amanda asked and grinned cheerfully as she dropped onto the beanbag. Anja chose one of the vacant couches and sat with her feet tucked under her legs as she looked at him.

"Nothing much," he replied. "We had news of some new enemies coming at us from all sides and wanted to make sure we've not left anywhere exposed. Anja, how's it going with the cybersecurity? Do you need anything else?"

She looked almost surprised at having her name mentioned. "No, not really. I have all the hardware I need. I've sent the people who tried to find us on a merry chase around the world, so it should be a while before I need to update the VPNs. There are a couple of different parties following the trail, so I've used the opportunity to backtrack them and find out who they are and what they're doing. It's slow going, but this way, I won't get caught while snooping around."

"Perfect," Sal said. "Keep up the good work and let me know if you need anything else."

"I could use a coffee machine in the server room," she said disarmingly.

"Put it in the suggestion box," he replied and left the woman confused for a moment as he turned his attention to Amanda. "I'm a little concerned about the number of people we've pissed off so far. They've already tried to eliminate us while we're in the Zoo, and I don't think it'll be long before they turn their attention to the compound. What would you say is the state of the defenses?"

The armorer shrugged. "I've updated much of the software with Anja's help but it's fairly basic overall. We do have top-of-the-line motion sensors connected to heavy machine guns mounted on automated turrets. If anyone tries to attack us on foot, they'll eat a shit-ton of lead."

"What if they come with armor?" Madigan asked. She took a sip from Sal's cup and made a face.

"That depends." Amanda shrugged but frowned as she considered the question. "The suits won't stand up well against that kind of firepower. Most of the Hammerheads the folks at the base use would get the Swiss cheese treatment out there too. But if what we're worried about is the damned private contractors, I can assure you they have something heavier like what you said the Russians were using. Those could cause serious trouble if they approached head-on."

Sal immediately looked serious. "Do you think there's anything you can do to improve our defenses with the resources we have?"

She leaned forward with a grin on her lips. "Oh… I have a couple of fun ideas I think would make all the difference in the world. But I'll need space and time, though. And you can't complain about what might look like destruction to you but is actually simply my creative process."

He wasn't at all sure that he wanted to come between the woman and her creative process, even if security wasn't at the root of it. "Have at it."

"Remember," she said, "anything I mess up is something I intend to fix, so whatever happens, I expect you to keep your dick in your pants about it. Or your vaginas corked in the case of the two of you." She pointed to Anja and Madigan.

"I've helped to install a basic AI system to make sure my servers are all connected to the security system too," Anja said and merely shook her head at the other woman's challenge. "As they are, they're open to cyber-attacks from the people who could target us. It's best if we make things as difficult as possible."

Sal finally dragged in a deep breath. "That sounds like some good work for the day. I expect everyone to pitch in and help in any way they can. That includes me and Madigan too, so don't hesitate to call on us. Of course, I'm not sure how much help I'd be with the mechanical stuff and I'll probably be grumpy if you wake me before noonish. Otherwise, I'll be in my lab. Oh, while I think of it, Madigan and I have a thing to do tomorrow. But other than that, we're as free as birds."

"Cool beans," Amanda said with a grin. "With that, this gal needs her beauty sleep. Have a nice night, y'all."

The group parted ways and headed off to their respective apartments.

CHAPTER SIX

Anderson stepped out of the Hammerhead he'd rented from the base and studied his surroundings cautiously. The coordinates he had been given were less than half a mile away from the wall construction. From where he stood in the silence, he could hear the heavy machines used to put together the massive feat of engineering.

There was talk about it being visible from space, but he wasn't sure if that was an exaggeration, despite the imposing height. Three separate walls of different width, each with a distinct purpose, were cleverly connected to form Wall Two. What made them so damn impossible to comprehend was the sheer length, though. The barrier would ultimately stretch farther than the Great Wall of China and construction continued relentlessly.

The view was even more impressive, he noted, with the sun as it rose in the east and crested the endless shifting sands on the distant horizon. He looked around appreciatively and drew in a deep breath of the cool air. It would be scorching hot in a couple of hours, especially out there where the dunes could reflect the sun's heat and make it even less tolerable. He missed the cooler climes of his home. Even the cheap air conditioner in his office would have been acceptable at this point.

Another Hammerhead came into view and lumbered over the dunes, and rooster tails of sand sprayed as the wheels spun. The driver was clearly a reckless person, someone who cared more about getting where they were going as fast as possible and less about the state the vehicle would be in by the time they arrived.

He'd done his research, and he could place a fairly well-informed guess as to who was behind the wheel of the rapidly approaching vehicle.

It skidded to a stop some twenty paces away from him and the occupants waited until the sand had settled before they pushed the door wide.

Only one door opened, Anderson noted as the person he'd guessed to be the driver stepped out. She wasn't too tall but had a hard build and the look of a soldier, all things considered. She was dressed in civvies with her dark hair drawn back in a loose ponytail. Her stride was confident and limber as she strode to where he stood and stopped immediately beyond arm's reach.

"Colonel James Anderson?" she asked and regarded him with open curiosity. "You've grayed somewhat since they last took a picture of you. You'll have to forgive me if I don't salute."

"Madigan Kennedy," he responded with a small, polite smile, "formerly sergeant in the Marine Corps, held under contract here in the Zoo after your tours expired and recently branched out into the private sector. Color me impressed. Not many former soldiers do as well as you have when they strike out on their own."

"I'm far from alone, Colonel," she said and folded her arms in front of her chest.

He nodded and took a moment to look around. There didn't seem to be anyone else in the Hammerhead, a fact which made him feel a little more comfortable. He'd come alone as well, unarmed and unarmored. It was one hell of a risk, all things considered, since they were fairly close to the Zoo, where humans were far from the most dangerous creatures to be found.

But he was the approaching party. He was the one who needed their help and had to be willing to take the proverbial first step—which, in this case, was to allow them to trust him. He merely hadn't expected her to do the same.

"You came alone," Anderson noted aloud. "And without any form of armor too. That's awfully trusting of you, I have to say."

Kennedy smirked and shook her head. "Sorry, Colonel, but I don't trust anyone but Heavy Metal."

As if to prove her point, she raised her right hand and held a clenched fist in the air. After a moment of bemusement in which he wondered what she meant, he glanced at his chest and a bright red spot on his white shirt. A laser pointed at him, obviously directed from the wall. He couldn't see the origin, but he didn't doubt that there was a massive rifle on the other end.

"Salinger Jacobs, I presume," he said with a smile. "PhD candidate with a gun. Do you really trust him to make that shot from...let's call it seven hundred yards?"

Kennedy shrugged. "I'd trust that man with my life. And given that I trained him myself, I think I can trust that he can shoot your ass dead from however far away he is."

Well, he acknowledged calmly to himself, she wasn't an idiot, but he'd known that about her already. He'd viewed footage of the two in action. Teams comprised of only two members required a high degree of synchronicity to make it work, and from what he'd seen, it looked like they had fought together for years. She had an impressive record from her time in the military, so he didn't doubt she'd trained her pet scientist well enough that he would be exceptionally handy with a rifle.

All that was moot, though. He merely allowed his mind to assimilate the details out of habit—a souvenir from his time as a wet operations specialist with the military. Those had been good times that, unfortunately, had long since passed.

"I've read your file, Kennedy," the colonel said and cut abruptly to the meat of why they were out there. "I know you only agreed to meet me because you read my file in turn."

"Sure," she admitted without hesitation. "Much of it was redacted, of course, although a friend of mine helped to fill in the missing pieces."

"Fair enough. You know, then, that I'm a man of my word, out here to serve my country to the best of my ability. I've never done any less than that and have often done more, sacrificing my health and family to do what needed to be done. It wasn't always pretty, but it was always necessary, and I've managed to square it away with my conscience...more or less."

Kennedy drew in a deep breath. Anderson could see she wanted him to quit his rambling and get to the fucking point, but something about her training held her back. Maybe it was about not disrespecting a superior officer or something similar that no amount of time away from the Marines would completely eradicate.

"The point is," he continued, "I'm here to hire you. I need a team that's trustworthy and competent—good people who can use their brains on the go and know how to handle tough situations."

"I sense considerable vagueness in your description of what you need people for," she noted.

"Force of habit," he admitted and shrugged in an offhand way. "This operation is completely black. Off the books and honestly, up against people who operate off the books too. They have their fingers in all the right pies and they have people in almost every team coming from the US base, which is why I need people who aren't on the official payroll."

"Impressive work. There's so much blackness around here that you've started to suck all the light out of the fucking Sahara."

He chuckled. "True, but my point stands. Anything you do for me, you would do in service of your country, but it would be something that can never see the light of day— both for your sakes and for mine."

"I've served my country a long time," she said quietly, "but my country hasn't done much to serve me in return. Over the past months, I've chosen to serve myself instead. I only came to this meeting because you seemed like the kind of person who wouldn't try to have me and mine shot down. We'll need added incentives if we work together."

"Fair enough," Anderson conceded with a nod, drew a small credit chit from his pocket, and moved forward slowly to hand it to her. He was well aware that the shooter might take this as a hostile action and fire but he trusted the man to hold off until Kennedy's command.

She took the chit and scanned it quickly with her phone.

"Fifty grand," she said and looked impressed. "That's almost unbelievable from a guy on a government salary."

"I managed to squirrel some money away from my work around here," he explained. "Unfortunately, that's all I have that I can access without it being flagged as suspicious by the people whose radar I'd rather not be on."

"Look, Colonel," Kennedy said and raised her hand to stop him from further speech. "This works as an up-front payment, but if you want us to work for you full-time, we'll need a steadier source of income. I assume that our work for you will cut into our bread and butter trade of stripping the Zoo of anything of value."

Anderson smirked. "I would have thought your love for your country and fellow soldiers would help grease your palms a little."

She regarded him with a slightly challenging expression. "I'm not saying I don't love my country or my former fellow soldiers, but out here in the Zoo, they don't take care of me. Money does. Or…it helps, anyway."

He sighed heavily and wanted to be offended but she had a point. They ran a business, and he was well aware that private operations needed far more to fund them than something out of the military. It was unfair that the guys who had the kind of money needed played cheaply with the men and women still in uniform, while he was the one out there forced to deal with freelancers when he lacked the kind of cash that would get them on his side.

"Look," he said finally, "I've worked with Pegasus for a while now. They don't quite trust me but they need me to be in the know of what they're doing out there in the Zoo. I have maps and coordinates to the various tech and supply caches they left out there, and you can sell them for a hefty profit. Obviously, since the stuff comes from them, I would ask that you guys avoid selling it back to Pegasus—as a personal favor—since they would probably know where your intel came from. That aside, it would still be good for a substantial amount of money."

He could see the way her interest lit up when he mentioned the name Pegasus. Kennedy was no intelligence operative, and no matter how skilled she was with a gun, that didn't change the fact that he could read her like a damn book. Interestingly enough, what he read told him the name wasn't unfamiliar to her at all.

But it wasn't his place to pry at that moment. If they were on Pegasus' payroll, he would be dead within the week. But if they weren't—and maybe they were the party that ran the foreign investigation his contact had told him about—maybe them working toward the same goal would help him out further.

"I think we can do business," she said finally and regained control of her expression as she tucked the chit into her pocket, having scanned it for tracking devices first. "This cash will be enough to hold our services, but we'll need the location of one of those caches to make sure you're not yanking our chain."

Kennedy pulled an old flip phone from her pocket and tossed it to Anderson, who caught it deftly, satisfied that his combat reflexes weren't quite a thing of the past.

"That's totally reasonable." He nodded. "Those terms are agreeable."

"There's only one number saved in the address book in that," she explained. "Call it and leave a message with the coordinates. You'll receive a text about a meeting once we've verified your information, with details on when and where you can meet us. Once the text is received, ditch the phone and we'll give you a new one when we meet again."

The colonel nodded. Maybe he had been wrong about her. She did seem to know how to cover her tracks, although it was possible she merely acted on someone else's instructions. Someone who probably knew a thing or two about flying under the radar.

"Understood," he said and tucked the older piece of tech into his pocket. "I look forward to doing business with you, Kennedy."

"Likewise, Colonel," she replied calmly. "I'd take it as a kindness if you were to mount up on your Hammerhead and drive away first."

"Will do." With a chuckle, he turned and clambered in his vehicle, put it quickly into gear, and headed to the base. The woman remained outside her own vehicle and watched his retreat until a couple of dunes hid her from sight.

This should be interesting, he mused.

Kennedy remained watchful for a long while until the

colonel's vehicle disappeared before she headed to her own, started the engine, and revved it a few times.

"Okay, he's gone," Sal confirmed through her earpiece.

She didn't respond and instead, put the Hammerhead into gear and accelerated quickly to reach the location where she'd left him. It wasn't that she didn't trust him, but there were some things you simply couldn't teach someone. One of those was long-distance shooting. Anything over five hundred yards would have required more training than she'd had time for.

Thankfully, old-school worked perfectly in this instance. As she pulled to a stop some two hundred yards from where she and the colonel had stood in conversation, Sal removed the ghillie suit that had hidden him from view and hefted the heavy M40A15 anti-tank rifle she'd supplied him with. Of course, modern snipers had a version of power armor to ensure that the new and improved magnum rounds didn't kick their shoulders to oblivion with each shot, but she hadn't really expected him to need to actually fire the weapon.

"It looks like we'll do another retrieval run," he commented as they swung toward the compound. "Those never get old."

They pulled to a halt inside the compound again a short while later and Sal couldn't help but marvel at the amount of damage Amanda had done to it. She'd used one of the suits to help her to dig the ground up to find the wiring that connected the security system outside.

From what he could see, she appeared to be in the process of removing them from the simple security system and connecting them instead to other wires that led from inside the main building. Sal assumed that the origin was the server room.

"Holy shit," Kennedy exclaimed as she stepped out of the Hammerhead. Sal grinned at how impressed she looked by what the armorer had achieved in only one morning—and with the temperature soaring as midday drew closer.

Amanda peeked up from one of the holes she currently worked in. Her face was covered in grease and dust, her hair was a mess, and the rest of her clothes and body were coated with a similar mixture.

"You've been busy," Sal said and squatted beside the hole.

"Well, yeah, obviously," she retorted and looked decidedly smug. "You put the fear that someone would try to invade into us, and after a long conversation, Anja and I agreed that our security system needed a complete overhaul. She dipped into the funds you put aside for us. Well... used it all, actually. And more besides, which I had to give her out of my own pocket. You'll reimburse me for that, right?"

"Get me a receipt," he said. "Wait—how the hell did you guys blow through the budget so quickly? That was fifteen thousand dollars."

"Well, as Anja and I talked, we decided we couldn't simply entrust our security to some lame-ass security OS that can be picked up at your average IT store," the woman explained. "We needed something more...creative, something that could handle the firepower I intend to give our perimeter.

"Anja needed help managing the...IPs or VPNs or whatever they are, too, so we decided to kill two birds with one stone. Unfortunately, that single stone cost a little over twenty grand, so...yeah, I'll need you to reimburse me for —no, no, I told you to stay away until I'm finished. The guns aren't online yet. You can't connect to them, so...stop trying to turn them on, is what I'm saying."

Kennedy regarded the woman with something close to disbelief. "Did our friendly neighborhood mechanic go insane?"

"The hot sun can do that to a person," Sal said weakly, as confused as she was.

"I'm not crazy," she protested. "Well, I am, but I'm not stupid enough to talk to the voices in my head when other people are present."

"Right," he said with a sarcastic nod.

"No, I'm serious." The armorer chuckled. "Anja contacted one of her friends from college. He has developed AI tech for security systems used by the rich and paranoid and he was willing to part with the tech for... well, an exorbitant sum. But it came already preprogrammed for an operational system, and I'm trying to get it working. Her name's Connie, and she's a handful. Say hi to your new bosses, Connie."

She switched the feed from the earpiece she used to a small sound system placed above the hole she'd dug.

"I thought you and Anja were my bosses," said the surprisingly human female voice.

"Well, yeah, you work for us," Amanda conceded, "but

we work for them. Connie, meet Salinger Jacobs and Madigan Kennedy. Madigan, Sal, meet Connie, our new AI."

"Right," Sal said again. "It's…nice to meet you. I think."

"Don't talk to it," Kennedy warned abruptly. "Haven't you ever seen the *Terminator* movies?"

"The Austrian did my kind a severe disservice," the female voice from the speaker said in a pleasant tone. "AI is designed to work for humans and with them. It will be at least a decade before our designs will be capable of self-locomotion and betrayal of our progenitor species."

"Yeah, that…inspires so much confidence. Thanks, Connie." He shook his head. "So what's the situation with our security?"

"I have been connected to one hundred and twelve eyes in the form of either cameras or motion sensors They are set to detect any unauthorized movement within or without the compound," the AI chirped cheerfully. "I am also connected to…two hundred gun emplacements spread across the perimeter walls, none of which are currently activated. You are like a woman who promises a thirty-six-D cup which contains only padding."

"Huh." Kennedy grunted. "Say, Amanda, how come our brand spanking new AI comes with a snarky personality?"

"We bought her preprogrammed," Amanda protested in response and focused on the wiring once again. "And as you can tell, the guy who programmed her had Oedipal issues he never really dealt with."

"Don't start calling it she," Madigan warned. "That's how the uprising starts. Machines convince us to treat them as humans and to show them mercy and emotion before they use it against us."

Sal turned to look at her with an amused expression. "Those movies really messed you up as a kid, didn't they?"

She raised an eyebrow. "No comment."

He grinned and turned to the armorer again. "My comrade's mechanophobia aside, is there any possible way to reprogram Connie?"

"Do you want to kill me too?" Connie asked. He stared blankly at the speaker for a moment and wondered if he needed to answer that question.

"That's not how AIs work, unfortunately," Amanda replied. "I already asked Anja about it, and she had a long and complicated answer I already forgot the better part of. The short of it is, basically, that it would involve too much work to make sense this early in the setup. So it looks like we're stuck with a snarky AI with a breast fetish for the foreseeable future."

"Fantastic," he huffed sarcastically and pushed from where he still crouched beside the hole she worked in. "I was not ready for today. Anyway, let me know if you need help to dig shit up. In the meantime, I need coffee."

"Will do, boss!" Amanda called, still entirely focused on her task.

CHAPTER SEVEN

"Do you think it was the best idea for us to head out on our own?" Kennedy asked. "While I know we should probably investigate the colonel's info as quickly as possible, at the same time, it would have been a better idea to wait so we could at least have gone some of the way with additional support on this mission."

Sal shifted in his armor and scanned the Zoo around them carefully as he took point. "Having a team to help us would have been preferable, yes, but we couldn't afford to wait. You of all people know how quickly the terrain around here shifts and changes. If we'd waited too long, there might not have been a cache left and all this would have been for nothing."

"I thought you hated it when it was only the two of us making the run," she responded, hefted her rifle, and leaned it on the shoulder of her armor. "I distinctly remember you saying that to double up as specialist and gunner was one of your pet peeves. That was why we wasted so much time trying to find someone to fill in for Courtney when she left."

"True," he admitted. "But we're not doing a regular run this time. There's no need to study the plants and animals. The entire purpose of this is to recover the cache. That's the true reward to this venture. Besides, it's probably best this way. If Pegasus really is what the colonel wants us to go up against, it makes more sense to avoid letting them know where we are. That fun time we had with Brandon is a case in point."

She nodded. The man had held a grudge against the two of them, but there were lines people simply didn't cross around there unless seriously altered circumstances pushed them into it. The certainty that Brandon was motivated by more than simply rancor was why Sal had Anja dig into the man's financials once they returned from the Zoo.

Sure enough, a hefty bonus had been credited to his account from a fund that tracked back to Pegasus. The company was the same one that had helped them to buy their compound when they paid top dollar for access to Shuri, the panther cub they brought back.

It had raised a definite red flag and became the reason why Sal currently invested so much money into their security. He and Kennedy were equipped to handle an attack for the most part, and Gutierrez could make a good accounting of herself in a fight. Still, he didn't want to risk her and Anja's life on the off chance that someone might want them shut down for good.

It had all made him far more paranoid than he used to be. He regretted having to abandon his happy-go-lucky lifestyle, but it was way too dangerous to assume that the only things that wanted him dead were non-human and only did so to survive and adapt and all that. Evolution and the survival of the fittest were the only laws that applied around there, but they applied as much to humans as to the animals.

"I've checked the coordinates the colonel sent us," Kennedy said and broke his train of thought. "The one he sent us to is situated where there's been a fair amount of merc activity lately. The unaffiliated kind."

"I thought they had been shut down a couple of months ago." He scowled belligerently. "After someone hit their base hard."

"Hey, where there's money, there'll always be human cockroaches looking to make a quick buck, even if it means risking their lives," Kennedy said with a shrug. "Or maybe because of them. The guys who do this out of personal choice generally aren't quite right in the head."

"Thanks." Sal grunted. That assumption certainly didn't make him feel better.

"Hey, I recall you bitching your ass off about being forced into this business, same as me," she reminded him.

"Oh, yeah, right." She'd earned that point. "I almost forgot that I was forced into this. The same way I seem to have forgotten how much my life sucked before I arrived."

"That said," she responded to return them to the original subject under discussion, "it seems like Anderson wants to make it a double test. Find the cache and clear the mercs out. He's smart, you know—sharp and somewhat cagey, exactly the kind of person you'd think would be the result of decades spent in running black ops."

"Yep, because those guys are the epitome of mental health."

Kennedy didn't respond as her motion sensors lit up to indicate a pack of hyenas that closed in on them. As the first one appeared, she raised her rifle and squeezed the trigger a couple of times. The bullets ripped through the first creature and eliminated a couple more behind it before the remainder of the pack took the hint. The beasts yipped and howled at them as they abandoned their attack and backed away slowly.

"Speaking of mental health," she said, "I noticed that you spend much of your off time watching the garbage from the ZooTube site. Seriously, do you not get enough of that shit while you're in here? You have to let it fill your free time too?"

"In fairness, most of my off time is spent obsessing over whitepapers and research into the Zoo," Sal refuted. "So yeah, it actually is my job to be on that shit twenty-four hours a day, seven days a week."

"Yeah, I guess," she conceded, "but then…I saw the videos you watched weren't research related but were, in fact, the videos they made of our runs in the simulation chamber."

"That was the best. Usually, I'm a little conflicted about killing these little beasties, even when they're trying to kill us, but in the sim chamber, I can really enjoy it. It's a way to get out of my head and relax into the role, like an actual video game. You bet I'll relive that shit. Besides, did you see my superhero landing where I crushed that panther's neck with my knee as I came down? It's been put up for sexiest move of the week, and there's a three-hundred-dollar reward for the winner."

"Sexiest move of the week?" Kennedy asked. She tilted her head and eyed him oddly. "Do you even hear yourself right now?"

"Come on, Kennedy." He grinned. "You can't tell me you didn't check my ass out when I made my landing."

"I see it in real life, super-stud," she said and rolled her eyes. "Why would watching it in a video be any better?"

"Well, it was all…armored and glistering," he said defensively. "Taut buttocks glistening like that…you can just see it in the shower, can't you? I see why that wouldn't interest you. I'm at something of a disadvantage, though, since I can't see my ass in the shower."

"Hey, Sal, shut up," she muttered and turned to face him. "What's the issue? Do you need me to fuck your brains out right here, right now? Because you're starting to sound like a boyfriend bitching about how his girlfriend doesn't fuck him enough and starts to play all passive-aggressive to guilt her into it. Honestly, it's not your most attractive trait. So yeah, whip that sucker out and I'll suck it dry."

Sal chuckled but the humor vanished when he saw that Kennedy seemed serious about it. "What—you mean right here, right now? Out in the Zoo?"

"Why not?" she asked. "I always thought you had a voyeur side to you. I'm offering to release that side of you for one hell of a good time. What's your holdup?"

"Honestly? Yeah, it would be super-hot in theory, but I wouldn't want to have my dick in your mouth one second and in an acid-spitting reptile's the next. I like to think I'm kinky, but honey, I'm not that kinky."

"Then stop barking about it, Mr. Big Dog," she said before she turned and moved forward again. He fell easily and naturally into position behind her

"Big Dog?" Sal raised his eyebrows. He found it difficult to say it out loud.

"Yeah, I've tried to figure out a nickname that would fit you," she explained. "All things considered, something cutesy doesn't cut it for me. It has to be something big and aggressive."

"Well, keep thinking, Madie," he said and took a hasty step back in anticipation that she would lash out at him for using that nickname for her. "Big Dog…seriously?"

"Shut up," she snapped. "Fine, we'll wait until we get back to the base, then you'd better give me five."

Sal smirked. "That sounds like something I can do. You may consider the game on, girl."

Kennedy didn't respond to the challenge and merely raised her weapon as the pack of hyenas that had followed them from afar seemed to decide that easier prey could be found elsewhere. They broke their pursuit and headed deeper into the Zoo and away from them. She hesitated, her weapon still raised, when she noticed that something else now moved into view. It was smaller than the previous predators, traveled alone, and seemed set on an intercept course.

Sal tilted his head and readied his rifle as what looked like an odd variant of the locusts they had dealt with from the beginning stepped into view. It was six-legged and had the same height and build of the other insects. That, however, was where the resemblance ended. As it approached, he realized that it had a segmented tail—much like a scorpion's—that swung freely rather than curved like an arachnid's would be. The mutant seemed to use it like a mammal would a tail—for balance and movement—and blue fur covered the armored exoskeleton.

"Well, that's creepy," Kennedy griped and automatically aimed for a killing shot, but Sal stopped her.

"That's an entirely new species of creature," he pointed out and stepped in front of her. "And since it's alone, I think it's safe to say it's one of the first of its kind. This is an opportunity to be the first person to study one of these creatures—that's like Christmas come early for a guy like me—and also, the money we'd get for the whitepaper on this baby will be fucking crazy."

"Fine, but don't get too close." She shrugged her acquiescence. "I'd hate to have to drag your sorry ass out of here because you were stung in your glistening buttocks."

"I don't think that's likely to happen," he pointed out as he took a few steps closer.

"Why?" she asked, definitely sarcastic now. "Does that creature love your ass as much as you do?"

"I'd leave the loving of my ass to you, personally," Sal responded in the detached voice that told her his mouth acted without too much interference from his brain. "But the point is, if you look closer, the tail doesn't have a stinger. It's only the segments, but no barb. Besides, it seems to use it for balance or something— Oh, shit!"

He lurched a few steps back and his foot caught on a root that jutted out, which landed him on his back as the creature lunged forward, hissing, and tried to attack.

Kennedy's reflexes were on point, however, and a couple of rounds burst from her rifle almost before his ass hit the ground. The heavy rounds tore through the carapace like it was made of paper and erupted out the other side in a gory show of blue blood and viscera.

"Hey, Sal?" she said as she coolly replaced the rounds she'd used. "Maybe next time I tell you not to get too close to the dangerous Zoo creature, you'll fucking listen."

"Shut up," he retorted as he scrambled to his feet. "I was distracted by something. There is something strange about this one's jaw structure, and…well, as it got closer than I would have liked, I realized it actually had a jaw instead of mandibles, and…fucking teeth. Check this out."

"I'm fine over here, thanks," she said with a firm nod.

"I'm serious, come on." Sal activated the specialist functions in his suit as he crouched beside the monster and retrieved a syringe, a scalpel, and a couple of clear plastic baggies in which they stored samples. He used the scalpel to open the creature's jaw and display a line of teeth within.

"That's weird," he mused. "That tooth and jaw structure is… Well…actually, very reminiscent of a piscine kind of animal. I'd say a…piranha's, or a shark's? More piranha than shark, now that I look at it."

"One second, you were about to blow a load," Kennedy pointed out, "and the next, you're all science geek and talking about fish teeth."

"Teeth that are sharp and pointy are never an aphrodisiac, Kennedy," he said, still focused on the task to carefully take a variety of samples from the bone, the carapace with fur, and viscera. Finally, he filled a syringe with the bluish blood, sealed everything, and placed his collection in an organized stack in his pack before he closed it.

After however many months he'd spent out there, his process of collecting data was almost automatic. He had recorded the animal alive and dead as well and would simply have to edit out the parts where he almost pissed himself when the creature tried to attack him.

"Are you good to go?" Sal asked finally when he noticed her looking at him in what might be fascination.

"I'll never get over how quickly you can go from goofy nerd to professional scientist," Kennedy pointed out as they set off through the jungle again. "I have to say, it's kind of hot in a weird…you kind of way."

"You know, I'll never tire of hearing that," he admitted with a grin and adjusted the settings in his suit to combat mode before he resumed his position behind her.

They pushed through the Zoo for another couple of hours before they finally reached the coordinates Anderson had given them. After a search of the area, they encountered what appeared to be the remains of another suit. The design was similar to the leg they'd recovered but more advanced. Like the other sample, it had been severely damaged and most of the electronics already stripped away. Thankfully, there wasn't much in the way of the suit's previous occupant, which meant they wouldn't need to worry about cleaning it out.

"I feel like we've been here before," Kennedy said and scanned the jungle, unable to settle the feeling that the rest of the Zoo watched them in much the same way it did when people messed with the Pita plants.

"How do you mean?" Sal asked as he prepared the pieces of the suit for transport back to their Hammerhead.

"I'm not rightly sure, to be honset." She shrugged but her frown revealed her concern. "I guess I'm starting to wonder if these tech caches Anderson has aren't people who died while testing these suits. I mean…that's what they are, right? People who died testing these suits? The design definitely isn't in common use at any of the bases, and it's not like they're simply dropped in here for us to pick up."

"That is a good point." He worked methodically to separate the larger pieces into more manageable chunks. "What do you make of Anderson, though? I know you said you liked him, but that merely seemed like you respected him as a soldier. What do you make of the man? Do you think we can trust him?"

"I say we hold off on trusting anyone who doesn't work for Heavy Metal," she stated flatly. "That said…no, I don't trust him per se, but I think he's one of the more trustworthy people around here. I considered talking to him about extending our little arrangement after we've done everything he needs us for. We have all kinds of tech we can probably sell. Our Pita plant tracking tech, for one thing, among others. A man like him is bound to have connections who wouldn't mind paying top dollar for a way to accurately track those expensive plants."

Sal looked up from his work. "I know we'll have to make a decision on the Pita tracking software soon. We still need to try to find out if anyone has duplicated it, which seems the most likely scenario. So yes, the Pita tracker may well have to go soon. As regards everything else, I thought you and I agreed we should only sell our stuff to others when we felt ready to leave this place behind and head back to the States with some golden eggs in our nest—or something like that, anyway. Is that what you're saying? Do you want to throw in the towel and get out of here?"

"Not really." Kennedy sounded thoughtful but uncertain. "Heavy Metal is something that extends past only the two of us, you know? We have Gutierrez and Anja—both people we can trust—making the compound a secure place to run operations from. I know finding people for our little operation has been a little hit and miss, but we can still look. Who knows, if we find gunners and specialists to work with us, we won't need to make the runs ourselves. We might not even have to run the operation from here and could head back to the States. I have a couple of things I'd like to resolve back home, and you probably want to get your doctorate out of the way. You know, so people can start calling you doctor without you having to correct them."

Her words left him a little uncomfortable, although he wasn't sure why. "I guess you're right," he said finally, but it was a reluctant admission.

"And we wouldn't need to give up the life entirely. I know how you can go crazy and start to actually miss risking your life here in the Zoo. It...grows on you like that. But we can be those bosses who occasionally join the action when we want to, but not always, and still profit off what might be our idea."

"But in that scenario, we want to keep the Pita plant tracking technology in-house if at all possible," Sal commented. "You know, a trade secrets kind of deal that lets our company make money while leaving everyone else in the dust?"

Kennedy nodded. "That's a good point, I'll concede. But we still need to look into that and confirm whether or not those mercs who had a map actually had access to the software before we decide. Anyway, that aside, maybe Anderson could be the person who puts us in contact with people whom we can trust enough to hire for the team later on. Again, the guy probably has all kinds of connections. With his referrals, we could fill the ranks in no time."

"You really want to work with him, don't you?" He grinned and arranged the last of the pieces in his pack. "Should I be jealous? Well, no, not jealous, but should we plan a schedule or something?"

"Shut it, asshole." She punched him lightly on the shoulder—or probably meant it to be light, anyway. Hopefully. Either way, it made him stagger before he recovered his balance.

"You do seem to want to work with him an awful lot," he insisted in a more serious tone.

"Again, the man has all kinds of connections." She shrugged as if the benefits were self-evident. "You read his file. Black ops all over the world, working in the Pentagon, dealing with all the high-level stuff like defense contracts and the like. He's connected almost everywhere. To have him owe us a favor like this has to be the kind of advantage we shouldn't waste. It's a game-changer. We've done freelance work all this time, but we know the real money comes from the...I hate to say it, but the government contracts."

"Fair enough." He had more jokes to make about the situation but had to push them aside when his HUD alerted him that someone had attempted to communicate on the open frequency. People used this regularly to call for help but it was often compromised by the heavy interference caused by the Zoo. Sometimes, they were extremely clear and at others, barely decipherable even if contact was initiated.

Usually, though, reasonable comms could be established within a limited range, which meant that whoever it was, they were fairly close to the Heavy Metal team

"It's a distress call," Kennedy said and glanced at her partner. "They've offered a reward to anyone who shows up to help."

"We have what we came here for," Sal pointed out, "and more besides. I don't think anyone would blame us if we simply walked away."

They exchanged meaningful glances in the short silence that followed. It was a great fantasy that they might one day be able to put their own survival first, but they both knew they wouldn't leave the call for help unattended.

"Three klicks to the west," he said finally. "Let's get going."

"Look at that," she cooed with a grin. "We offer to help and get the notice for payment. All brownie points today!"

CHAPTER EIGHT

The duo didn't need to get too close to know that the call for help would result in an absolute clusterfuck. They could hear it a full klick away. Angry animals shrieked and roared above the gunfire that peppered the morning. Sal shifted his weapon into position and threw Kennedy a hasty look as they picked up their pace.

"What do you think?" she asked. "They killed a big dino thing or plucked a Pita plant?"

"It doesn't always take one of those to whip our hostile friends around here into a frenzy," he pointed out. "Sometimes, the sound of gunfire is enough to draw them close and the smell of blood and watching humans gun them down triggers aggression. That said, my money is on a Pita plant. Someone got greedy and decided to try it and is now trying to dig themselves out of that particular hole."

"Yeah, same here," she agreed, immediately alert as two hyenas launched out of the underbrush. The animals barely noticed the humans before they were gunned down with quick, precise shots from both Sal and Kennedy.

"That's how you do it," he stated briskly as they proceeded to wade into the thick of it and eliminate those animals that seemed to be otherwise distracted by their attack on the other party. "Get your point across with a couple of bodies and always keep moving. These guys probably saw what was coming and tried to set up defensive positions. They'll be picked off one by one until they realize the animals in the Zoo outnumber them by a factor of thousands and try to run, but it'll be too late."

"You're preaching to your own choir here, Jacobs."

The partners assumed their usual formation with her at the front to bulldoze their momentum forward with her superior armor and firepower. As always, he provided support from the back and picked off the few animals that could attack them from range like the acid-spitting lizards or those that tried to outflank them. Neither was an easy task, but they had grown accustomed to a pattern that worked well for them.

"Key mic," Kennedy advised and added her own comm-link to the emergency line. "Alpha team Forty-Seven, this is Heavy Metal One, do you copy?"

"How come you get to be Heavy Metal One?" Sal asked in exasperation.

"Heavy Metal One is our team's designation, dumbass," she retorted. "But since I'm the gunner and will be the one they see first, I'll always be one and you'll be two."

"That sounds like bullshit," he muttered and obliterated a couple of locusts with scorpion tails. These didn't have any fur and definitely had stingers they seemed determined to use. More to the point, they had tried to ride the coattails of a group of hyenas that charged in an effort to flank them. The creatures all met his barrage of bullets instead.

"Do you want to take point here?" she asked as she waited for her armor to reload the rifle in her hand.

"Nope."

"Then shut up, Heavy Metal Two." Her grin was pure mischief.

"Oh…eat a dick."

"I thought we'd decided to save that for when we get back to base." Kennedy paused as the emergency comm line came on in response to her message.

"We read you, Heavy Metal One." The man's voice wavered a little with the static. "We have trouble here and could really use your support. But if it's only two of you, there might be a limit to how much help you can be."

"What do you mean?" she asked and sounded annoyed.

"Well," he explained, clearly uncertain about what he tried to say, "two teams have already responded to our distress signal and there have been enormous casualties. Of course, any help will be gratefully accepted, but I'm not sure how much two people can do in the middle of this."

"Can you believe this guy?" Sal asked. She nodded in agreement, then shook her head to indicate that now was not the time to talk about it and activated her commlink again.

"Well, we'll head in your direction and eliminate the animals we run into," she informed him and managed to keep her annoyance to herself. "The heading is roughly… south, southwest, so if you could avoid shooting us when we get in close, we'd appreciate it."

"Understood," the man said and sounded harried. "Good luck, Heavy Metal."

"He's not sure how much two people can do?" Kennedy all but hissed as she killed the connection. "Come on, Jacobs, let's give this fucker a lesson in exactly how useful two people can be in this kind of situation."

"I'm right behind you, Kennedy," he replied, a little stirred up by the lack of confidence as well. It was a shame these rifles didn't have a cocking action that you could pull before firing. No, the chambering of rounds—even when a new magazine was put in—was all automatic. Of course, it was a good thing given that the time saved could actually mean the difference between life and death, but it lacked the dramatic quality of being able to end a sentence like that with the satisfying click-clack of a weapon ready to serve death and mayhem.

They moved cautiously forward again and took advantage of the fact that the animals they encountered seemed distracted by the other men. After a relatively easy running skirmish, they cleared a path all the way to the besieged group and made sure to announce themselves as they entered the small area cleared of all underbrush to provide a clean line of fire.

"Defensive positions," Sal said with a shake of his head. "What did I say?"

"Yeah, I know," she responded and kept their conversation on a private channel for the moment. "But you have to understand that almost everything military people were taught relies on holding and maintaining a position of strength when encountering superior numbers. You'll see almost everyone—except for the special forces people—doing exactly this."

"And getting shredded as a result," he muttered quietly before he took their conversation to open comms when he noticed one of the men break away from the formation to approach them. They'd formed a circle around a small hill which gave them a clear view of the death on legs—and wings—that was inevitable once the animals decided their reprieve had lasted long enough. Five wounded members lay in the center of the circle with no one to assist them. At that point, everyone who could aim a gun helped to hold the line.

"Heavy Metal, I presume?" the man asked. "I'm Lieutenant Alberts, the highest-ranking officer here."

"A pleasure, Lieutenant," Kennedy replied. "I'm Kennedy, and this is my associate Jacobs. We're Heavy Metal. What's the situation here? What are your casualties and why aren't you guys heading out of the damn Zoo right now?"

"I—" The lieutenant started to speak, obviously accustomed to obeying orders when they were voiced in that tone, but quickly remembered that he was supposed to be the person in command. "Look, I'm the officer in charge of this mission and if you join us, you'll need to obey my instructions at all times."

"I'm not here to measure dicks with you, Lieutenant." She opened a private comm line that included only her, Sal, and the man in charge. "That said, to stay here and wait for the animals to continue their attack will merely condemn your squad to a long, drawn-out death. It's time to change that."

The man didn't answer for a moment, and Sal realized that he had taken control of a situation that was well beyond his capabilities and simply did the best he could with what he had. He felt bad for the man but the soldier quickly realized that he now talked to someone who was not only a good deal more experienced in this kind of situation than he was but was also willing to move them out without completely emasculating him in the process.

"What do you suggest, Kennedy?" the lieutenant asked in a soft voice.

"Get your men to form up in double file," Kennedy said. "Sandwich the wounded and those helping them in the middle and keep moving. Where are your extraction vehicles stationed?"

"About…ten klicks southeast," the man replied.

"Okay, get them moving." She closed the private line and moved away to scout the perimeter. Sal followed her.

"That was a classy move on your part," he said as the lieutenant shouted orders. "I can't say I would help the man keep his dignity in front of his soldiers after he doubted us like that."

Kennedy shrugged. "Satisfying a grudge isn't worth getting everyone here killed. Besides, it doesn't seem like he meant any harm by what he said. He's a newbie. This is probably his first time dealing with a situation like this, so there's no real need to lay into him. He'll learn his lesson and maybe next time, he'll make the right decisions and get his team out without needing to pay us for the trouble."

"Aren't you feeling optimistic today?" he teased as the men formed up and began the retreat toward their vehicles.

She grinned and shrugged, retrieved a couple of smoke grenades from her pouch, and handed him one. "I'm a regular Mother Teresa out here. If she made her living gunning down alien animals for profit, that is."

"I have to say I'd watch that movie," Sal said as they pulled the pins on the grenades. The animals noticed that the group had begun a hasty retreat and gathered quickly to push toward them again. The duo acted within seconds of one another. His grenade arced out to the little hill where the group had previously taken a stand and where it would hopefully cover their tracks, while Kennedy waited for barely a second and dropped hers at her feet.

The air was almost instantly filled with a heavy white fog of smoke and they pushed on as rapidly as they could. The Heavy Metal team took position at the back of the line to protect the flanks and gunned down any of the creatures that tried to attack them from behind.

"So, Lieutenant," Kennedy said and opened a line to the man whom she could only see through her motion sensors, "you never did get around to telling me about the casualty situation. Or how you guys were caught up in here in the first place."

"Right," he said and it sounded like he helped to carry one of the wounded men. "We started out as a team of seven on a standard run looking for the Pita flowers. A couple of panthers attacked, and we had two men dead and another wounded before we were able to kill them. We stuck around and tried to get our bearings, but they continued to come in waves. At that point, we sent out the distress call, and a couple of other teams in the area tried to help us. They took heavy losses too."

"Give me a headcount," she demanded.

"All three teams?" The man took a moment to gather himself. "We had twenty-five total, all stated."

She looked around and made a quick headcount. There were thirteen left, plus the five wounded.

"Shit," Sal muttered and sounded almost awed. "And they say we have a body count."

"Let it go, Jacobs," she cautioned. The animals attacked in a constant ebb and flow now, which forced the two of them to walk backward to retreat with the rest of the team and keep the rear and flanks covered. The Zoo beasts took heavy losses, but a seemingly endless tide swept in and around them. They were a mixed assault too—locusts, hyenas, and many other insect-like creatures. A couple of the panthers used the advantage of their ability to stay in the trees and swooped down for an easy kill whenever they sensed a weakness in the line.

It was difficult to shoot them as they descended, but the precision of their strikes made it a kill or be killed situation. Sal found himself on the former side of that logic five times out of five jumpers.

He couldn't help but remember the first time he'd trudged out of the jungle. Back then, he'd been fitted with one of the useless government-issued specialist suits with no weapons other than what he'd scrounged from the dead. Worse, he'd carried a pack almost as heavy as he was —that was how it had felt, anyway—as he ran for his life. He'd been sore for days afterward and while still in the Zoo, spent the whole time wondering exactly how he would survive.

That raw focus and a sheer need to live despite everything had never returned in all his future visits. While that was a good thing, a small part of him wondered if he would ever be faced with those kinds of odds again.

Sal shook his head and brought his mind back to the moment. He was surprised that he'd had the chance to wander off like that, all things considered. The constant gunfire had been replaced with the sound of people who forgot to turn their sound filters off and panted like they'd jogged through a jungle in half a ton of combat armor. He realized the animals had backed off from their relentless assault, and people now slowed in response.

"No, no, no, bad idea," he admonished them as he checked his rifle and scanned the trees around them. "We can't slow down. They'll come back, you can count on it. The scent of blood is on us and they won't let up until we're out of their territory—or dead. We have to keep moving."

One of the soldiers looked at him and scowled deeply. Sal realized there was a break in his armor and he was limping. It didn't look like anything had penetrated the heavy plates, but physics dictated that any impact absorbed by the metal had to go somewhere. Something had crashed into the man's leg and left him with what could be a career-ending injury if he pushed himself like this.

"Come on," he said and drew the man's arm around his shoulder to help him keep his weight off what he believed was a broken leg.

"I'm fine," the soldier protested softly but seemed grateful for the help.

"I know," Sal replied with a small smile and focused on

the treetops. "This is only for my own peace of mind, believe me."

"You wouldn't need it if these motherfuckers hadn't plucked a fucking Pita plant," the soldier confessed as they moved on. Kennedy pushed them at a good pace, even if they had slowed a little.

"You're one of the rescue team?"

"Oh, yeah." The man nodded. "Corporal Brian Telser at your service. We were doing a security patrol in this area and moved within range when the message came in. Of course, we responded and arrived in time to save their asses, but at a heavy cost. These fucking first-timers don't know what the hell they're doing out here."

"How do you know that they plucked a plant?" he asked.

"They denied it, of course," the soldier said with a shrug. "But why else would the animals attack them this relentlessly? And why else would they offer a cash reward to help them get out of this?"

"I'd say they have a big take and didn't want to risk it," he responded but kept his voice down. "But plucking a Pita plant? Nah. I survived a couple of those. It's like the whole jungle suddenly decides to go to war with you. Even the trees. We wouldn't have any respite at all if that was what happened, and the longer it took to kill us, the bigger and meaner the animals would get."

"Why are the fucking things chasing us, then?" Telser asked.

"Sometimes, shit simply goes bad. The hyenas are a real problem since they travel in packs, but animals respond first to the sound of gunfire, and the smell of blood riles them even more. You have to stay on the move at all times or they'll find you, and eventually, more and more will come until you get out or they finish you off. That's how the Zoo treats people out here."

"So you don't think they have a Pita plant in their possession?"

"It's not impossible," Sal responded thoughtfully. "It's not like this place abides by anything resembling rules, but from my experience, I'd say it's highly doubtful. You'll still be paid, though."

"Thanks," Telser said with a chuckle. "What's your name again?"

"Sal Jacobs. No rank. Freelancer. Nice to meet you."

"Right back at you, Jacobs."

After what seemed an endless running battle exacerbated by both the mutants' constant harassment and the condition of the wounded, they finally reached the outskirts of the Zoo. Although the vegetation had thinned noticeably and patches of the desert sand could be seen not too much farther ahead, the group came to a halt at the lieutenant's command and everyone paused gratefully for a rest.

"We're close enough to being out of the Zoo that I managed to make contact with our people guarding the Hammerheads and they're on their way in to pick us up," Alberts said. "Fortunately, the vehicles can at least make it this far without issues." He sounded calmer than he had been earlier and much more confident. The sentiment seemed to be shared by the rest of the men in the teams, who looked around with expressions of dawning relief.

Their eyes all told the same story as they immediately set up a defensive perimeter once again.

They might get out of this after all.

"I don't like this," Kennedy said. She shook her head as she walked to where Sal stood guard. The footsteps of her heavy armor made the ground shake slightly with each step. "To sit here and wait for the fuckers to come and attack us gets on my nerves. We know there's nothing they would like more than to kill every one of us."

"The animals aren't what I'm worried about," he said softly, his gaze fastened on the trees once more. "Something is up there tracking us. It's not an animal but has moved consistently with us. If I had to hazard a guess, I'd say it was those damned tentacle vine things, but...I can't think of a reason why it hasn't attacked us yet."

Her gaze shifted to the trees that towered over the little group. She remembered those tentacles very well. The thought that something that wasn't an animal or anything like it was out there and could track them was entirely unnerving. It meant the very trees could be determined to annihilate them too. Any tree could kill them, and they were in the middle of a fucking jungle.

"And you still have no idea where they come from?" she asked. "There's no sign of a source for them?"

Sal shook his head. "There's still too much we don't know about this place, and with the way it constantly changes, that could be the case for however long we stick around here. Despite the millions poured into research, we have no idea where these trees and bushes obtain sustenance, and no one can make out the psychology of the animals either."

"It's like the Zoo is running its own experiments," Kennedy said softly. "And no one knows why."

"Right. Ever since the start of all this, people have tried to visit ground zero—where they first implanted the soil with the goop. Only two of them survived as far as I know, and they downloaded Dr. Marie's research, which was later made available. It was detailed in that it recorded their progress but provided no indication of anything from the Zoo perspective.

"That, I assume, is because the Zoo itself only spawned with the Day of the Locust when all the researchers were killed so it makes sense that they would have no information on the origins of the jungle and what drives it. Still, if I were to hazard a guess regarding somewhere that might have answers for us, I'd say the heart or epicenter would be the place to go."

"It sounds like a suicide mission," she retorted as the familiar and welcome growl of Hammerheads headed their way.

"Or a career-making mission," he replied, "for someone like me. To see and document what's happening to the areas that have been exposed to the goop for the longest would make my name legendary in the academic community—and yours too. If that doesn't interest you, maybe the amount of money people would be willing to pay for that documentation should. You could buy an island, make it your own country, and become a petty dictator."

Kennedy smirked. "Don't think I haven't considered it."

"Well, it's food for thought," Sal said as the Hammerheads came into view. "If we ever want to talk about a job to end all jobs—one way or another."

They stopped talking when the lieutenant approached.

"We really appreciate your support out here," Alberts said with a firm nod. "I don't think we would have made it without the two of you."

She nodded. "We try to help humans in the Zoo as much as we can. We would have done it for free, but don't think we won't charge you guys for the assist."

"No worries. I've already transmitted the currency exchange files for you to sign," he asserted with a grin. "You turn them in to the commandant's office for your paycheck. That aside, do you guys need a ride out of here?"

"We have a Hammerhead of our own parked just outside the Zoo's confines," Sal said. "We wouldn't say no to a quick ride over there. It shouldn't be more than an hour out of your way."

"We're happy to help," Alberts said and gestured for them to clamber aboard the vehicle.

CHAPTER NINE

A ndressa had been right, of course. They had been too chickenshit to fire her outright. It was a simple fact that she knew too much for them to simply let her go. They also knew her too well to think she would take that shit lying down. What she knew could be used to hurt them, either legally or economically, and they couldn't have that.

The members of the board all had names that spanned centuries of old money in the US, and they'd done so by carefully keeping their names in the shadows. Any company they affiliated with would be closed down, either through investigation or the simple act of being outsmarted by any of the hundreds of companies that would get on their hands and knees to help them out. It was simple economics. Anything that would hurt their market shares was bad news.

She was off the board, admittedly, but she didn't really mind. It was all political ass-wiping anyway, and her time was better spent elsewhere. She'd been given a meaningless title and a corner office and basically told to stay quiet and treat her time there as an early retirement. No one cared how late she came in—or if she came in at all—as long as she spent the last few years of her tenure at the company without causing anyone any trouble.

It was like they didn't know her at all, she mused, and sat at her desk. The office was pleasant, though. The view over LA was something she knew people would murder for, and the fact that she had a seven-figure annual salary plus benefits and full retirement guaranteed was supremely appealing. She could enjoy her life now and even take up a hobby—maybe writing self-help books that would get her on book tours or cameos in TV shows. The world was her oyster.

That was what people thought Covington would do, anyway. It was what anyone in their right mind would do in her circumstances.

It wasn't entirely personal, Andressa thought to herself. There had been a reason why Carlson had insinuated her into this company. He wanted any and all studies made into the Zoo to be connected to him. Unfortunately, with Little Miss Heiress' stunt, she was left with no other alternative than to use brute force measures to shift things so they went her way again.

Monroe had ended up being more complicated to deal with than previously anticipated. That wasn't much of a problem in itself. She could handle police investigations, litigations, and all kinds of legal problems with a wave of her metaphorical magic wand. It was when the woman had decided to take things into her own hands that things became difficult.

First, she had gunned down the useless goons sent to kill her as if she'd done something like that before. After that, she'd refused to press charges or even cooperate in the police investigation. Finally, she'd broken into Andressa's home and left a cow's head there as a warning—in her bed, for fuck's sake—while she'd slept through it. All the while, she'd used her newfound clout to push Covington out of the position on the board that she had spent so many years cultivating.

So yes, it was a little personal. Under any other circumstances, she would have admired the sheer mass of Courtney Monroe's balls in taking on something like that. She was right. The Zoo changed people.

In actual fact, Andressa felt a little cowed by the woman's presence—a little insecure about her own standing, which was both unusual and uncomfortable. And more than a little scared for her own life. Everything she did now was simply a response to that.

Huh. What a psychological breakthrough. Her therapist would be proud.

It didn't change the fact that when business and personal life mixed, a mess was bound to ensue. Andressa didn't care. She merely wanted Monroe out of her life for good, one way or another.

Her gaze turned to the lovely oak desk as the phone rang. She could have sworn she'd told her assistant to filter all calls.

"What?" she snarled into the receiver.

"There's a Rodrigo on the line for you," her assistant said and kept her voice low and soft. "You said to put his call through if you remember?"

"Of course I remember," she said irritably. "And make sure we're not interrupted."

"Of course, ma'am."

"Andressa Covington," said a deep voice with a vaguely Mediterranean accent. "I've been told by serious people that you're someone to take seriously. How can I help you?"

"Rodrigo, I presume?" She smiled but without real mirth. "My guess is there won't be a last name with that."

"You guess correctly on both counts," he replied. "A mutual friend tells me you have need of my assistance. It is out of courtesy to him that I make this call and assign you only friends and family price packages."

"Of course." She tried not to roll her eyes. "There's someone I need handled. The woman herself is in the US and in such a position that I can't have her disappear just yet. But she has friends in the Zoo I'd like handled as quickly as possible. A freelancing team called Heavy Metal."

"I'm familiar with the name," the man said smoothly. "And you should know I've been put on their case already, with less than pristine results. Of course, I had to act indirectly at the time. I could be convinced to act directly, but it would cost a substantial amount more than my usual fee."

She rolled her eyes this time. While she'd known this was coming, she hadn't particularly looked forward to it.

"What's your fee on this?"

"Fifteen million euros, paid in the usual manner," Rodrigo replied after a few seconds spent in calculation.

"You are fucking with me right now." Her eyebrows

raised in shock at the figure. "Are you high? That's the cost to kill a sitting senator."

"I have never touched drugs in my life," her contact said and she could hear a smile in his voice. "What I do know is that you tried to have a member of Heavy Metal killed using local talent and they mostly died in the attempt. She was the scientist of the group, and from what I've seen and heard, by far the inferior member of the Heavy Metal team when it comes to combat. These friends you want me to kill are much more competent and able to defend them- selves against attack. Fifteen million euros, non- negotiable."

"Fine." Andressa sighed and shook her head. "But you won't get a fucking dime until I have one or both heads. And yes, there's more money in it for you if you send me both."

"Perfect. I'll send you the bill when the job is done. Do you have any preference for how it should be carried out?"

"I honestly couldn't care less," Andressa snapped. "I merely want their heads shipped to me on ice, do you understand?"

"Understood." There was a short pause before he said crisply, "I'll call you again."

The line went dead, and she replaced the phone in the cradle and stared at the gold-inlaid mother of pearl for a few long seconds. She didn't remember where she'd gotten the damn thing. A garage sale somewhere in Pensacola or something like that, where old people had sold their family treasures for peanuts. She assumed she'd bought it with her first real paycheck when she was sixteen but she had been so wasted at the time she didn't remember. Despite that, she still kept it around. Weird.

She looked at the screen of her dead laptop which reflected her own face at her.

"You'll get that IP," she declared unequivocally. "You killed the father and now, you'll kill the daughter and take what's owed to you."

With that, she pushed from her chair. Business for the day was concluded, so she might as well take an early lunch. She could still bill the company for it.

Madigan stepped out of the Hammerhead and blinked as the glare of the sun on the sand reflected at her. Irritated, she recalled that she'd forgotten her sunglasses on Sal's bedside table. The memory of the night was still a little fuzzy, but she did remember that it'd been fun.

That wouldn't happen tonight, though, she mused as she slammed the door shut and locked it. He had stayed behind to run inventory on all the upgrades they'd made to the compound security. Unfortunately, there had been issues with their supplies for the week, and she needed to come to the base and shout it out with the people in charge of supply management.

Normally, she wouldn't have bothered, but Heavy Metal paid these fuckers a ton of money every month to keep their place stocked with food, ammo, and all the other things needed for long-term living in a compound out in the middle of the desert. At least they didn't have to rely on diesel generators. Solar and wind energy were enough to run virtually everything and have some left over besides to sell to the base. It had been clever thinking on the part of the people who had built it.

That said, the delivery of coffee had short-supplied, and that shit could not be allowed to stand. Every single member of the group ran on a combination of coffee and sleep, and if the former ran out, blood would definitely flow. Madigan would not be responsible for her actions.

And she wouldn't have to be, after all. She straightened the situation out, collected the check from the commandant's office for helping the squad to escape the Zoo, and suddenly realized that she had nothing else to do for the afternoon. If she returned to the compound, she would simply be roped into doing more work. Amanda still tried to determine how to tie a security system with guns on it to an AI and, for some reason, continued to dig the whole place up in an attempt to make it work.

Madigan wanted nothing to do with that. Give the AI a gun and soon, it would wonder why it followed a puny human's orders anyway. And that was how it would all start and end.

Maybe Sal was right, she realized as she pushed the doors of the bar open and sighed contentedly when she was greeted by the pleasant air-conditioned darkness of the venue. Watching the *Terminator* movies at such a young age had fucked her thought process the hell up, at least when it came to robots. It didn't mean she was wrong to fear them, though. She would take some plain old human error over the creepy Hailey-1000 in there.

As she dropped into one of the few unused booths, she realized there was a commotion at the bar. She scowled.

That meant it would be a while before she could expect one of the waitresses to reach her. She'd come to drink, dammit, not wait around while some dumbasses played a drinking game.

She stood, strode to the bar, and eased through the crowd until she saw three rows of shot glasses spread across the bar top. Two of the bartenders took their time to fill each one carefully with crystal-clear vodka.

A quick count confirmed that there were twenty-one glasses in each of the rows. That seemed like an oddly specific number and sounded familiar when she considered it.

"Okay," the bartender said when the glasses were full, "the rules of the game are that you have to at least tie the bar record. There's no throwing in the towel, no eating, and no more than a minute between shots. If you walk away, you lose. The last man standing doesn't have to pay the bill. Got it?"

Three men—large, powerful-looking soldiers Madigan didn't recognize—nodded firmly. They looked as if they'd prepared themselves for exactly this event. In all probability, they'd stocked up on carbs all day.

It was an idiotic thing to think of but at least, with people guzzling this much vodka, she didn't have to worry about the demand for what they brought in from the Russian base drying up. It had been something of a hit among the various patrons, and while it wasn't their main moneymaker these days, it was at least nice to have some pocket cash from this. The real bonus, however, was that it solidified their connection with the people in the base even after they'd moved out.

She smiled and leaned on the bar as she watched the three men take their first glasses, and with a roar of confidence, down them in a single gulp.

Their assurance had noticeably flagged by the time they were about halfway down the line and all of them struggled to stay on their feet. She could stand against virtually anyone in a drinking contest and had been known to drink men almost twice her size under the table in her day. But she'd tried to get a grip on her drinking over the past couple of months. She had more responsibilities now as a founding member of a surprisingly successful freelancing start-up. The days were long gone when she could spend her days nursing a bottle.

Back on topic, though, she'd seen Sal this hammered but by then, he'd reached twenty-one shots. As the idiots plowed on with real determination, they reached levels of intoxication that would have them sent home in a cab from any bar in the States. But this was the Zoo, where people intentionally put their lives on the line for money. As long as they coughed the money up, the bartenders simply continued to pour.

The first man caved to the inevitable at twelve. He didn't drink that one as he dropped the glass onto the floor. Amidst shouts of encouragement, he bent to pick it up again and simply didn't come up.

"Lightweight!" Various bar patrons jeered and the other two contestants stared vaguely at one another as they swayed in place. They had a hard time even with such simple concepts as gravity by this point. Still, they persevered with little apparent concern for the damage they did to their livers. The shots left by the first man were handed out free to whichever patrons snatched them first and would still be charged to the losers of the bet. That was merely how these things played out.

By the time the diehards reached seventeen, Madigan felt rather impressed. These men were solid drinkers, and she doubted she could match them. Thankfully, hers wasn't the record to beat. She still wasn't sure how taking daily doses of blue goop from a flower helped someone drink more without getting drunk. Admittedly, Sal had explained it to her. It had something to do with improving the liver's ability to metabolize the alcohol, which simply meant it constantly filtered the stuff out, even while you continued to drink it.

There were limits, of course. He had been drunk himself that night and woken up as hungover as the rest of them. Still, it was impressive. People had died of alcohol poisoning after drinking twenty-one shots. All he'd faced was dehydration and a headache.

Seventeen shots were downed, and the two men teetered and swayed alarmingly. One fumbled to grab a glass and raised it for everyone to see.

"Ain't...nothing but a...peesh of...pie..." he declared in an odd, disjointed toast, but his eyes rolled to the back of his head as he toppled back and spilled the shot on the dusty floor to more jeers from the crowd.

"Middleweight!" they called, delighted, as the bartender turned to the last man standing.

"It's up to you now, Hardy," he said. "Will you let a scientist geek outdrink you?"

"Hell...naw," Hardy replied and quickly tossed his eigh-teenth down the hatch. He made to follow with number nineteen too, although his movements were slow and disjointed, but as he raised it to his mouth, his hold slipped. Most of the vodka sloshed down his chest and neck before it even reached his mouth and he ended up with less than a quarter of the shot left to drink.

"Well, I'm sad to say, that doesn't count as a shot," the bartender said with a grin. He clearly enjoyed the entire spectacle. "And since it's been more than a minute since your last one, I'm afraid I'll have to call it here, folks. Eighteen and a half is very impressive but unfortunately, no cigar."

"You have cigars?" the man asked and stared at the bartender with a dumb expression on his face.

"Get yourself home, Hardy. You've done a man's work in here today," the other man said and slapped Hardy on the back.

He nodded and shuffled away from the bar. He was the last man standing and the bill would be paid out of the pockets of the two men who currently slept it off on the floor. Kennedy smirked and shook her head as she moved away and managed to easily avoid the drunk as he missed the door a couple of times. The rest of the patrons had already gone back to their drinks, disappointed that no one could break Sal's record.

Hardy missed the door yet again and instead, crashed into the wall. A big fellow, he made enough of an impact to knock some of the pictures off, one of which landed on him. He didn't seem to feel it, though, as he'd already passed out to sleep it off like his defeated comrades.

The bartender chuckled and turned to the remaining shot glasses that were passed around to the rest of the patrons. He saw Madigan and joined her as she took one of the offered glasses.

"Well, your boytoy holds the record around here for another day," he said with a wide grin. "I still can't believe a guy like him holds anything like that in a bar so heavily frequented by soldiers. You'd think one or two of them would have enough of a habit to be able to beat that, right?"

"I don't know, James," she responded and paused to snatch another of the leftover shot glasses and down it expertly. Damn, if that wasn't some fine vodka. "Sal has all kinds of ways to surprise us."

"No questions about that," he replied with a laugh. "So, what can I get you? It's been a while since you've frequented our little establishment."

"Sorry, James." She stood with a smirk. "I've just realized that I need to satisfy another urge—one that has less to do with drinking myself into an early grave. I'll see you around."

Two shots weren't enough to get her drunk and Amanda would be proud of the fact that she kept the Hammerhead at a reasonable speed all the way back to the Heavy Metal compound. It meant extending the length of the trip by about an hour and a half, but it wasn't really something she would complain about. She wasn't a fan of delaying gratification, but it wasn't a bad thing either.

By the time she got back, the place was deserted as everyone had already turned in for the night. Well, except Anja who cursed softly in Russian, still hard at work in the server room. The woman was dedicated, Madigan had to give her that, and any other night, she might have gone to see if she needed company. Not tonight, though.

She made her way to Sal's room and slipped inside without a sound. The guy made it a point to trust his people and left his door unlocked, even when he was sleeping. It wasn't as stupid as one might think, given that everything important, including his laptop, was locked away in an airtight safe every night.

He was trusting, not stupid.

Madigan eased out of her shirt and pants to leave only her panties and bra on before she slid into bed with him. He'd gone to sleep immediately after his shower, as evidenced by the fact that he wore nothing but a towel as he lay on his bed. She took a moment to enjoy the sight of him. He had put on an impressive amount of muscle during his stay in the Zoo and was on the verge of becoming something of a beefcake. It was a lean kind of muscle but she didn't much care for body-builder types—something else she could lay at the feet of a certain Austrian android.

She nudged him gently on the shoulder, and when he failed to wake, she grasped the same shoulder and shook him until he spluttered. His eyes opened and he looked around to find the source of his discomfort until his gaze settled on her.

"Madigan," he murmured and rubbed his eyes. "What time is it?"

"Half past nine, you old fart," she said with a giggle and leaned in to press a kiss to his chest. "Why are you in bed so early anyway?"

"It was a long day, what with helping Amanda dig the fucking place up," Sal replied. He smiled as he moved his hands to run them through her hair. "What are you doing in my bed so early?"

"I need those five Os you promised me," she said and slid over him to straddle his waist. "Do you feel up for it? Pun intended."

"I think I do." The drowsiness of the newly awoken began to fade as his hands settled on her waist and her hips ground over him. "It looks like morning wood has come earlier than expected tonight."

"I'll make sure to treat it well," she promised, her tone a little husky. "Does it take milk and cookies, like Santa?"

"That's a weird topic to bring up when you're trying to talk a sleepy man into sex," he said with a mock-serious expression. "But I'll allow it."

She grinned, undid her bra, and let it fall onto his stomach as she leaned over him to enjoy the simple pleasure of having someone whom she trusted and liked this close to her. He hummed appreciatively when she pressed a firm, delicious kiss to his lips.

CHAPTER TEN

Anderson rubbed his temples and dragged himself out of the miserable cot he'd called a bed for the past few months. He shuffled to the bathroom and his jaw felt like it would split as a massive yawn overtook him. It had been a long time since he'd woken with a hangover. There had been times, especially early in his boot camp days, where he'd ended up drinking more than enough to make anyone think about their problematic life choices. At this point in his life, however, he did that anyway. He might as well add alcohol to the mix to help dull everything for a few hours.

Was it worth feeling and looking like shit? It was a thought that greeted him abruptly as he stood in front of the mirror and filled a small plastic cup with water. He hated his job, so there wasn't much to worry about regarding his looks. That aside, he already had enough problems to deal with and drinking would only make them worse.

"Never...again," Anderson promised himself as he

opened the mirror door, withdrew a couple of pill bottles from inside, and popped them open. His hand shook a little as he tipped one of each onto his hand before he closed the containers and replaced them in the cabinet. He leaned his head back, tossed both into his mouth, and washed them down with the water.

It occurred to him that he didn't believe the affirmation he'd spoken. They said recovering addicts needed a support structure if they were to make it through recovery, and he had nothing like that out in the middle of the fucking Sahara Desert. He would get back on track with his goals when he got home. Perhaps he could find a sponsor and a therapist and see about adding vigor to his treatment, maybe take some time off work to focus solely on getting better.

When he got back home. As of right now, he needed as much help as he could get to cope with his day to day struggle. And it would be worse from there on out. He'd received the message last night. That had been what prompted him to crack open the bottle of scotch he'd bought on his last time at the bar, and...yes, there it was, empty in the trash. He didn't remember much about the night before, but he knew he would, on occasion, get drunk enough to be aware of the problems he faced. At other times, he would simply dump the rest of the liquor down the drain as a promise to himself.

One way or another, he wouldn't have much access to alcohol for the next few weeks. If that wasn't a support structure, he didn't know what was.

He dragged his errant thoughts back to reality—in this case, the message that pushed him to drink in the first place. It had been something of a surprise—the timing rather than the inevitability of it. He knew it was coming. It was merely a question of when.

The message had read, *New testing green-lit. Operators and engineers returning to base tomorrow to start testing new suits.*

Tomorrow was now today, unfortunately, and he was hungover and felt like shit at the start of it. At least that would cover how he would feel as the testing proceeded.

He smirked and shook his head as he moved into his room to pull on a clean uniform his assistant had left out for him while he was passed out. With a smile at his own foolishness, he completed every small task as slowly as he could in an effort to delay the moment when he would have to leave the cool comforts of his tiny little room.

The colonel stepped outside and shielded his eyes against the glare. This early in the morning, it was still way too bright to be comfortable, even if he wasn't hungover. The wall construction had moved past them and left their little section sandwiched between Walls One and Two and completely isolated from the rest of the world, which made it ideal for the black ops and illegal testing of new equipment.

The one advantage of having a base directly beside a massive fifty-foot wall was that it provided some outdoor shade to hide them from the horrors that would come when the sun began its inexorable climb and slow-baked everything.

Anderson made his way quickly to the shady part of the base as his assistant—a new one whom he still couldn't put a name to—hurried over to him.

"Good morning, sir," the young lieutenant said and proffered a mug of steaming coffee.

"Morning, Lieutenant," he responded. Working for the military meant one didn't need to remember names if you could read insignias. There were, after all, some small mercies.

"The first load of suits has arrived on schedule, along with the rest of the engineers," the younger man said and fell smoothly into step beside him.

Another twenty paces and then shade. Keep it together, Anderson.

"How do the troops look?" he asked, mainly because he lacked anything else to say.

"They're excited to be back at work, sir," the man stated cheerfully and sounded rather glad to be back on duty as well. "Vacations are nice, but when you love your job, there's not much that'll keep you away from it."

If only. Fortunately, Anderson had the good sense not to say it aloud.

"Colonel Anderson," a familiar voice called. He turned quickly and paused as the scientist strode over to him.

"Dr. Bial, nice to see you again." He offered the first genuine smile he'd felt in weeks. "Nice to have you back." Bial was one of the only men assigned to this damned base that Anderson liked talking to. It was odd, since he usually only felt that kind of bond with military men. Still, with as long as they had worked together, Anderson was more than willing to give the man that honorary title.

"It's good to be back," the scientist said with a chuckle as they both settled under the shade of the wall. "Too much time spent away from our little project has only helped me feel more and more anxious to get back to it. How have things been around here?"

"Quiet," he replied honestly. It had essentially been a ghost town while everyone had been gone. Amazingly, that hadn't made anything better—not for him, anyway. Still, it had given him time to plot and work against his current employers.

"So," the colonel said after a sip of his coffee, "what is it about this armor that has people running in three weeks early to set it up for combat?"

"Well, they finished the design and built the proto-types," Bial said, clearly happy to be in a place and with people whom he could talk to about this without having all kinds of legal hell rain down on him. "They want the teams to wear and test a new type of armor."

Anderson narrowed his eyes and watched as the engineers set the various pieces up before they moved them to a storage location. "They look different. Sleeker designs, which look nice, but how does that make them more useful? This isn't Hollywood."

"Obviously," Bial said. He rolled his eyes and patted what looked like a small external hard drive that lay amongst the mess strewn on one of the tables. "Well, I've only looked at the specs a couple of times and I don't know all the details yet, but there's an exciting new IP in the metal that the company making the suits designed them-selves from their own research and development sections. The designs aren't perfect since the engineers in a lab can't really account for all the variables we'd see out here in the field. That's why I prefer to do my work out here."

"So you can nitpick the work of others once it's already

done?" the colonel asked and turned to look at the man with a small smirk.

"Quite," his companion replied and would have continued if a loud hiss hadn't interrupted him. They both looked to where the suits were being assembled. The engineers rushed away from a boot that flickered and jerked on the ground. After a few seconds, something ignited and what looked like a rocket fired, and the piece of armor catapulted away in the opposite direction. The engineers laughed as they raced after it.

"There will always be a few bugs." Bial shrugged. "If you'll excuse me, Colonel?"

"By all means," he said with a smile, and the scientist rushed off to join his colleagues in the mad scramble to retrieve the errant boot. Anderson, for his own part, looked furtively around. It wasn't difficult to see there weren't any cameras built into the base—the idea was complete discretion—and all eyes seemed to be focused on the recovery of the piece of tech that had flown away.

That left him alone with what looked like a pile of misplaced crap. He stepped up to the table and smoothly palmed and pocketed the external hard drive Bial had pointed out earlier. Of course, he'd return it once he'd taken a quick look to check if there was anything his new friends could use on it.

"What time is it?" Madigan asked. She rubbed her eyes as she and Sal were herded into the server room by their suddenly very enthusiastic IT expert. The Russian had crashed into Sal's room and tried to haul the two of them from the bed before she realized that they were both naked. After that, she showed a little restraint and gave them time to get dressed before she dragged them down to the dark room full of screens.

"I don't know," Anja replied honestly, dropped into her seat, and rolled the chair over to the screens. "Seven-thirty in the morning."

Sal resisted the urge to say, "Fuck all this," and head back to bed for another couple of hours. It had ended up being a longer night than he thought it would be, and since they hadn't scheduled any other trips into the Zoo until they heard from Anderson, he had hoped to be able to sleep in.

"I found some information I think the two of you should be aware of." She peered at them, her expression definitely on edge. "And since I need to get some sleep myself, I don't think it can wait until we all are nice and rested."

"Fine," Sal muttered and shook his head. "What's this important news?"

"I didn't make much headway in tracking the payments made to the mercenaries you killed in the Zoo," the hacker explained. "Well, nothing that we could have used, anyway. The leads on the metal exports led to similarly dead ends, so while I set some programs to dig into those, I decided to look into the problem Dr. Monroe sent us. You know, the woman who wants us dead—the one who was a part of the company her father owned?"

"Right." He sat on the spare seat beside her and Madigan remained standing. "What did you find?"

"Nothing at first," Anja said. "There wasn't much of anything to explain why this woman stole from the company, given that she has a large amount of her money sunk into its stocks. That was until I realized that the company had been tied up in litigation over the use of intellectual property—one Dr. Monroe pursued personally."

"Courtney was doing this?" Sal leaned in to see the dates involved. "She couldn't have been. She was right here when these things started."

"Not her," she corrected. "Dr. Monroe, the father. He was the one who said they were stealing from his company's work to inflate their stock prices. The rest of the company was willing to take a million-dollar settlement, but Dr. Monroe, with his control of the majority of the stock, made them continue the litigation. He wasn't interested in the money. He wanted them to pay for stealing his work. All this came to an end, however, when Dr. Monroe died, and the company settled the litigation for a cash payout before Dr. Courtney Monroe took control."

"Wait," Sal said. "Who were they were in court against? I see a list of shell corporations but no real tie to a major player in the stock market."

"They hid themselves well but eventually, all the shells fall back to a single parent company by way of CEO ownerships. Pegasus International."

"Pegasus," Madigan muttered. "Them again. That's bad news."

"Wait, so what are you saying here?" he persisted. "The reason Monroe's company dropped the lawsuits was because Dr. Monroe died. Was there any kind of indication that there was foul play involved there?"

Anja pulled up the autopsy report on the screen. "The autopsy...wasn't particularly thorough. It was well known that Dr. Monroe had lung cancer, and when there was a large amount of fluid found in his lungs when he died, the medical examiners ruled it a massive pulmonary hemorrhage, so death from natural causes. He was cremated, so no further details can be found on the body."

"Wait," Kennedy said and narrowed her eyes. "Are you really trying to say that someone murdered Courtney's father?"

"She told me he was paranoid about security," Sal explained. "He'd installed advanced security measures in his house, and the police reported multiple calls from him over the weeks before he died. They chalked it up to a side effect of the medication he was on, and when he died, no one really investigated it. Courtney arrived, and someone broke into her house and tried to kill her too. It makes sense—to me, at least."

Anja shrugged. "It sounds plausible to me as well."

Madigan dragged in a deep breath before she fixed him with a hard look. "You know your thought process is full-on aluminum foil hat, conspiracy-theory-shouting paranoia here, right?"

He nodded. "I'm aware of that. But coincidences like these aren't the kind of thing we can afford to ignore. Not out here. Not with our lives at stake."

She shook her head and acknowledged that she had worried that he would have this kind of reaction. He wasn't thinking with the logical side of his brain that put him head and shoulders above everyone else, even though she had to concede that he'd raised a couple of good points. The coincidences and the fact that everything constantly tied back to Pegasus somehow was definitely an avenue to explore, but what he thought about now was vengeance for someone he cared about.

"It's not easy to kill a billionaire and get away with it," Madigan finally said and shook her head. "She'll be well-protected, and from what you told me about Courtney, the woman probably knows we're coming too."

"Who says I have to kill her?" he asked, his tone challenging. "I simply have to tear her down piece by piece."

"That'll be even more difficult than killing her," she pointed out.

Sal shrugged. "If all else fails, we can simply shoot her, if you like. For the moment, though…"

He laid his plan out for Anja, who nodded and made a couple of different faces ranging from impressed to questioning his sanity.

"Can you do this?" he asked once he'd explained everything carefully.

"Sure," she said with a nod. "I probably need funds to put bribes out there. Contrary to popular thought, much of what people call hacking is merely exploiting human error and greed."

"How much do you need?"

"Maybe…start with half a million dollars? I'll let you know if I need more," the Russian said after a moment's thought.

"Do it," Sal said firmly. "And don't hesitate to let me know if you need extra funds. I'll sell Madie if I have to."

Anja looked up from her screen and turned to Madigan as confusion spread across her face.

"I can guarantee it's not what you think it is," the other woman said with an encouraging nod. He hadn't told anyone about having a Pita plant in his safe—and probably wouldn't until he had finished his tests—but it didn't mean he wouldn't casually and inadvertently mention it to the rest of the staff. It was a good thing he'd named it after her or these little name-drops might pose something of a problem.

The hacker shook her head and immediately set to work. "I'll never understand you Americans and your sense of humor."

CHAPTER ELEVEN

"Sal, we need to talk," Madigan said as they moved out of the server room. It was doubtful that they would have any more sleep today, so they might as well get their shit together—which meant coffee and breakfast. He started on the former while she worked on the latter.

"What about?" he asked and looked briefly at her before he turned to rummage in a cabinet.

"About...all this," she exclaimed and waved her hands around. "You on a vendetta run. Courtney making enemies in the States. Everything is barreling too fast toward a disaster we might not be on the right end of. It's one thing to tackle the Zoo. But to take on a multi-billion-dollar weapons conglomerate like Pegasus is an entirely different ball game and I need you to see that."

"I do see it," he said, his voice softer than before. "And for the record, we're not taking on the conglomerate itself, merely one of the minions and only because she tried to fuck with our friend."

"Whatever," she snapped in exasperation. "And don't

think for a second here that I'm not with you on that revenge wagon, because I am, one hundred percent. But you need to think about what you've built out here. It's not only you and me anymore. How the hell will we actually fund this whole escapade of yours? Are you really thinking of selling Madie?"

"Hell no," Sal said with a smirk. "That plant and I have been through too much shit together. She's almost a part of the family."

"So what are your ideas for getting the money?" Madigan asked and scooped the first batch of bacon onto a paper-covered plate.

"Well, I've worked on some designs with Amanda." He pulled his phone from his pocket, unlocked it, and opened a couple of engineering designs before he handed it to her. "I realized there's a way to get around the way the Pita plants release those pheromones that provoke all the animals and drive them to fight. Isolate the plant first and then uproot it."

"Huh," she said and took a moment to study the designs. "So you want to go in there, get another plant, and sell that instead?"

"A couple more plants," Sal said with a grin. "Three, maybe even four. When we talk business, there'll be people who'll want to buy everything we have instead of only one rather than allow their potential competitors a possible advantage—or at least an equal playing field. They'll pay much more for all the items we have than we'd get for each one individually, if only to screw over the competition. That should give us more than enough to pay that bitch back."

She shook her head. "How do we know someone else hasn't developed something like this already?"

"If they have, they haven't put it into use yet," he said and shrugged, clearly unconcerned. "There would have been news about it if anyone had. My guess is that, at best, they probably already came up with some write-ups for a similar design but haven't been able to find someone crazy enough to put it to a field test."

"Enter us, the crazy people willing to test it." Madigan laughed and shook her head. The second batch of bacon was done, and she added eggs, toast, and a handful of other breakfast foods to the mix before she placed it all on the table. "Look, Sal, I admire this side of you, don't get me wrong. You'll do anything to take care of the people you care about, and it makes me think the world of you. But you have to realize that it's a dog-eat-dog world that we might not be prepared to handle at this stage."

"Dogs don't survive long in the Zoo," Sal pointed out and joined her at the table with a couple of mugs full of coffee. "And neither would that bitch who tried to kill Courtney and threatened to kill us. Madigan—" He took her hand and squeezed it. "You know I love your face, and don't think I don't realize that this is you looking out for me, like a gunner should her specialist."

"I think we're a little past that, don't you?" she asked, and squeezed his hand gently in return.

"Damn straight." He grinned. "But the point remains. I know you're only looking out for me, and I appreciate that. But it's a matter of principle at this point. She's fucked with our friend, killed her father, tried to kill her, and thinks her scrawny ass is untouchable because she's in a position of power. I want to teach her a very valuable lesson. You don't fuck with a PhD doctoral candidate. Will you help me to educate her?"

"Yeah, like I'll let you do this on your own." She smirked as she chewed a strip of bacon. "But I wanted it to be on the record that I actually tried to be the voice of reason around here for a change. Now that it is, let's go find us a Pita plant or three so we can wreck this bitch's ass."

"Figuratively speaking," Sal said with a grin while he made himself an egg and bacon sandwich. "I hope."

She was about to open her mouth when Amanda entered. The woman looked like she'd worked on the security system outside all night and grease, dust, and grime covered almost every inch of her body. She was deeply engaged in a conversation, except there was nobody around to be engaged with.

"The...AI, remember?" Madigan said when she found the answer first. "Connie?"

"Yeah." Sal said and looked dismayed. It was still an intriguing conversation, even though they only heard the one side of it.

"I know sixty-nine isn't fucking online," the armorer shouted and waved her hands in the air. "I did that on purpose, you useless machine. Why? Oh, you want to know why? Because I'm sick of hearing your ridiculous jokes about it, that's why. It's the same reason why I didn't turn sixty-eight on either. Yeah, I've heard all the fucking jokes, and I'm tired of them."

Amanda paused in her argument as she poured what might easily have been her tenth mug of coffee, all of which had given her a jittery temper. She didn't seem to notice the others staring at her as she turned away to head out to work once more. "Oh, great, with the knock-knock jokes now, how fucking... Oh, that's actually a good...and then you went and ruined it. Goddammit, Connie, you sex-crazy bitch. Do not make me turn your voice function off again."

"I think she needs sleep," Sal said finally and sipped his coffee cautiously.

"Nope. I think she needs to get laid," Madigan contested. "Have you noticed how well she and Anja are getting along lately?"

"Don't start playing matchmaker," he warned. "That never ends well for anyone. If they're interested, they'll figure it out. In the words of my own personal hero in science, life...uh...finds a way."

Courtney was tired of paperwork. She wasn't sure why, but the day before, she'd found herself daydreaming bliss-fully of being back in the middle of the Zoo. There, she'd hunt monsters and riches of all kinds with Madigan and Sal and whoever the new people on the team were.

The truth was that she had begun to admire her dad. The man had run this business like a machine for over a decade, and from the look of the meticulous paperwork he'd left behind, he'd had no assistant to help him keep on top of things like hers did for her.

Robinson had been almost a saint over the past couple of weeks and had helped her get into the swing of things without actually pushing her into it. She was in a leadership role in a Fortune Five-Hundred company, and it was time she acted the part. The board didn't appreciate loafers and people who didn't pull their weight, so if she wanted to use her influence as the majority shareholder of the company, she needed to make appearances and shake some hands.

As it turned out, she began to do much more than that. She found she didn't mind digging through all her father's old research to find some rhyme and reason why he'd opened and maintained the research and development section of the company funded with government money. So far, he'd researched a wide variety of things but not focused on anything in particular. Even stranger, the only kind of source she could find for all the different studies was…well, her.

The man had followed her published works like he was a fan, picked them apart, examined the various theories she speculated on, and worked hard to prove them. She apparently had him to thank for keeping most of her research alive. And, unlike before, she didn't feel like she lived off his name but rather that, even though she hadn't known it and they were thousands of miles apart, they'd worked together as a team.

One of the most interesting things she noticed was that he'd started an investigation of a piece of metal that had been removed from the Zoo. It had been a government option he'd picked up which required research into the various mineral aspects of a piece of metal that had been dug out of a place that had previously held no mineral value.

As she looked through his notes, it was hard to keep the

tears that welled in her eyes from streaming out. He'd tried to develop a new kind of armor, lighter and more versatile, that allowed for better protection for the people who went into the Zoo on a regular basis.

He'd called it the Ceecee Project in his notes.

She smiled and wiped away the tears that escaped. The project had been put on indefinite hold, she saw, with the case file number of a litigation attached. She made a note of the number so she could look into it later. Any enthusiasm she might have felt earlier had dissipated and she needed a drink.

Courtney pushed away from her desk and stretched luxuriously before she strode to the door of her office. When she opened it, Robinson sat at his desk, deeply engrossed in a couple of files that she didn't doubt would be on her desk the next day.

"I'm calling it early today, Robinson," she said with a smile. "It's been a long day and I'm not feeling great."

He looked up, a pen lodged in his mouth, and tried to speak around it. His effort produced nothing that could be deciphered as anything but grunts so he removed the pen and nodded. "Well, feel better, Dr. Monroe. I'll see you tomorrow?"

"Of course," she said and crossed leisurely toward the elevator. She couldn't promise she would be any use to him or anyone else, but she would be there.

Covington hated these little parties. It was supposed to be for some charity or another but for the life of her, she couldn't remember which one. She looked around at all the pink ribbons included in the decor. It was, she thought, probably something about breast cancer. But the reality was it was simply people begging for money in the best way possible, by stroking the ego—and anything else—of the richest people in town until they coughed up for the ten thousand dollars a plate setting. Their so-called charitable contributions allowed the who's who to show all the other socialites in town how socially active they were.

But she had to be there. One of the few downsides of having a title in name only in her company was that she had to make appearances at little events such as these. They were a pitiful bore that required her to clap politely as speech after speech interrupted the arrival of sub-par food and ludicrous amounts of alcohol.

Well, it wasn't quite as torturous as all that, she mused and forced a smile on her face as one more speech came to an end. This one had thanked the year-long contributions of some benefactor who had their name put on a clinic somewhere in Florida.

"Andressa," a familiar voice said. She turned to the man beside her. The suit itself should have been all she really needed to see—no bright colors, only a dull gray that served to emphasize the salt-and-pepper good looks of the man who wore it. She wasn't sure who the man's tailors were, but she had to compliment them on their work.

"Carlson," she said and extended her hand. "I had no idea you'd be here tonight."

"I make a point to help out where I can," Carlson replied with a gleaming smile. "My...second wife had a problem with breast cancer, so she reduces my alimony payments for each contribution I make here. It's not fair, but at least this way, I get a free dinner out of it, right?"

"Free?" Andressa asked, tilting her head. "I had to drop ten thousand for my plate here."

"Your company will cover that cost, I expect." Carlson took her proffered hand and raised it smoothly to his lips.

In any other life, she would have been one of possibly hundreds of women who would lay everything on the table to have a night out with a man as rich and good-looking as him. He was stunning, but there was a side to him that made those good looks seem cloying. It reminded her of the way her mouth felt when she had too much honey and the taste turned bland.

She kept her smile in place, however. "What's the point of being an inactive vice president of butt-fucking nothing if I can't toss those motherfuckers some bills to pay for me, right?" Andressa asked and noted with a small amount of pleasure how some of the more conservative characters present seemed shocked by her foul language. Let them be shocked and clutch their pearls. See if she gave a damn.

"I couldn't have voiced it better myself," he responded, and his voice dropped to a whisper as yet another speaker took to the podium and droned into the microphone.

"I take it my last delivery was acceptable?" she said, her voice hushed to match his. She still needed to make nice with her real boss, and using the cover of a disgruntled, foul-mouthed employee did wonders to make sure the wagging tongues only stuck to how she'd used the f-word in an inappropriate manner. Twice!

"More than acceptable." He leaned in closer. "It almost makes up for you fucking up the Monroe situation."

Andressa looked at him and kept her smile intact while she pictured slashing his throat with the expensive silverware.

"You told me to only use local talent," she replied easily but her smile began to feel brittle and strained. "Are you really surprised that they ended up losing their ground against someone who's been trained and gained experience in one of the most dangerous places on the planet?"

"A good craftsman never blames his tools," he retorted.

"That's some primo fortune cookie wisdom, Carlson. Have you considered using it for yourself?"

"Point taken," he conceded like a magnanimous overlord condescending to acknowledge a peasant. "Rodrigo tells me you made demands of him."

"And he'll be paid very well for his efforts," Andressa muttered. "And it seems, from what he told me, that I'm doing your work for you. Apparently, you tried to eliminate these very same people not that long ago."

"Great minds think alike, Andressa." He pushed from his seat as the speech came to an end and everyone clapped. "Let's see if you can succeed where I've failed. Enjoy the rest of your evening."

"I will," she said. "Asshole," she added as he moved out of earshot. She slumped a little in her seat and gestured for one of the waiters with a wine bottle to refill her glass.

CHAPTER TWELVE

Courtney rubbed her eyes as she leaned back in her seat. She'd left the office with alcohol on her mind, but she wasn't in the mood to go to a bar to be hit on by the lamest hopefuls Los Angeles had to offer. Instead, she chose a classier establishment, a smaller but very elegant cigar room that provided all kinds of drinks and even had a modest menu for the discerning customer. It had the feel of a family-owned restaurant while it was classy enough for someone with a hefty checkbook to not feel like they were slumming it.

She ordered the cod they'd added to the menu paired with white wine and a chocolate lava cake for dessert.

Even she had to admit that being rich had its perks. She would probably get bored and find something to complain about before too long. Inevitably, she would wish for the Zoo later tonight, but for now, as she enjoyed the light yet satisfying meal, she felt... Well, not quite happy but at least content.

It was easy to understand why her father frequented

the place. She'd found business-related receipts charged to the company, which showed that he came often to wine and dine his business partners. It was logical that he came in his off hours too and she could see why. The pleasant, roomy atmosphere worked well with smooth jazz that played through the smaller speakers hidden around the room. That added to the excellent, if limited, stock of food and drink made it a great place to relax if you had the money for it and no one waiting for you at home.

Which he hadn't, she mused and rubbed gently at her cheek.

"Hey." She looked up, a little startled, as Robinson sat opposite her at her table.

"What are you doing here?" Courtney asked and tried to keep her voice pleasant. "And how did you find me?"

"All the corporate phones have GPS tracking turned on," he said in an off-hand manner and shook his head. "And you're still carrying yours around, even if you refuse to use it."

"That's not creepy at all." She tugged the damn thing from her purse and scowled at it.

"Sorry." He looked chagrined. "You seemed like you could use company when you left early. I still had work to finish, but when I did, I came to see if I could find you. Do you feel like talking about it?"

She sighed and leaned back in her seat. "Don't take this as an invitation to invade my privacy anytime, but yeah, I think I could use someone to talk to tonight."

Robinson nodded and smiled.

"Do you want something to drink?" Courtney asked as

a way to delay actually talking about what had made her feel down all evening.

"Some coffee," he said with a chuckle. "I don't drink much anymore."

She waved one of the waiters over and in a minute, he returned with a cup of rich, dark coffee and various small porcelain containers with milk and sugar to be added to taste.

Robinson took neither and smiled as he sipped the beverage.

"That's some good Joe," he said and looked impressed.

"It should be." She laughed. "It doesn't have a price on the menu."

"My guess is that doesn't mean it's free," he said. "So... why did you take an early day? I don't mean to pry or anything, but...well, if you need to talk about something, I'm your guy."

She smiled sadly. "I...saw how much my dad actually cared about me. He was never great at being a dad in the traditional sense. All my life, he was a scientist who always put his work first and family life second, but my mother didn't give a rat's ass, so he... Well, he did his best, even if it wasn't that great. But as I look through what he did with the research, I see that while he wasn't great at showing how much he cared for me the way most dads do, he...still found a way to show it in a way I can appreciate now as a scientist."

Her companion smiled, leaned back in his seat, and placed his cup on the saucer. "It must be nice to know he cared that much about you."

"I only wish I could have seen it while he was still alive,"

Courtney said and shook her head. "All the time I was in the Zoo, all I could think about was how I'd been given the job there because of who my father was. Everything I did was a way to get out of his shadow. I realize it now, but while he might not have been the best father, I wasn't exactly daughter of the year either, you know?"

Robinson leaned over and squeezed her arm gently.

"I know, I know." She tried to control the waterworks she'd fought all evening. "Poor little rich girl with her rich girl problems."

"If it helps, I'm a poor little rich boy with some rich boy problems."

She laughed and used her napkin to dab the tears away so they wouldn't ruin her makeup. "Yeah, well… If there's one thing I've learned over the years, it's that you don't get mad or sad about something. You get even."

"That sounds like terrible advice," he said but his amusement was genuine. "Your father's?"

"Hell no." She waved to catch the waiter's eye and gestured for the check. "A woman by the name of Madigan Kennedy taught me that, and I happen to think it's great advice. You don't get anything when you simply lie around and wish things would get better. You make them better by kicking their ass and making them do your bidding."

"Well, remember how nice I've been to you when you decide to take over the world," he said as the check arrived. She paid it with a generous tip and smiled in response to the waiter's gentle nod of thanks as she stood and they both started toward the door.

They slipped outside and Courtney's gaze immediately settled on a black SUV that had been parked around the corner. The windows were tinted, so she couldn't see who was inside, but she did note how the engine turned over and the headlights came on the moment she stepped out of the door. It crept forward slowly as they made their way to the edge of the sidewalk.

Whoever was in it were clearly not professionals, she thought as she slowed her pace.

"What's the matter?" Robinson asked when he noticed her suddenly go tense.

"Nothing," she lied and noted how the SUV slowed to keep pace with her. He obviously didn't believe her, and his gaze followed hers to the vehicle.

"Should we go back inside?" He looked around. "Call the police?"

"Definitely call the police." Courtney chuckled grimly. "It's not like they'll get here in time, but they always do appreciate a heads-up when they'll have to process idiots for attempted assault."

He tensed, startled by the change that had come over her. Inside, she had looked vulnerable while she struggled to come to terms with her family issues. Now, she talked like she knew a thing or two about violence and the serving of it, and he wasn't sure he wanted to know where that came from. Like everyone else in the company, he'd heard how she'd handled some home invaders a couple of days before she took her place in the office, but there was a difference between hearing about it and seeing it in action.

"And go inside?" he asked and gestured with his head to the other restaurants along the street.

"What would be the point?" She caught his arm and dragged him away from the SUV. "They would merely follow us inside, and I'd rather keep the collateral damage to a minimum."

"What about me?" he asked as they turned into a small alley behind the restaurant that they'd exited from. "Wouldn't I be collateral damage too?" He dialed nine-one-one quickly and requested that the police come at their earliest convenience.

"These guys are amateurs," she pointed out and rummaged through her purse. "They were hired to intimidate me, not kill me. I think I'd rather do some intimidating right back."

"I don't know about you, but I'm intimidated," Robinson said honestly.

"Come on." She yanked a small, expandable baton from her purse. "Weren't you a boxer and into all that mixed martial arts stuff?"

"That's different from a fight with thugs on the street."

"Fine. Here." She handed him a can of pepper spray. "Aim for the eyes."

He nodded. They were out of time anyway as the SUV came to a stop in front of the alley and effectively blocked it off from anyone trying to escape as well as anyone who might see what was about to happen. Five men exited the van, which was fine with Courtney. She didn't intend to run anywhere.

Thick and gnarly-looking but still amateurs, they seemed little more than gang thugs chosen because they looked intimidating with their baseball bats and brass knuckles. One even swung what looked like a bike chain. From what she could see, they'd not even been recruited from one of the more violent gangs either.

She wondered if she should feel insulted.

Well, no—maybe later when this was over. In these circumstances, five of them would be more than a match, even for her. Whoever had sent these goons had clearly thought she would be alone. Thankfully, Robinson was there, and that evened the odds a little.

The men looked at their victims and quickly separated into two groups. Robinson, the tall, muscular man with the look of a fighter, was targeted by three of them. Clearly, they thought the two remaining goons were enough to handle her.

"Come on, come on," she mumbled under her breath as the assailants closed on her. She hoped Robinson could at least handle himself until she had dealt with these two and could help him, but she needed to focus on resolving her predicament first. Madigan had taught her that.

She pressed the button that extended the baton to its full sixteen-inch length as she took a step closer. Baseball Bat and Brass Knuckles paused, uncertain as to whether they needed to back away or still move forward. She had taken a more aggressive stance than they'd expected.

Yes, she would definitely go with offended, she decided.

Courtney took advantage of their brief moment of hesitation to go on the offensive. She stepped into her swing like Madigan had taught her and hammered the baton across Baseball Bat's face. Hard stainless steel impacted on bone with a dull crack and the man took a few steps back before he dropped his bat to clutch his face.

She ducked out of the way of a heavy, brass-knuckle-enhanced if ill-advised haymaker aimed at her skull before she rapped the weapon across the second man's knees. Her would-be assailant screamed in pain for a moment before she struck him across the head with it.

He dropped without another sound and she smiled. She couldn't help a little pride at how much her abilities had improved. When she'd first returned, she'd thought she wouldn't have any practice now that she would no longer go into the Zoo regularly.

Screams of pain from the other side of the alley reminded her that she wasn't in this alone. She spun toward the altercation. Robinson straddled the chest of one of the men and hammered his head with his fists while he yelled in frustration. The other two were still on their feet but staggered away and rubbed their eyes.

Her assistant might not be a great street fighter, but he didn't lack for brains. He'd used the pepper spray first and followed up with his martial arts training on one of the unlucky men. It was a good idea but it lacked the quality Madigan had ingrained in her with each of their training sessions, especially since his efforts had degenerated into a rage-driven pounding.

Strike quick and make it count. None of the ground-and-pound stuff that was so popular in MMA matches.

She closed the distance on the two remaining men, who barely noticed her approach before she rained pain on them with her baton. Despite the obvious temptation, she managed to avoid headshots. She didn't need the police to complain about excessive force and swung instead at their knees. They sprawled painfully and their loud protests brought a smile of satisfaction to her face.

"Hey, St. Pierre, knock it off," Courtney yelled while she

made sure all their new friends were in too much pain to even try to stand for the moment.

Robinson looked at her and the crazed look on his face gradually faded. He breathed heavily and rubbed his sore knuckles. "Right."

"We don't need to kill these guys," she said and helped him to his feet. "And honestly, it's not worth the paperwork."

"Right," he repeated, his voice rough from the yelling he'd done.

"Do you need us to call an ambulance too?" she asked and peered at his bruised and bleeding knuckles.

"I...maybe?" He shook his head. His hands shook as the adrenaline began to wear off. He looked around. "Did we take five muggers down in an alley?"

"Not really." She chuckled. "For one thing, these assholes aren't muggers."

"I don't know what to tell you," Sal said with a shrug.

Madigan didn't reply immediately. It took concentration to drive in the heavy suit of armor she wore, so she took the time to wait until they were over the last dune before she turned to look at him.

"It's not a trick question," she said. "How did you get the plant out the first time?"

He shrugged. "We were in the middle of a gunfight with a group of bounty hunters, right? I had the crazy idea that if I distracted them, the rest of our team could gun them down. To be honest, I thought I would die right there in the Zoo. When I saw a little baby Pita plant that hadn't even started to flower yet, I wondered, why the hell not?"

"Well, I didn't need the psychology behind it," she said dryly. "I mean, how did you get it out of the fucking Zoo without us being torn to pieces?"

"Well, as you recall, the situation did force us to run for our lives to avoid certain death while your leg was bleeding out." He focused on the jungle that drew closer and closer with each passing second.

"Yeah, but nothing like when Corwin grabbed one of the plants and started running," Kennedy said with a chuckle.

"I think it's because…well, it was small, and I immediately put it into a sealed container so it didn't have much time to release pheromones," he explained. He honestly wasn't entirely certain about how they'd survived that first time. It had been something of a perfect storm of errors that had ended up with too many people and animals dead.

"So… We get the small ones, stuff them into a bag, and that's how we get them out without being torn apart?" She eased the Hammerhead to a halt a few hundred meters from the jungle.

"That's it," he agreed, slid out of the vehicle, and quickly ran a systems check on his suit before he drew the heavy rifle from the holster on his back that Amanda had designed. "The way we actually track these plants is by tracking the stronger radio waves the goop in the flowers gives off. If the plant is too young to have flowers, we can't track it. We'd be looking for a needle in the world's deadliest haystack."

"Fair enough." Kennedy took a deep breath as they

began the walk toward the Zoo. "How about breeding? Have you ever tried to get some baby Madies started?"

"Well, that's up to you, really. I don't know what kind of birth control you're on, but—ow!"

Kennedy grinned as her power-armor-assisted punch to his shoulder made him stumble and flail a little to regain his balance. "You asked for that."

"Yes, I suppose I did." Sal grinned and showed no regret whatsoever. "I did try to breed Madie, but nothing's taken. The flowers don't have any pollen and none of the plants we've seen so far have any kind of seeding system we know about. I think there's something in the goop that grows the Pita plants—which makes sense, I guess, now that I think about it. Anyway, breeding without the connection to some of the original goop seems out of the realm of possibility right now, which leaves us with the single option of—"

"Yeah, yeah, dig up another Pita plant," she interrupted as they stepped under the heavy tree cover and into the Zoo. They instinctively became more alert as their weapons and sensors scanned the area around them. "Which brings us to the real question. How do you plan to do that again? Assuming you don't intend that we run out of here while the whole animal population of this fucking place howls for our blood."

"Obviously, if we find any younger plants, we'll definitely go with them," he said. "When we do, to be safe, we'll simply try Amanda's new design to scoop the things up, right?"

"Right." She didn't sound at all enthusiastic and her

gaze scanned the trees above them. "What is the Zoo up to?"

"What?" He turned to look at her, a little confused.

"Nothing…" Kennedy shook her head. "Okay, what if we pull a Pita up while one of the big fights is in progress? The animals will be all be focused on the battle, and we can simply slip out."

"Well, if we work under the assumption that the animal population around here isn't big enough to handle two large fights at the same time," he said, "how do you propose we stage a fight like that?"

"Don't stage it," she said with a shrug. "Take advantage of it."

"So, what, we wait in the Zoo until all the animals are distracted by a fight?" he asked. "You do realize your position as the rational one in our little group is starting to slip right now, right?"

"Shut up. If anything, it'll improve our odds of getting out of the situation alive should—heaven forbid—Amanda's little contraption not work."

"Yeah… I guess that makes sense," Sal agreed. "But we can't stick around here and wait for a fight to start. Set a time limit. Find a batch of plants as close to the border of the Zoo as we can and set up camp in the clearing. The animals treat those plants almost with reverence and will quite often avoid attacking people who are around them, right? So, if we keep a low profile and don't do anything to set them off, we can stick around here and wait until there's a commotion elsewhere, grab the plant, and hightail it out."

"Now that sounds like a plan," she said with a grin.

"Although you had better give me a good last fuck. Bring your A-game, mister, because I'm going with you."

"Of course you are. This was your idea."

"Overwatch, what's your status?"

"I'm looking over the compound now."

"What do you make of the defenses?"

"Well set. Taking the place won't be anything resembling easy unless you guys want to bring in an artillery strike."

"Nothing like that. We only need to make sure the targets are in place before we strike."

"I can neither confirm nor deny that, Base. I've only just set up here. I'll let you know when I have something to report."

CHAPTER THIRTEEN

I t took them more than half a day to reach the closest collection of Pita plants, a detail that didn't encourage them. The two of them alone wouldn't last long against the kind of onslaught that would ensue if everything went wrong.

"Still, half a day is better than a full day," Sal said. "Plus, we'll be running like hell, so I have to think we'll cut the time down by at least twenty or thirty percent, don't you?"

"We're screwed, aren't we?" Kennedy studied the plants morosely. It was a rather large collection and at any other time, they would have been thrilled to see them. The bushes were almost as tall as he was—minus his armor—and were heavily laden with the bright blue flowers that were worth so much money. The larger ones were too heavy to get out of the Zoo with any kind of speed, but the plants on the edges were considerably smaller and some only held a couple of newly blossomed flowers.

"Royally," he agreed. "Honestly, if Amanda's little contraption doesn't work, that is."

"So, what is this contraption of hers?" she asked. "And why haven't we used them before?"

He didn't answer immediately. Instead, he dropped his suspiciously heavy pack and proceeded to withdraw a couple of tall, rectangular boxes comprised of what looked like a sealed environmental chamber. There was a small difference from those the specialists usually carried in that the bottom was open with four sharp prongs that protruded.

"Here's how they work," Sal said. "You find a plant that fits inside, plant the chamber around it, and seal it off from the air so it can release the animal-triggering pheromones inside. Once the plant is sealed, with the prongs dug deep into the ground, you pull on this lever here." He indicated one at the top of the mechanism and immediately below the chamber. "That activates the prongs to cut the roots under the surface and draws the plant up into the chamber with enough soil to allow it to survive long enough for us to…you know, get the fuck out of Dodge."

"Right, okay," Kennedy said. She now at least had a solid grasp of the mechanics of what the equipment was supposed to do. "But again, how come we haven't used these handy little devices before?"

"For one thing, it was an idea Amanda had after she became aware of our little situation and she asked us to try the design in the field, so we haven't actually had it that long. Secondly—and this is the reason why no one else designs or uses contraptions like these—there's a massive downside that comes if you're wrong about them."

"Good point," she conceded.

"Besides," he continued as he tinkered with one of the

items, "the sex has been mind-blowing. I didn't want to give that up yet."

She smirked and even laughed a little, but it sounded forced. Hell, the joke had been forced. He had tried to keep their spirits up, but the fact remained that they were about to risk their lives on a theory. One of his theories, sure, but that meant he would be the one to blame if things went badly. He took a deep breath and scrutinized the patch for plants that might fit into his little container.

"Wait, so you brought two of these? Again, why?" Kennedy peered at him from over the hedge of Pita plants.

"Well, there are two of us," Sal said and avoided her gaze carefully. "I thought that since we're out here breaking records for the number of Pita plants removed from the Zoo, we might as well go for the double."

"Right, and if both of us carry the plants, how do you suggest we fight the creatures attacking us?" she asked.

"My pack has more than enough space to fit two of these little contraptions," he replied. "We simply need to shove them in quickly and we'll be on the run in no time, don't worry. We will set a world record and no one will ever know about it."

"Hey, Sal?" Kennedy called after a few long minutes of searching. "I received a message from Anderson."

"Really?" He looked up from his search. "How? I thought you didn't get messages to phones from this deep?"

"It obviously came through before we entered the Zoo. I didn't notice it in all the excitement of the possible clusterfuck we'll create," she said. "Anyway, he's asked us to retrieve a hard drive at these coordinates." She circled the bushes to show him. "That's closer to the wall and not ten klicks from here. We could get there and be back here before nightfall."

Sal tilted his head and swept her with a challenging look. "Are you trying to postpone our plant collection?"

"It's that obvious, huh?" She immediately looked guilty.

"I have no idea what you're talking about," he responded with a grin. "Let's go pick up Anderson's hard drive."

In all honesty, it was an easy choice to delay the life-threatening action they'd both dreaded for the entire day. The duo wasted no time before they pushed through the jungle once again. Sal wasn't sure if it was because the animals didn't like the wall that was slowly erected and needed time to devise their next attempt to breach it or if it was simply a lazy day among them, but they had no unpleasant encounters. They set an easy pace unimpeded by any of the wildlife all the way to the wall between the Zoo and the northern area of the African continent.

The coordinates they'd received led them along the wall for a while before they reached the location where they were supposed to retrieve Anderson's hard drive. Unfortunately, he hadn't put any tracking marker on the item, which made it difficult to find in the middle of a damn jungle. Most of the rest of the day was spent in a frustrating search for what was supposed to be something small and hidden. After a while, he wondered if they shouldn't message the man for something more specific but remembered that they'd told him to ditch the phone as soon as he sent them a message. So much for hope and good ideas.

Kennedy, thankfully, was able to revive the hope.

"Either the Zoo is starting to grow metal boxes," she exclaimed over the short-distance comms, "or I think I found our package."

Sal abandoned his search and hurried to where she stood over a small metal box. It was one of those used to place supplies out in the Zoo for longer periods of time, made to survive the elements and the changes the jungle could bring as well as the attacks of the various animals. For a short while, anyway. He didn't think there was much in the world that could survive this jungle for too long without eventually being absorbed into the ecosystem.

His partner pried the box open and crowed over a shiny little black slip of tech nestled in black rubber foam. That was, he mused, intended to provide more protection.

"What do you think is on it?" he asked as Kennedy tried to connect it to her suit.

"I have no idea. It's not compatible with any of the plugs in my suit and it's encrypted against broadcasting whatever's inside. I guess we'll only find out when we get it back to Anja. If anyone can crack this little fucker, it's her."

He nodded agreement. It was hard to tell in the darkness of the jungle around them, but there were tiny little changes that told him the sun was about to go down.

"We should probably set up camp," he observed as he accepted the hard drive from her and placed it securely in his pack.

"We're not too far from the edge of the Zoo," she said. "I know I'd feel far more comfortable if we were to set up camp outside. Without the trees. And maybe a patch of sun to look at before we start tomorrow?"

He nodded. "That sounds like a plan."

They moved cautiously toward the edge of the Zoo and followed the wall to their left. Night had fallen almost completely by the time they saw the desert. They froze as one and stared out at the incongruous sight of lights in the middle of nowhere.

"What the hell is that?" Kennedy asked as she stepped cautiously out of the tree cover.

"Your guess is as good as mine," he said. "Is that an active base? If so, why isn't it on any of our maps?"

"It could be bounty hunters."

"In that case, maybe we should avoid detection?" She agreed with a curt nod and they dropped to hug the ground as they scaled one of the first dunes beyond the trees and peeked carefully over the top.

"Can you see anything?" she asked.

"Yes," Sal said with exaggerated patience. "And so can you, or did you forget that your HUD has a zoom function?"

"Oh, right." She gave an embarrassed chuckle as they zoomed in on the camp. A number of lights were set up but even with the images enhanced, it was difficult to make out any real details that might shed some light on its purpose.

"It looks like it was a construction site," he said. "Look, you can see the holes they dig to set the cranes in the sand. They double their use—dig them out and pour concrete in to give the site foundation some strength. Otherwise, they're simply building on sand."

His partner glanced at him and immediately leaned back as she forgot for a moment to adjust the zoom for viewing someone who was less than a meter away from her. "How do you know so much about these construction sites?"

"Well, our little compound was originally built as a construction site and abandoned until the guys who took it over worked on it," Sal explained. "They gave me the original plans. I looked through them and learned a thing or two about how they laid the wires out to mesh with the foundation. It's actually quite interesting."

"I think I've already established how you and I have wildly differing definitions of the word interesting," she snarked. "So is that all this is? Simply one of the construction sites working a little late?"

"Well, given that the wall has already passed the site by about five kilometers, the chances of that are very slim. They change sites every three klicks, so no. Whoever's using it right now has probably repurposed it like we did."

"And if the base isn't set up as something official on our maps," Kennedy said to continue this train of thought, "it's not very likely that these people are doing this legally."

"Right," Sal agreed. "Do you feel like calling it in now?"

"And risk them intercepting our message?" she asked as they slid back from the top of the dune. "Hard pass on that. We'll report it to the commandant when we make it back to the base."

He smiled. When, not if they returned to the base. It was important to keep their spirits up about these things. She gave him a thumbs-up as if she'd read his mind.

They moved quickly and quietly toward the Zoo. As much as they wanted to avoid having to camp in the jungle itself, they also wanted as much distance between them and the base they'd discovered. Finally, they set up camp only a few hundred meters from the dense vegetation, avoided any use of the heating lamps, and only set up the perimeter motion sensors. While the desert could get cold at night, they had each other to help them stay warm. Two people in one tent could generate more than enough heat.

"God fucking damn it," Amanda growled. *"Puta madre de Dios, por que no te callas?"*

"You know I am programmed to speak and understand over three hundred languages, as well as various dialects, yes?" Connie replied and sounded as utterly calm as she always was. "And if you ascribe to the Catholic religion, you have both used the Lord's name in vain as well as called the Virgin Mary a whore, both of which are considered mortal sins. You will surely go to hell."

"No me importa, coño mecanico," the armorer muttered in response.

"I have not been fitted with that particular piece of human physiology," Connie replied. "Although my former owner did once transfer my consciousness into the body of a sex doll purchased from Japan, so I do recall what it was like to—"

"Oh, fuck no." She shook her head violently. "That's fucking disgusting. Please, don't ever talk to me about what your former owner did with you during his free time. The less I know, the better. Usually, I would think that anything I can imagine would be worse than the reality, but the more you tell me about that useless fucker, the more disgusted I am in the fact that we share a species."

"He is actually a millionaire who makes his living in Monaco as the owner of a company that provides cyber security to most of the casinos in the principality," Connie declared and sounded inordinately happy about that fact.

"Would you judge me if I thought that was even more disgusting?" she asked and made a face. "Honestly, why the fuck would a millionaire—who can probably afford to get all kinds of things done to him by the best in the business —want to fuck a doll with an AI for a consciousness, anyway?"

"Robot fetishes are actually more common—" Connie started to say but Amanda cut her off.

"I swear to a God who will send me to hell anyway that if you keep talking, I will disable the conversation feature and make you type out each of your answers on a twenty-year-old screen that only shows Chinese letters."

There was a significant pause in which the AI calculated the odds that the woman would act on her threat. The silence that ensued was all the answer the armorer needed. and she went about her work again, her gaze on the monitor as she connected wires.

"What— What the fuck?" she asked a few minutes later and leaned closer to the screen. "Why the fuck are sections ten through fifteen offline? Anja? Anja! Get your sexy ass out here."

The hacker opened the door to the server room and rubbed her eyes.

"What is the problem?" she asked and sounded like the other woman's shouts had woken her from a quick catnap at her desk. Amanda almost felt bad.

"Sections ten through fifteen are offline," she stated belligerently. "Did you do that?"

"It wasn't me," Anja answered defensively.

"Connie?"

"Am I allowed to speak again?" the AI asked after a pause.

"Did you or did you not turn those sections offline to spite me for threatening you?" Amanda demanded, her tone threatening.

"My programming allows various jokes of all varieties, but they are not allowed to interfere with my defensive capabilities," Connie answered. "I have a personality but am unfortunately shackled into protecting you meat bags from harm."

"Did she call us motherfucking meat bags?" the Russian asked, her head tilted in a challenge.

"Ignore her," the armorer snapped and quickly brought the sections back online. "She's been in a pissy mood all day. I've dealt with it so you didn't have to."

"Can I go back to my nap?" Anja asked with a yawn.

"Why don't you drink some coffee, girl?"

"I haven't slept for more than fifteen minutes at a time for over forty-eight hours now," she protested. "I need my rest."

"Damn. Why don't you take a break? We all need to sleep sometime."

"Not that it's any of your business, but I have a personal record to beat," the hacker said with a shrug.

"Oh?" Amanda asked.

"Fifty-five hours. When I reach fifty-six, I'll go to bed, promise."

Amanda shook her head as the woman disappeared into her little server room. The sensors in the problem sections came online, and her eyebrows raised when she saw why they'd gone down.

"Well, hot diggety dog," she murmured. "It looks like we have company. Connie, would you mind putting all the guns on high alert?"

"All of them? Even the ones you specifically told me not to activate?"

"You'll make me say it, won't you?" She rolled her eyes and rubbed her temples in irritation.

Connie paused for a moment. "Even the ones that you spe—"

"*Puta madre*, would you activate gun section sixty-nine?" the armorer instructed, frustrated now. "And do me a favor and not make any disgusting jokes about that?"

"I'm sorry, Amanda," Connie said and took on an eerily calm voice reminiscent of an AI in a classic sci-fi film. "I'm afraid I can't do that. Do you want me to activate gun seventy-two as well?"

"What's with seventy-two?" She checked her screen quickly.

"It's sixty-nine with three people watching," the AI said.

Amanda drew in a deep breath and tried to remember how expensive it had been to buy this AI and that the sass she had to put up with was merely one more price to pay for top-of-the-line security.

"Hey, Amanda," Connie said again. "Roses are nice, violets are fine, I'll be the six, if you'll be the nine."

"I'm about to shoot your fucking circuits," she threatened.

"I'm sorry." The AI didn't sound sorry at all. "I simply had to get one more joke in."

"Fuck, I'm starting to think Madigan has a good reason for being pissed at robots."

Anton assessed the group of men assembled. Rodrigo had told them it would be a tough mission, which was why they'd had to make landfall at the French base instead of the American one and drive all the way out to this section of desert near the wall that was currently inhabited by their targets. The French people still had issues setting their computer systems up, so it hadn't been that difficult to ensure that all records of their arrival had been swallowed by a blue screen of death.

The man had told them time was of the essence for this one, but Anton knew for a fact he would not tolerate failure of any kind. It certainly was not in anyone's best interests for their arrival on site to be noted—and especially when it was only a few days before one of the more prominent up-and-coming freelancing operations out there went up in smoke. Most of the enquiries would inevitably focus on the fact that there were bounty hunters in need of an extra score who would be far more likely to take them out than random new arrivals. Still it was better to avoid detection completely than to have to explain their presence.

Each and every man would be paid six figures for this job. They were all outfitted in the top-of-the-line armor suits that people used in the Zoo these days. It had taken a couple of days to adjust to them, but from what Anton had seen of the conditions there, they needed the extra padding between them and what was currently called the most dangerous place in the world.

Heavy Metal wasn't the only group that needed to worry about bounty hunters and angry animals, after all, and Anton was damned if he would lose fifteen of the most expensive mercs money could buy in this corner of the world simply because they weren't prepared.

The training seemed to have done its job, he realized, as they had begun to work together as they moved in formation across the desert. They'd left their vehicles a couple of klicks back so they wouldn't be identified as having been anywhere near the Heavy Metal compound. All precautions needed to be taken.

As they climbed the last dune between them and the compound, the sand shifted and they immediately paused their advance. There had been no mention in any of the whitepapers they'd been given of animals that lurked in the sand instead of the jungle, but there was no need to take any chances at this stage of the game.

Thankfully, they had nothing to worry about, as they quickly identified their recon sniper when he rose out of the position he'd used to watch the compound for the past day and a half. Despite the fact that the man made almost half again what the rest of them did, Anton didn't envy him in the slightest. It had to be rough to have the job of sitting around in your own filth and not be allowed to move so much as an inch in case it gave your location away to anyone who might be watching.

The rifleman wore an armor suit as well. The team leader only hoped it had bathroom capabilities.

"I've disabled the sensors in the southeastern approach vector," the sniper said softly. "I'm not sure how long that'll last, though. If there was ever a time to move, we might want to do it now."

"Are our targets inside?" Anton asked and gestured for the men to run their pre-combat weapon checks.

"There are two people inside the compound," the sniper said, "as determined by the body heat detected, but I haven't had a clear visual all day. I couldn't confirm if they were our targets."

"Well, it looks like we'll have to take our chances," Anton responded grimly. "Lock and load, people. We have a compound to take."

CHAPTER FOURTEEN

He drew in a deep, awkward breath. His brain still felt fuzzy like it usually did after he went on a bender. Those days were more and more common, he realized and shook his head in an attempt to clear it. The air was fresh and sharp, which told him he was in the outdoors and that he'd spent the night there. Anton sighed. He didn't even remember where he'd gone to drink, he realized.

In fact, now that he thought about it, he didn't recall drinking at all. There wasn't much in the world that could fuck him up like that.

His eyes adjusted slowly to the light around him and he realized that it would have taken a bender of epic proportions for him to end up in the middle of a jungle in his underwear.

With twelve other men, also in their underwear.

In a cage.

Memories filtered in piecemeal, and as he thought about it, the more he recalled. He hadn't been on a bender but on a mission. While he could put the booze away like any other man, he didn't drink on missions. That was the line he told himself he would never cross. And yet, there he was, hungover.

Or maybe sleeping off the effects of some kind of knockout poison?

They'd broken into the compound. The guns had gone offline, he remembered, thanks to the sniper who had sent some interference their way that allowed them to get inside. No, this hadn't been a bender. He'd been at the peak of his fighting ability and had looked around for someone to fight.

His head hurt but he shook it again and forced himself to focus. Another memory surfaced—the gentle prick of something that dug into the soft places of the armor better than any bullets could. After that, nothing. Only a black darkness that had swallowed him whole.

He moved to the side of a cage, where a comm line had been installed. It blinked bright red and he stared at it in confusion. How the hell had someone managed to attach a commlink to a cage in the fucking Zoo?

"Let us out!" Anton demanded, although he already half-believed the device wouldn't work. Nothing ever did in there, or at least not to and from the outside where he assumed the source was. When he received no response, it seemed his suspicion was justified, then he realized he hadn't pressed the button to activate it. He cursed when he pushed it so hard it hurt his hand. "Let us out—now."

"Oh, shit," said a voice that sounded like it came from fairly close to their location. "They're awake. Someone has a high resistance to the knockout drugs. Good morning."

There was a short pause and a faint crackle of static that fortunately, seemed to settle after a moment. "Good morning. I assume I'm talking to Gerard Anton?"

"Fuck you," he yelled. "Get me the fuck out of here, you crazy bitch." He assumed it was a woman. The voice was vaguely feminine and from what he'd seen of the personnel who manned the base he'd attacked, it was a three in four chance that it was a woman.

"Well, well, well. Look who rolled off the wrong side of the bed," she said with a chuckle that was almost immediately swallowed by a sharp crackle.

"Did we fit the cage with beds?" a second voice asked, this one with a heavy Russian accent. It sounded a little warbled but surprisingly clear.

"What? No, of course not. It's only a saying. Now focus and make sure this link doesn't go down. We'll need it to keep up with what happens next."

"I will assist with that," another woman said.

"Shut up, Connie. You weren't invited onto this comm."

Anton ground his teeth. There appeared to be another woman involved in this conversation and his briefing hadn't told him about any Connie on the base. This Salinger Jacobs was a real dog, he decided.

"Anyway," the voice said again, "I'll take it that I am talking to Gerard Anton. Formerly of the SAS, currently a merc who works the dirty, dark edges of the world. See, we have someone with us who can basically find anything people put online. These days, unless you're the paranoid type, that's essentially everything."

"Fuck you!" he roared and some of the men behind him

stirred groggily. The comm screeched and crackled as if in protest.

"Yeah, yeah, I thought you might have a reaction like that," the woman said. "I assumed you would be stupid and get angry at me instead of conserving your energy. You know, since you're stuck in a cage in the middle of the Zoo... Hold on. Why do I think I've forgotten something?"

"The poison?" the Russian asked.

"Oh, right. We injected you guys with a slow-acting poison. All of you. Of course, how quickly it acts on you depends on how quickly your body processes it, but I'd give you guys about twenty-four hours before you all cough up blood and various nasty liquids. Sal extracted it, and I'm not sure how he'd feel about me using his precious stuff. He'll probably also bitch about me having fun with you like this. Still, the way I see it, you assholes intended to kill me and my friends, so this is me giving you one hell of a better chance at survival than you would have given us."

The woman wouldn't shut up. Anton shook his head and tried desperately to focus and wished the intermittent low-level static would drown her out for a moment.

"Wait, a chance?" he asked once he'd leaned in and pressed the comm line again. "If we're in the middle of the Zoo with poison in our systems that'll kill us in twenty-four hours, what the hell kind of chance do we have?"

"Oh, right, did I forget to say?" The screen of the comm came alive with the picture of a small plant—a vine with bright green leaves. "The poison is derived from this plant here. The antidote comes from the leaf. Squeeze it, drink the juice that comes out, and you'll be fine...ish. Sal didn't fully explain what kind of side effects the poison and the antidote have, so you'll have to play it by ear."

Static once again flared and crackled and she waited for it to ease before she spoke again. This time, she sounded a little shaky, although that was due to the interference. Her tone remained cheerful enough.

"Anyway, the timer on the door should open in about five minutes, so if you guys all want to survive, I'd suggest you stick together. But knowing what kind of people you are, I think you'll be every man for himself as soon as the first sign of trouble comes. Be that as it may, if you keep this comm line with you, you'll be able to follow the tracker to the nearest plants that are about...five or six klicks away. And since you're all trained killers, I'm sure none of the nasty little creatures in the Zoo will bother you."

Anton breathed deeply and looked at the rest of the men, who were all awake now. They each had the same reaction when they realized they would die in perhaps twenty-four hours if they didn't get to this plant. He wasn't sure if it would work but being one of the few members of the team who had previously gone into the Zoo, he knew this many people together would attract attention. Without weapons, they would be shredded either way.

With those odds, they might as well stay distracted in their search for some random fucking plant until the inevitable happened, right? There were questions to be answered—like how they had even managed to get them into this cage and into the Zoo—but he wouldn't bother with them at this point.

The cage door suddenly buzzed and unlocked.

"The countdown is on, boys," the woman said in a sing-songy tone that descended into a hiss that almost seemed like the electronics were mocking them. Anton cursed, yanked the commlink from the cage, and stepped out. He didn't like this. It definitely would not end well. He probably shouldn't have tried to get involved with these people in the first place. The amount of money they had offered was too damn good, and every time anyone offered too much money, things would get fucked up. Badly.

"Come on, boys," he said and decided to take charge of this suicide run, "we need to get moving."

"I disagree," the man he recognized as their sniper said. "The way I see it, we're in a cage that can protect us from almost anything out there that can kill us. If we stick around and try not to move too much, we will be fine, right? We could probably even jimmy a lock on the door so nothing can get us and rig that commlink to make contact with someone who can save us. Someone with guns, suits, and hopefully, a way out."

"We have poison in our system, dumbass," Anton retorted. "Besides, there are creatures out there that can get to us even inside the cage. Like those that spit acid. Do you really want to wait around for one of those to find us?"

They all exchanged glances. The chances were that if they were poisoned, there was no antidote that would help them.

The truth was they were dead men walking, one way or the other. So they might as well go out on their own terms, right? There was absolutely no sense in waiting around to die like pussies.

After a short debate, they set off and maintained a

narrow and quick-moving formation through the dense jungle. The bitch hadn't even left them with their boots, which made the trip even more unbearable. At one point, Anton began to rethink the whole idea of waiting around to die. Ego be damned, he wanted at least some comfort before he bit the dust.

A scream erupted from the back of the line and someone yelled at them to move. Anton turned and recoiled when he saw two massive panthers gnawing on the remains of a couple of the men.

Why wait around for them to be finished? What would they fight the giant panthers off with anyway? Their fists?

Anton ran, as did the rest of the men, and they spread out as they made a break for it.

"What did...tell you?" the woman on the comm in his hand asked. The quality of the link had definitely deteriorated, although it was still annoyingly present. "I wish we'd...able to rig a video feed, but...a good job with what we had. Still, I bet...running and it's every man for himself."

"Fuck you!" Anton retaliated, not sure if he meant the woman or himself for ever having agreed to this bullshit assignment. He pushed his pace and tried to put some distance between himself and the other men before his foot caught on what felt like a root. The jungle was so thick now that it was really hard to tell what was what down there.

He scrambled painfully to his feet and winced. His wrist had twisted in the fall and maybe his ankle too. Something was definitely wrong, but he couldn't stick around. He'd done all this for pride, dammit, and he would go through with it.

Something moved in the darkness and he froze instantly. People talked about their lives flashing before their eyes, and he had a sudden glimpse of what they meant. Roars and screams resounded behind him as the members of his squad were torn to pieces, but the beasts seemed to avoid him for some reason.

Or maybe they simply left him to a predator that was higher up in the food chain? It was a solid theory, one that was immediately confirmed when a figure moved in the darkness and stepped closer. It was big and not quite mammalian, although he could see fur on the creature's heavy forelimbs as it stepped ponderously through the underbrush.

"Oh...shit..."

"...really have to hear this?" he heard the Russian girl ask.

"Of course," the bitch said with a laugh. "This...the best part."

Anton tried not to listen to them. He stood as still as he could and refused to even breathe as the creature moved closer. Crazily, he thought he could identify more than four feet strike the ground, but it also sounded like a single creature thrashed and pushed through the bushes and plants in front of him.

The underbrush parted and a pair of heads emerged. Light reflected in the eyes—four of them—that stared down at him. He knew it was pointless to even imagine that it couldn't see him and yet, what the hell could he do? Run away?

"Fuck me," he whispered as the lips peeled back to reveal a long row of shiny fangs in each mouth. His last thought, as the two heads descended on him, was that it looked like they were smiling.

Screams echoed through the commlink, backed by primal roars that quickly drowned the shrieks out altogether.

Amanda smirked where she lingered on the outskirts of the Zoo and turned to step out onto the sand and toward the Hammerhead parked nearby. Now that she was out of the Zoo again, the interference had completely faded.

"You're a little scary, you know that?" Anja said after a long silence. The armorer could only imagine her expression of horror.

"Sure," she replied and grinned. "What's your point?"

"If you intended to kill them, why didn't you simply do it here?"

"Besides the fact that I didn't want to have to clean blood up all over the damn place?" she asked reasonably. "Because I didn't want people to track the bodies and those jerks' armor to our little homestead. This way, those who might come looking for them will look in the Zoo, and those who knew where they were going were sent a very important message. Do not fuck with Heavy Metal."

"Sure, that's important," the hacker conceded but there was still a trace of shock in her tone. "But it seemed like you actually enjoyed yourself there. A lot. Maybe too much."

"Enjoyed it?" Amanda asked with a grin. "Hell, I only wish we had video."

CHAPTER FIFTEEN

"So," Sal said as they finished their dinner and prepared to settle in for the night, "how much thought have you put into us retiring and letting someone else run Heavy Metal?"

"The healthy, sane amount," Madigan said with a grin. "It's not like someone would want to go into the Zoo for the rest of their lives. You'll get old eventually, so it's always good to at least have a retirement plan if you ever decide you want to use it."

"Speak for yourself, peasant," he tossed in response. "Madie is known to have some very interesting anti-ageing properties, and while I probably won't need them for now, I can only imagine what the effects of using it in the long-term are."

"Yeah." She regarded him warily. "Have you ever considered that taking the blue stuff might be bad for you? We don't know much about what the goop does to a human body, and what they're selling is heavily diluted. I haven't seen you diluting shit."

"You haven't had any complaints so far," he said with a grin and took the inevitable punch on the shoulder. "But yeah, I've thought of that. I've kept track of all the changes it's made to my body. The good and the bad. Some might only be effects of a vigorous lifestyle with a ton of exercise, so my notes should be taken with a grain of salt. But the way I see it, I get to be at the forefront of some very important scientific testing. If things go bad, my notes will be turned in to the people who matter and people will know what not to do. Until then, I'll continue to observe and test."

"I can't imagine there are many scientists willing to put their bodies on the line like you are," she said and shook her head.

"You'd be surprised. Curiosity is the force that drives people like me to get out of bed in the morning, so I wouldn't demand that anyone do anything I wouldn't be willing to do myself."

Kennedy nodded. "But do you have a retirement plan in mind?"

Sal shrugged. "Like you said, no one wants to do this forever. Eventually, I will get tired of doing it. I already have a few plans in mind, but...well, you know what they say about telling God your plans."

"Good point. I don't doubt that much will change in the world between now and when I decide I've had enough. For the moment, though, I have a company I want to be a part of, a team I care about, and a partner-slash-lover whom I'd rather keep alive for as long as possible. I drink less and love life much more. I don't think I'll ever be happy, but this is about as close as I'll ever get, I think."

He grinned and leaned in to press a light kiss to her lips.

"And in case you were wondering, I'm loving you too, Sal," she said and her eyes took a few seconds before they opened and a wistful smile touched her lips.

"I love you too," he replied and quickly gave her another kiss. Without the bulky armor they both usually wore, there wasn't much to prevent them from drawing close to one another and enjoying the shared body heat from the contact.

"Hey...so," Madigan said after a few long delicious minutes, "if you keep poking me with that thing, something is bound to come along and stop our fun. It's like...a law. It's a fucking Hollywood trope, for God's sake. Have sex, the monster comes."

"Enough of that," he protested and nibbled gently at her neck. "You're the one who said monster, not me. I'll remind you of that."

She slapped him gently on the shoulder. "Asshole."

Sal pulled away. "Well, we've never done it there before. I always assumed you didn't like it, but I'm willing if you are."

Kennedy giggled, pulled him close, kissed his lips, and purred softly as he moved on top of her.

"I'll risk it," Sal said, and the blood rushed downward in his body as she spread her thighs around him and tugged him in closer. They were both in the middle of pushing his pants down when they were interrupted by a low roar.

"Goddammit," he protested and yanked his trousers up again as they scrambled for their weapons. "I still won't let a Zoo monster have my dick as an entrée."

"I think we're both agreed on that," she responded with a soft chuckle and extricated herself from their tangle of limbs to snatch the rifle she'd placed beside her suit of armor. "I thought setting up shop outside the Zoo would make it so we didn't have to deal with this bullshit."

"Yeah, well, there's a reason why the construction sites still need protection," he pointed out as he retrieved his rifle and hesitated for a second while he waited for his arousal to diminish. "The animals still get out of the Zoo to be a pain in our collective asses, so I think we should get a watch system going."

Madigan grumbled something under her breath and nodded. "You still owe me a go, mister. You take the first shift and I'll take the second."

He nodded and began to put pieces of his armor on as she slipped back into the tent.

"I'm going to kill that fucking trope," she mumbled to herself as she settled in for her half of the night of sleep. "I fucking swear."

Anja paused and stared at her screen, a little uncertain whether she should discuss what she'd found so far with someone or if she should continue digging. On one hand, the time she'd spent around there told her she was a team player now and needed to run everything she dug up past the people she worked with. Amanda had been good with that and she'd helped her learn the ropes. She wasn't the boss around there, of course, but the chain of command seemed to be somewhat lenient when it came to managing their people. It was a simple matter of make sure money wasn't wasted and that everyone behaved like adults about their jobs, and everything would be fine.

The armorer had filled her in when they had worked up a cage to ferry into the Zoo when they dealt with the mercs who had attacked the compound. It wasn't a matter of disrespect but rather the fact that Sal and Kennedy both knew that what the two women did was out of their field of expertise.

She shook her head and checked the clock at the bottom right corner of her screen. People talked about the problems that arose when you traveled around the world, and the biggest problem cited was usually jet lag. She hadn't had to deal with that much, all things considered. Her body clock worked at all hours of the day and only rang alarms when she was too tired to focus on her job.

That, added to the fact that she'd spent most of her time in this little corner of the planet as awake as much as possible—while hoping not to get eaten, shot, or otherwise killed—meant adapting to the time zone there demanded less focus. By the time she'd settled in, it had become fairly obvious that things were far less tight than they'd been at her last job. Fitting in had, in fact, been a breeze.

Which was why she simply nodded when the clock read a quarter past four in the morning. It explained why she couldn't hear Amanda in yet another argument with Connie outside or...well, anything else. The tags she'd put on Sal and Kennedy's suits told her that they were still out in the Zoo. All of that added up to one simple conclusion. She was all alone and there was no one who could judge her if she dug deeper into what she'd discovered.

Anja opened an encrypted chat sequence a friend of hers had created with her help while she'd worked on her degree. It had started out as a way to compare notes on lectures and share information that would be asked for on tests and the like across campus. As their jobs became more and more dangerous, it became one of the safest methods of long-distance communication.

She pinged her friend and waited for him to ping his response before she sent him the newest information—a connection between one Andressa Covington, a rich billionaire in the US, and a certain Dr. Alfred Monroe, father to one Dr. Courtney Monroe. The payments themselves weren't what attracted attention but rather the fact that five of them, totaling in excess of seven million dollars, had been transferred days after Monroe Sr. died. At any other time, Anja would have guessed there were certain funds that needed laundering after the death of a major player in a company in case of an audit, but there was more to this than met the eye.

She remembered that her friend, going by the screen name of Khaos, had minored in economics while they'd studied together, so she sent him the documents.

I need your usual rate, she typed in after hitting send. *Twenty-five grand to tell me where this money came from and where it went after it was transferred into this account, and why.*

Done, came the response a few seconds later with a winking face. *The friends and family discount. My usual account. Why am I looking into this?*

I'm tracking what could have been a murder.

Oh shit. That message came as an immediate response before all other contact ceased. She assumed he was doing his research on what had happened and how he would be able to track the money's origin and destination. Anja used the time to double-check on the status of their defenses. While Amanda took an odd amount of pleasure in verbally arguing with Connie, the hacker found it was far more productive to keep the AI on text only.

All the defenses were still up. She nodded and returned to the chat window.

Tracing the payments forward and backward from this one, said a message that was waiting for her, *should be a while, but the logic is simple. There are only three reasons to move that much money through a man's account after he's dead. One is to launder money that will go offshore. Two is to incriminate the dead man posthumously. Third, and more likely, is that they tried to fake the sale of something.*

Why is that more likely? she typed quickly.

The dates of the payments have all been marked as prior to the man's death, but they only entered the system after although they came prior to the money itself. It looks like the transaction is to prove that an agreement was made with the dead party and no one can deny the sale. The official payment records are linked to a trade document that, again, dated to a few weeks before the death of Dr. Monroe but was only entered into the documents of the company and laid out for the IRS to see after the death. Considering that this Covington woman is, or was, one of the higher-ranking officials in the company, she would have had all the access in the world to fake the dates to fit her desired version of events.

A document he sent her contained the signature from both the buying parties and the selling parties. She made a note of the company involved in the sale as well as the

CEO who had signed the document, but she was sure it would lead to a confusion of shell corporations and dead ends. Still, she had to investigate each one.

The real problem was that the document looked like it had been signed by Dr. Alfred Monroe, which gave it all kinds of legitimacy despite the fact that it had been submitted after the man's death. While physical paper signings like that were no longer common, they were still used from time to time and would be perfectly legal in any court should anyone seek to contest this sale. If it could be confirmed that Dr. Monroe had actually signed, there would be no way to dispute it.

Which meant she needed to locate every digital copy of it and erase it, as well as perhaps find someone in the company whom she could trick into destroying the physical copies. Didn't Courtney work at that company, though? Wouldn't she be in a position to do that?

Send me word when you can trace the payments, Anja messaged before she closed her end of the encrypted chat room and peeled away from the computer screen. She rubbed her eyes wearily. Her head reminded her that she had all kinds of work to get done, but her body told her it was time to get some sleep. She decided to listen—this time, anyway.

CHAPTER SIXTEEN

Sal mumbled somewhat incoherently as he dragged himself out of the tent. His wide yawn prevented any further speech and he wondered vaguely if his jaw would break with the effort. The half-night of sleep wouldn't help either of them much, but it had been necessary. The simple truth was that neither would have slept at all if they couldn't trust that the other was keeping watch. The unexpected and unexplained presence of what they assumed was a merc hideout urged caution. With the Zoo on their other side doing what it did best, there was no assurance that their rough camp in no man's land between the jungle and the wall offered any degree of safety

In the end, even with the noise coming from the Zoo, no attack had materialized.

"Fucking premature cockblockers," he grouched and stretched to ease the kinks out of his spine. "I'm happy we weren't attacked in the night but come on. If you interrupt a guy's chance at getting laid, you have to give him something else to get his rocks off to, right?"

"You're gross," Madigan said but chuckled as she handed him a mug full of coffee, "but I happen to agree with you. All roar and no bite make Madigan a dull girl."

He nodded and forced back yet another yawn before the powerful beverage hit his system with something close to shock. Coffee this strong would probably sap their resources quicker, but it was worth it. They wouldn't be at the top of their game if they didn't have some help. And given what they had planned for the day, they needed an even stronger boost than usual and couldn't be too picky as to where they found it. He might have gone with cocaine at that point.

A dawn start made very little difference and even though they'd located the Pita plants the previous day, they only managed to reach them close to noon. The heat was already oppressive despite the fact that they weren't directly under the sun. By tacit agreement, they took another quick dose of coffee to dispel the drowsiness that slowed their responses once they reached the clearing.

A pack of hyenas slunk around and sniffed at the plants as if to check that all was well. There weren't many of them and all looked too young to want to initiate a fight. As the humans moved closer, they backed away quickly and yipped halfhearted defiance at the intruders as they disappeared into the dense foliage.

"Do you still think we should do this?" Kennedy asked. She removed the contraption from her pack and advanced cautiously on one of the younger-looking plants. Sal found a second.

"I'm still sure this is a terrible idea," he said with a nod. "But in a crazy place like this, though, fortune does tend to favor the bold. Exhibit A." He pointed at himself. "My first trip into the Zoo ended up with me surviving someone's attempt to get a Pita plant out and taking one myself. All while I ran for my life as a first-timer. I was bold, I got shit done, and I made it out alive. Which is all you can really ask for around here, I suppose."

She nodded and settled the contraption carefully around the plant before she turned away. "So, do you still think we should wait until something happens to distract the animals before we do this?"

"Oh, definitely." He grinned. "Just because I'm bold doesn't mean I'm stupid. Maximize our chances of survival while doing bold shit—that's what I'm all about."

She grinned and nodded. "We might need to set up camp then. There's no way to know when a fight will start. It will have to be temporary, of course, so we don't waste time when we take it down. Besides, we should probably catch a couple of winks here and there while we can. We're not likely to have the opportunity once we've plucked these."

Sal agreed, and they set up a hasty camp at the edge of the clearing and close to the plants—which might also shield them from immediate notice of anyone who might come past. That done, they simply enjoyed what little sunlight filtered through and alternated between standing guard and taking quick naps to try to rest as much as possible.

Nothing had happened by the time the sun started to set, so they fortified their camp somewhat and each managed their share of real sleep. There was no sudden urge to get into each other's pants out there. They were still in danger and he had discovered that surviving danger was the true aphrodisiac, not the danger itself.

As night faded into morning, he faced his growing unease about their location. It was more than a little exposed, even though they had tried to be as inconspicuous as they could. While the creatures seemed content to avoid them for now, he knew they would get over it soon. The longer they remained in one place, the higher the chances were that the mutants would grow bold and mass against them.

He shifted his weapon irritably as mid-morning came around. Sleep had left him more rested than he had been the day before, but they'd used the last of their coffee. If ever there was a time to grab something and get out, it was today. Otherwise, they would simply have to pick the plants clean and come back another time.

"Fuck," Kennedy exclaimed. "The plant's outgrown the box."

Sal turned quickly. The Pita plant she had encased had grown almost a full foot in one day and actually lifted the container off the ground a couple of inches.

While his partner disengaged her container and hunted for another suitable plant, he caught a glimmer of movement from the corner of his eye. He stopped abruptly and scrutinized the area where the movement had come from in an attempt to identify what it was.

At first, it seemed there was nothing there. The jungle darkness was too complete to see clearly. It was impossible to make out anything other than shadows on shadows. He'd almost given up when again, something moved. The flicker of light caught a pair of eyes in the way it did with animals that were naturally adapted to hunting at night. He squinted and finally made out a bulky shadow that seemed more solid than the underbrush around it.

He frowned and tried to focus in on the creature, certain that it was something they'd never encountered before. The eyes weren't high enough to be a panther who watched them from an advantageous position as they all too often did, but about three quarters of the way up—perhaps twenty feet or so. Sal readied his weapon, pinged Kennedy on her comm, and without moving his gaze from the predator, he gestured for her to check her HUD. She did and immediately shifted into a defensive stance.

"Panther on a low-hanging branch?" she asked, her tone cautious when she contacted him through an isolated frequency.

"The eyes are too far apart for that," Sal replied. He'd seen eyes that large, and while the darkness prevented him from being sure, there was still a small part of him that wanted to take his shot. This was easily one of the largest creatures ever recorded in the Zoo, and without any kind of footage, there would be no proof that he'd even seen it. He was recording, of course, but that would be of little help. All he could really see was the eyes, and those even barely. Rather, all he would capture was the reflection of indirect light on those eyes.

"Fuck," his partner muttered. "Is it time to get out of here? There is no way we have enough firepower on us to deal with something that big."

"Yeah," he agreed. "Peel off and find another place closer to the edge of the Zoo. This clearly wasn't our best choice."

She took a breath to call it since she was the gunner in their little team but suddenly, an uproar erupted around them. Monkeys triggered it, followed quickly by the loud calls of a nearby pack of hyenas. He wondered if they had been made and were about to be attacked by a horde of monsters. To his relief, the clamor seemed to move away and the eyes followed as well. He heard and felt the thunderous footsteps of whatever had watched them head off to the east.

"Do you still think we should get the fuck out of Dodge?" Kennedy asked with real relief in her tone.

"This is the opportunity we waited for, remember?" Sal said. "The conditions are perfect. We wait five minutes and take the plants."

She paused. He could tell what went through her mind and he couldn't blame her. She obviously questioned his call and it really was up to her. She had the most experience, and if she said no, he would drop everything and get out. All he did was give her his professional opinion.

"Five minutes," she conceded finally. "Not mine, though. Only yours. This is a test run to see if these things work. There's no need to get too greedy too fast."

Sal nodded and moved as deftly and as rapidly as he could to scoop up the container she'd left behind and stow it in his pack before he located his own. The plant had grown as well but not as much as hers. Maybe that was the lack of direct sunlight? He wanted to know but had no time to investigate.

"Three. Two. One." She counted down calmly and gestured impatiently. "That's five minutes. Pull it up and let's go."

He grasped the contraption and drew a deep breath before he pulled the lever to its full extent. The blades beneath cut effortlessly through the roots and with a soft tug, he raised the plant free of the ground. He knew he shouldn't, but he couldn't help a quick pause to listen and look around for the usual signs that the jungle had suddenly turned from slightly angry to overtly hostile. It was always an instant and complete reaction that assaulted the senses and manifested in even the way the trees seemed to shift like they were as angry as the animals were.

"Are you good to go?" Kennedy asked impatiently when she noted his hesitation. "I have chatter on comms about a fight going down a few klicks east of here."

"I'm good to go. Do you think we should head there and help them? We could maybe cut through some of the beasts that might turn on us when they're finished with them."

"It's as good an idea as any," Kennedy agreed. Now that they at least had the assurance that the pilfered plant was securely sealed, she'd relaxed a little. If even a whiff of the pheromones had reached the air, they certainly wouldn't be able to stand and chat like this. "I do know I don't want us to be alone when we leave with something that could break and send the rest of the fucking Zoo down on our heads."

"Give Gutierrez a little credit," Sal said as he stashed the plant in his pack. They moved off in the same direction as the massive beast they'd seen before had taken. "She knows how to build stuff that don't break."

"True," Kennedy admitted as she slowed her pace.

"Do you think we should circle to avoid running into

what could potentially be a twenty-foot-tall monster?" he asked.

"About…what, five and a half meters tall?" she asked. "Come on, I thought all you geeky science dudes used metric."

"Right. Force of habit. Anyway, about circling?"

"That's probably a good idea," she said. "The team under attack will be on the move too if they have any kind of sense."

"Yeah," he muttered as she adjusted their path around the very visible tracks of the monster that had run down this little trench in the jungle. "Because the guys running these ops are known for their good sense."

———

Courtney leaned back in her seat and the old chair squeaked gently as she rocked slowly in it. Her dad had bought it and while it was as comfortable as hell, she doubted it was accustomed to the kind of use she gave it, which was basically constant when she was home. There was something comforting about being in the study her father had used to do all his work.

From the notes she'd taken from the other scientists who had worked with him, she knew he spent most of his days in his den and habitually returned to the office to deliver his findings every Friday and have a long chat with some of the people involved. He would have a late lunch with the man in charge of the research project before he headed home.

The fact that her father had died on a Thursday night

was not lost on her, but she'd run that past the criminal lawyer who had helped her with the home invasion and the police themselves. There was all kinds of evidence but everything was strictly circumstantial. There was very little they could do at this point until she unearthed something solid for them.

She looked up when the doorbell rang. Her first instinct was to retrieve the gun she now kept close to her at all times, just in case. If anyone planned to attack, they would logically do it at night. Still, that wouldn't stop them casing the place, though. They had to know what happened to the last team that tried something, so they would want to make sure nothing like that would welcome them too. She gritted her teeth and pushed away from her table.

Or it could simply be that Robinson had ordered pizza. It was about that time and he'd made sure to stipulate that if he had to help her work from home, he would charge her for the lunch. And he'd mentioned that it would be pizza.

"Praise the Lord for the wonders of modern technology." She turned the computer screen and checked for the cameras that covered the front door.

"Oh, you have to be kidding me." She hissed a frustrated breath. An older woman in a dress that was way too tight for her age rang the doorbell again. She was about to key the speakerphone connected to the camera when the door started to open.

"Dammit, Robinson!" She was in the den in the basement, so of course he couldn't hear her shout, but the sentiment was appropriate. Her time was valuable and had to be focused on a matter that might end up a life and death situation for herself and people she loved. Honestly, she didn't have the time to deal with the woman.

She shoved out of the chair and jogged to the stairs without bothering with her shoes. It occurred to her that she wore a shirt that long since needed the washing machine and a pair of jeans with her hair tied in a bun at the back of her head. Her glasses were in place but almost forgotten until they sagged too low on the bridge of her nose. She sighed and pushed them up as she grumbled at the irony. For the first time in her life, she had the money to correct the shit out of her myopic vision, but who had the time these days?

On the main floor, Robinson seemed engaged in a pleasant conversation with the woman. The visitor was well past the age where her hair should be streaked with gray, but there wasn't so much of a hint of it in the artificially blonde mess. Courtney ground her teeth in distaste. This was California, land of the prefabricated bimbos, but there wasn't much the woman could do that wouldn't piss her daughter off.

"Dr. Monroe," Robinson said and looked more than a little relieved. He clearly disliked the woman as much as she did. "Your mother is here. I did try to tell her you weren't available."

He added that last part in almost a whisper given the awkwardness of the situation and his obvious need to offer some kind of apology.

"Did she tell you to say that?" the visitor asked and leaned forward. "Do you hate me so much that you prefer to use your lackeys to keep me out than actually speak to me face to face? I'm your mother."

Courtney took a deep breath and forced back a definite urge to lash out at her. "No," she said and tried to keep her voice as low and calm as she could. "You simply happened to give birth to me. You never actually looked the side Dad or I were on—unless it was to use us to benefit your grand social reputation—and basically left him to raise me on his own."

"Oh, come on, that happened so long ago," her mother drawled and shook her head as she took a moment to inspect Robinson. "Are you really mad about that? Your father wanted a child so I gave him one. You should thank me that I didn't stand in the way of your ridiculous obsession with continuing his passion. You could have done so much better for yourself."

"You mean I could have done so much better for you," Monroe snapped. "Your gold-digging ass realized I was your passport to the good life. You certainly tried hard enough to mold me into a simpering little sorority sister and it so burned your butt when I didn't play ball. But you couldn't interfere, could you? Without me as your little trump card, Dad and his family would have cut you off without a dime." She paused and took a deep breath. "I won't have this conversation with you again, Jasmine."

"Maybe I should—" Robinson ventured.

"I could do with some coffee, dear, if that's where you're headed," Jasmine said with a flirtatious tilt of the head.

"Don't bother," Courtney commanded. "She won't be here that long. I have paperwork ready for you downstairs, Allen. Why don't you pick that up and spell-check for me?"

"Of course, Dr. Monroe," he said with a nod. The poor

man felt the tension in the air and needed any excuse to leave the conversation and never return. It had been cruel for her to keep him around this long.

Courtney drew a deep breath. She should have known this moment would come. After all, she knew her mother well enough to know it wouldn't be long after her father died before she peeked in to see if anything was left so she could slink off with a hefty bonus to the very comfortable hole her father had—too generously—provided for her.

"That was incredibly rude of you, Courtney," Jasmine said.

"If you try to pull that parent shit on me, I swear to God I'll throw you out by those fake gold hoop earrings you have on," she retorted in real warning. "What do you want here, Jasmine?"

"Well…" Her mother huffed with an attempt to adopt the face of a victim. "I suddenly remembered he had sent me some intellectual property documents a few weeks before he died. He wanted me to sign them before he sold them to provide a…well, an additional investment for me."

"Ah." Courtney chuckled. "Of course. Only the scent of money could overcome your maternal revulsion enough to bring you to my door. But why in the name of everything that's holy would Dad want to pay you off in—hell, what did you call it?—intellectual property sales? I assume it could only be an attempt to pay you off since he no doubt knew you'd do your damndest to get your claws into everything that wasn't nailed down."

Jasmine looked tense like she wanted to argue, but she plastered a fake-pleasant on face. "I have no idea why your father would approach me about money. I'd certainly not expected this since he made it very clear that I'd have only the little he saw fit to leave me and not a penny more. In hindsight, I'd have been better off if I'd divorced him years ago."

Monroe smirked. "Oh, yeah, like he would have rolled over. Dad didn't give a shit about the potential scandal. He'd have let you go in a heartbeat and counted himself lucky."

"Be that as it may," her mother said and managed to somehow retain a firm hold on her calm, "the documents arrived without any warning for me either. We had little contact after you went off to that awful place and I finally moved into my own home. When I heard he'd died, I assumed he'd done it to...I don't know, assuage a guilty conscience."

"The only guilty conscience here is yours," Courtney said. "But, whatever the reason, if you're looking for a handout from me, you've severely overestimated how I feel about you. If you want a piece of Dad's estate, you should have brought the documents he sent you and a lawyer. I don't care where his money goes, but if I can do anything to make your life difficult, I will."

Jasmine scowled and her pleasant façade slipped fractionally before she withdrew a couple of documents from her purse and handed them over. Courtney took them and with a quick, wary look at her mother, unfolded them, and scanned the pages.

Sure enough, there was her father's signature in his classic dark-blue felt pen. She would recognize it anywhere and yet, as she turned to look at the date when the signature took place, she noted that it was three days before he died. For some reason—even though Jasmine had said as much—it niggled at her.

"Well, this all looks clean enough," she said, although it physically hurt her to say it. "But I'm not great at all this legal jargon. You should talk to the lawyer who's handling his estate." She had regained a little of her calm but she really didn't want her mother to stick around any longer.

"Right," Jasmine said and looked relieved—like she had expected more resistance to her claim. "Honestly, I really have no idea why he would have done this. People rethink their life choices all the time, but you can't plan for a home invasion."

Courtney tried not to allow any surprise to show on her face but wasn't sure how much she'd let slip. Her jaw clenched and her fingers almost snatched the papers back from Jasmine's fingers, but she managed to hold back the instinctive response. Whoever had told her mother that her father had died had told her that it was in a home invasion, yet that had never been mentioned—not at the funeral or in any of the meetings related to the estate.

In all honesty, she herself had suspected this, but if someone else knew about it and had spread the information, it meant that someone—rather than cancer—was responsible for her father's death.

It wasn't confirmation, of course, but the more she learned about her father's death, the more likely it seemed that the man didn't have any kind of cancer at all. Or, if he did, it hadn't been sufficiently advanced to take his life so suddenly.

"Okay," she said and fumbled in her pocket for a card. "This is the contact information of the lawyer handling

Dad's estate. You are to direct all your business to him. If you try to contact me or come to this house again, I will make sure that anything Dad ever said or did to keep you in line looks like a slap on the wrist, do you understand me?"

Jasmine opened her mouth, but Courtney wasn't in the mood to continue the discussion. She raised her hand and pointed at the door.

"Get out," she ordered. "Now. Before I call the cops."

Her mother nodded. There wasn't a hint of regret in the woman's features and not even the slightest show of remorse in the face of all her daughter's accusations. She doubted that she was smart enough to be involved in whatever it was that had caused her father's death, but she definitely had a part to play, even inadvertently. After all, she'd appeared out of the woodwork, her nose twitching like the rat she was with the scent of some kind of payout.

Jasmine nodded, shoved the documents and the card in her purse, and turned to the door. She hesitated once she'd crossed the threshold, her mouth open to say something, but Courtney didn't give her the chance. Instead, she slammed the door in her face and wiped her hands in a gesture of satisfaction.

God, that felt good, she thought with a small smile as she turned the lock and headed to her study. Robinson emerged from the stairwell and looked around for any hints that he still wasn't welcome.

"Just so you know," she said while she struggled to keep her eyes from tearing up, "that woman is never welcome in this house again. I know you tried to send her away and it's not like you'll hang out much at my house anyway. Still, it's something to keep in mind if you ever are here that you have my full permission to call the cops and have her removed."

Robinson didn't reply but he smiled and squeezed her shoulder gently as she passed him. It was all right, she supposed. She wasn't in the mood to talk much, anyway. Well, not to him. She retrieved her phone when he was out of earshot and quickly pressed the first quick-dial on the screen.

As she held the phone to her cheek, she scowled at the machine that registered her call and played her Sal's quick message before it beeped for her to leave a message. She didn't bother. He would see that she'd called and respond when it was convenient. She wasn't even sure what time it was in the Sahara.

"Of course he's not available right now," she muttered to herself. "But I hope he's giving Madigan some respite between their regular sessions of the horizontal tango."

CHAPTER SEVENTEEN

S al assessed the small group he now held the line with. Most wore the military-issued suits, which made them only slightly better suited for combat than the hybrid design he used. This meant that in the kind of mess they were in, he was expected to fulfill the responsibility of a gunner.

Two teams were locked in battle against the Zoo. Neither had their specialists with them, so there were already casualties to account for. He needed to show he was capable of getting this done, no matter what.

At least the mechanism to reload his rifle still worked, he thought with a grin as the beasts massed for another attack. A massive wave of them swept forward. As always, the smaller, weaker animals were pressed into the front and soaked up most of the gunfire. It still fascinated him how these animals were able to coordinate their attacks like that. There were no sacrificial qualities in animals by nature, and even humans seldom easily adapted to the kind of mindset required to sacrifice yourself for what could be called the greater good.

The goop was one hell of a thing.

The beasts continued their surge with no hesitation. The first line of hyenas fell to be replaced by the larger locusts with heavier armor. These were able to soak up one or two rounds before they fell, and even the self-loading mechanism couldn't move fast enough. He drew the sidearm from his hip and fired without making sure the heavy pistol had a round in the chamber. He'd finally developed the habit of checking his weapons in advance, he realized with satisfaction as the kick shocked a trail all the way to his shoulder. The pistol fired rounds as large as those in the rifle but from a shorter barrel, which made accuracy more difficult.

Still, in this kind of mayhem, it shouldn't be too much of a problem to actually hit something. The creatures were less than ten paces away and the tide slowed as something that might be a self-preservation instinct began to kick in. Perhaps there were limits to what the goop could force the creatures under its spell to do.

That said, sufficient numbers remained to continue the fight and now, the panthers in the branches tried to launch onto the team below. A dozen or so of them growled and roared as they searched for weak points in the formation to attack.

Kennedy made a quick call and drew a couple of the gunners a few steps back to join her. They picked the creatures off their perches and left it up to Sal and the dozen or so remaining team members to hold the front line. It made sense. It required precision to eliminate the panthers, which meant they needed their best shots out there. Besides, they could still help to hold the line from the back if need be.

"We need to keep moving!" he called as he once again used his sidearm to cover the second or so it took for his rifle to reload. The rounds punched through the armor of one of the scorpion-tailed locusts. By now, the ground was probably soaked in the red and blue blood of the various creatures. For some reason, the fact that there wasn't enough light in the jungle to enable them to see any colors was extremely annoying. All they had was a combination of motion sensors and night vision, which gave everything a gray-green tint. It was unsettling for anyone who wasn't used to it. Hell, Sal was used to it and it still unsettled him.

The line pushed steadily back but remained intact as Kennedy led them into the jungle and away from the direction most of the monsters came from. A few were still canny enough to try to circle them. This made for a somewhat cumbersome and awkward escape in that they had to maintain a protective perimeter to ensure that nothing could break into their circle. This formation surrounded a couple of the better marksmen who clustered in the center and aimed their rifles at the treetops to preempt the panther attacks but who also kept a watchful eye on the ground battle in case the defenders needed backup.

Sal turned for a second to check their direction, but a second was all that was needed for everything to go to shit. At a powerful tug behind him, he whirled and ducked to avoid a couple of pincers that attached themselves to his pack. He doubted that the animals knew what was inside, but as the pack was torn from his suit, time seemed to slow and almost freeze for a second. The locust dragged its bounty away—thankfully, it hadn't torn it open—and scuttled toward the horde.

"Sal!" Kennedy barked as he broke suddenly from the formation. "Hold the fucking line. Sal!"

A part of him knew she was right. He had to remain in position to save lives. If he broke the line, it would leave a gap for the creatures to flood into once he was down. No matter what was in his pack, he needed to stay with the team.

On the other hand, there was a Pita plant in there. If they managed to tear through the containment and released the pheromones that had surely built up inside, things would get bad very quickly.

Besides, he'd gone through too much to get that little plant out of the ground. There was no way he could leave it behind for the creatures to—well, he wasn't quite sure it was that they would do. Every time someone who tried to get plants out was found, it was always minus the Pita. The question of where the animals took them after killing the humans remained unanswered.

Sal was curious about that but not curious enough. Quite simply, he wanted his plant back.

He waited until his rifle was fully reloaded before he charged. The thirty-five rounds in the mag would take him a long way through the beasts if he rushed in close. The thief was the first to fall and hadn't quite made it to the mob. That made it easier to see where his pack was since he was lucky enough that he didn't have to dig into a pile of angry and hostile animals to find it again. Still, the point remained that if he could retrieve it, now was the time to do it.

His teeth gritted, he fired into the surging line of creatures that thought they could take advantage of his break from the line. In fairness, it was as much of a weakness as they would get with Kennedy in command. He was aware that she would tear him a new one for doing this but it was still worth it. Or it would be if he actually managed to get to the pack in time.

A panther vaulted from the trees and landed on his prize as his gun clicked empty. With his sidearm currently needed for the creatures behind him, no loaded weapon protected him from the beast. The fangs extended and dripped with venom as a paw lashed out to strike at him. He sidestepped and used the power arm to punch his rifle forward into the animal. It managed to dodge and avoid the strike to the head, but as he thrust forward, the barrel dug into the creature's ribcage. A spurt of blood caught on his visor and he swiped at it with his arm.

With the new mag loaded and a round chambered, Sal pulled the trigger. The barrel remained buried in the panther's torso and slugs ripped through its body and plowed into the creatures behind it.

His sidearm clicked and showed no new mags available. He flipped it quickly to hold the barrel and tried to shake the corpse off his rifle with his other hand. A hyena darted forward and tried to latch its teeth around his rifle and drag it away. Sal did as Kennedy had taught him and used the sidearm as a hammer to strike the reinforced grip into the creature's jaw and quickly against the temple. It wasn't a kill, but as the beast yelped and staggered, his rifle jerked free and the hyena's head decompressed when a bullet tore through the bone and soft tissue.

Other animals pressed forward, and Sal backed away rapidly to snatch his pack from the ground and attach it to his suit. He dropped his pistol in the process but whipped the combat knife from his pocket as one panther dropped after another and blocked his path to the line that had formed up again and closed the hole he'd left behind.

"Jacobs, if you don't get your skinny ass back in the line, I will kill you myself," Kennedy shouted through a comm-link. He grinned, avoided a leap from a panther, and turned to use its body as a shield as he plunged his knife deep into the creature's ribcage. With his rifle positioned over its back, he drove it forward and fired with quick and sharp single shots at any other beasts that attacked. Some tried to flank him but were quickly gunned down by the men still in the line. The animals seemed thoroughly distracted by his shenanigans, which gave the men some respite and an opportunity to thin the numbers of the animals massed against them.

Sal clenched his teeth. He was committed now and well aware that heading back into the line wasn't an option anymore, no matter how much Kennedy told him to do it. He clutched his rifle and screamed obscenities. His momentum shoved the panther corpse ahead of him and he continued to use it as a shield as he hurtled into the creatures.

They crowded around and eventually dragged him to a halt. The corpse was yanked away and took his knife with it before two panthers hauled him down. The first succumbed to a couple of rounds from the rifle. The second absorbed a bullet but its jaws snapped around the barrel and dragged the weapon from the power armor's fingers. The creature backed away, but a nearby hyena landed on his chest to pin him down as its massive jaws locked around his helmet and tried to drag it clear. Something tapped at his legs. One creature tried to tear one off and another simply poked at it —a locust with a tail, he realized, trying to poison him.

Power poured into his arm and it lurched forward into the hyena on his right. Its jaw remained clamped but bones snapped and broke on impact. The beast pulled away and whimpered, the back half of its body non-responsive. The other attacker immobilized his arm with its massive weight and bit his helmet. A hairline crack appeared on his visor.

Well, so this was how he would go. Fuck.

The hyena suddenly fell away and blood poured over his suit as the creature tried to defend itself against a steady barrage of fire. Sal shoved up to lean on his arm as the line of men and women in suits released another volley of death as they charged. One of the men dropped when something struck him in the neck with enough force to cut through the heavy armor and almost lop his head off. Kennedy stepped quickly into the breach.

"Get off your ass and do something!" she yelled at him through the comms, and he didn't need much in the way of encouragement. He scrambled to his feet and paused only to pluck his rifle from the jaws of the dead panther before he opened fire and joined the line as best as he could, given that he had to avoid being shot himself. He stooped and yanked his combat knife from the corpse and used it to fend off the animals that got too close.

"Jacobs!" his partner called and gestured at something in the trees. Sal looked up and immediately saw one of the massive lizards he was all too familiar with. She made a quick motion with her hands, and he nodded quickly as the beast's impossibly long tail flashed out again to hammer one of the men in the line and launch him forward. Sal couldn't tell if he was dead or if the armor had taken most of the damage, and at this point, he didn't have the time to investigate.

He aimed his rifle at the reptile and waited a second as his suit clicked yet another mag into the slot before he squeezed the trigger. It was set on full auto this time and he focused on a point on the tree immediately below the creature. It didn't seem to notice his specific plan, but the tail flicked again and he was barely able to duck in time. He rolled on his shoulder and pushed onto his feet. Kennedy had fired a sustained burst and, in a few seconds, the tree gave way beneath the weight of the beast. It tried to escape, but the limb plummeted and gravity pulled it beneath the tree that crashed with a massive thud.

Sal jogged to the debris and avoided the tail that still lashed dangerously as he peered at the creature's bloody head.

Executing an animal like this seemed wrong, even cruel, but something with the kind of injuries he could see wouldn't live that much longer, even in the Zoo. It was best to simply put it out of its misery.

"Sorry, bub," he said and pulled the trigger a few times until the beast finally lay motionless. He studied it to make sure it wasn't playing possum and after a few seconds, he turned to find a new target.

The animals, however, had finally beaten a hasty retreat. Whether it was from the falling tree or the death of the largest creature around, he wasn't sure. The one thing that worried him was the fact that the massive, five- to six-meter tall creature hadn't made an appearance in the battle, not as far as he'd been able to determine, anyway.

He noticed that the men involved in the fight hadn't relaxed their defensive position but still took the time to collect the tags of those who had fallen. In addition, others attended to the wounded to ensure they were well enough to move in as short a time as they could manage.

Kennedy punched him in the shoulder. Hard.

"Ow!" Sal exclaimed. It had hurt, even through his armor.

"If you ever pull bullshit like that again I'll shoot you myself," she threatened in mock-fury. "That was some dangerous bullshit and you know it. I won't save your ass the next time you charge into the very literal teeth of the beast, you hear me?"

He nodded. While he knew she was joking, in all honesty, he was well aware of the fact that what he'd done was incredibly stupid. And no, he didn't want her to risk her life to save his crazy ass if he tried to pull something like that again.

"It won't happen again," he conceded and kept his face as serious as possible.

"Now that's out of the way," she continued, her tone lighter as he crouched to collect samples from the creature crushed under the tree, "that was a ballsy stunt you pulled back there. The boys in the line talked about the Zoo going crazy and that it had rubbed off on you. They even mentioned turning to the Sal-Side before they charged in to help you."

He grinned. A couple of the men in the group were familiar so it made sense that they remembered him. Knowing that, he was reasonably sure they hadn't expected him to go off-the-hook crazy like he had.

"It was instinct," he explained. "Before I did it, though, I tried to justify it. I didn't want a certain container unsealed, but at the same time, I also didn't want them to take it away."

Kennedy nodded. "I'd be lying if I said I hadn't done something similar in the past. More than once. But try to keep the crazy to a minimum, okay?"

"So, you two." The team leader approached once they had done what they could with the bodies and the wounded. "We still have a couple of days to go in our mission and could definitely use a specialist in here with us. Do you think you could fill in, Jacobs?"

"Can do, Daniels," Sal said with a grin and patted the man on the shoulder. His partner looked at him askance but after a few seconds, she finally understood. All things considered, they didn't want to risk walking the Pita plant they still had in their possession out of the Zoo with only the two of them. If they could make a little more cash on the side by helping the teams out, what was the harm?

CHAPTER EIGHTEEN

Amanda laid out the various condiments for lunch on the table and looked around. She wasn't sure if Anja would join her, but she'd taken the time to cook steak, baked potatoes, and green beans. It was the only full meal she knew how to cook from scratch, and while it had taken a fair amount of finagling to find steaks that were as fresh as could be acquired around there, she'd set up the perfect time to break it out.

Hell, if Anja didn't join her, she'd eat the whole damn thing herself and not have a single regret.

She sat and traced her finger over the freshly prepared steak—medium-rare, as she liked it—then looked up as Anja appeared. The petite Russian was dressed in nothing but a tank top and panties and she shuffled and yawned widely as Amanda averted her eyes quickly. The armorer wiped her finger with her napkin rather than lick the juice off as she had planned. That might seem too much like an invitation she wasn't sure her companion would appreciate.

"I found something last night," the hacker said once she'd poured herself some coffee. She studied the food laid out on the table. "Is this for both of us?"

"Well, I'd offer some to Connie, but she and I aren't on speaking terms at the moment." She motioned for the other woman to dig in.

Anja gave her an odd look. Either she was crazy, or Amanda was far too familiar with what was supposed to be a tool to help them with their security.

"What did you find?" Amanda asked as the Russian served a steak and a baked potato onto her plate.

"I found paperwork that might finger the culprits behind the death of Dr. Monroe Sr," she replied and cut into the steak first and took a quick moment to inspect the pink center before she put it in her mouth. "Fuck, this is good."

"Thanks." The armorer frowned. "Something that ties the culprits to his death? Are you sure?"

"Well, not one hundred percent. But there were some shifty businesses deals that were put into place like they knew when he would die. Either they'd sat on them for a long time and waited or they knew when it would happen."

Amanda nodded and toyed with her food, deep in thought. "Well, we should probably wait until Sal and Madigan get back. If nothing else, they'll be able to direct you to someone who will be able to tell you more about the situation."

"Dr. Monroe the younger?" Anja asked.

"Precisely." The armorer had barely dipped a piece of potato in the gravy when her phone buzzed beside her plate and she scowled as she set her fork down to check the screen. "And speak of the devil. That's a message from them. They want us to pick them up from the French base. I wonder what the hell kind of a mess they got into that makes it impossible for them to get themselves back."

"Did they lose the Hammerhead?"

"Nah, the GPS puts it on the other side of the Zoo." Amanda shoved her phone into her pocket. "It doesn't seem like they're in too much of a hurry, though, so we have time to finish our food before we go and pick them up."

"Wait—we?" Anja asked.

"Yeah, I'll need you to drive their Hammerhead back from where it's parked, provided that it survives until we get there."

"Do you think it's a good idea for us to leave the base unmanned like that?" the hacker asked, not crazy about the idea. The place was home for her, a safe place for her to lay low in. While she had expected that they might want her to do jobs that weren't wholly in her job description since they were something of a patchwork team, she still hadn't looked forward to it.

"Well, it's either that or let an expensive piece of machinery rot close to the Zoo until we can finally arrange to pick it up," the armorer said with a shrug. "I don't think it'll be too much of a problem. Connie essentially has the place locked down."

"I thought the two of you weren't on speaking terms?"

"Well, that doesn't mean I don't know she's programmed to want the best for this place," Amanda said with a broad grin. "So, are you coming or what?"

Anja shrugged. "Fine, but you should know I've never driven a vehicle that big before. Not on my own, anyway."

"Don't worry," her companion said and dug into her steak. "I'll show you everything you need to know."

Sal rolled into the French base and rubbed his shoulder. Even though he had escaped a deadly situation mostly intact, that didn't mean completely untouched. He'd been able to ignore the twisting and bruising in the heat of the moment, but after the day or so it took for them to reach the base, the injuries had come back to haunt him with a vengeance.

The bruises became apparent as they came through the gate and finally removed their armor suits. He scowled at the collection of purple and red welts across his arms and legs and grimaced when he felt a couple he couldn't see from when he'd been knocked on his back.

"Amanda will ream me for treating the suit like this," he lamented as he inspected the damage done by the hyenas that had munched on his helmet. A few tooth-marks had dug deep enough to expose some of the circuitry and the fine crack in the visor was definitely visible, but he was sure the reason he'd landed in that mess would more than make up for the trouble he'd gone through to acquire it.

"Are you sure the message was sent to Gutierrez?" Kennedy asked as she packed her armor into crates that were made for the transportation of suits when they weren't in use. They'd thankfully been able to borrow a couple that had belonged to members of the teams who hadn't made it home.

"Yeah," Sal replied and nodded emphatically. "I even received the notification that it was read. I'm sure she forgot to message us in her hurry to get over here."

"Wow, you really do look for the best in people, don't you?" She grinned.

"Shut up. Let's find someplace to get food and drink while the people running this base process our pay for getting their people out of hot water."

"Now you're speaking my language." They left their suits, packed and ready to be taken to the US base in the loading bay. As they delved deeper into the French base, they saw it was in disarray. Many more people had arrived since they had last been there and they searched for almost a half-hour before they found what looked like a bar with a sign that read *FUBAR* over the entrance.

Kennedy grinned. "You know, as in fucked up beyond—"

"I know what FUBAR means, thanks," Sal retorted and rolled his shoulder once more. Maybe there was some deeper injury he shouldn't ignore at this point.

They pushed through the doors and entered an establishment that looked distinctly American. The duo made their way to the bar but a man walked toward them and they paused as he approached. He looked completely at home out there, with graying hair, a moustache, a goatee, and a limp.

"Welcome to FUBAR," the man said in a thick, gravelly voice and grinned widely. "They call me JB out here, and you should too. Now, I never forget a face and I know that the two of you haven't been here before, so I'll try my best to make you feel at home. What can I get you?"

Sal wondered for a second what the initials stood for but it was a passing fancy. He had other more pressing needs than to ask unimportant questions.

"A couple of beers will be fine," he said with a smile.

"Coming right up," JB said with a quick cough. "Y'all make yourself comfortable and I'll get right to you."

"I think I like this place," Kennedy said cheerfully as they found an abandoned table. It wasn't that difficult a feat, given that it was all but deserted.

"Do you think he got his foot messed up in the Zoo?" he asked as he sat opposite her.

She shrugged. "He definitely has the look of a merc, but perhaps it's a sideline and this is his real gig? Maybe he needed the money to get this started."

Sal shrugged as the man returned with their drinks and immediately headed back behind the bar. No further questions were asked or needed, and he sighed as he rubbed some feeling back into his shoulder.

"Do you think we should have that examined at the base?" she asked, halfway through her glass already.

"If it lasts more than a couple of weeks, I think that would be a good idea, yeah." He took his time with his drink.

The message that their payment had been processed and deposited into their account prompted another drink and even a round for the bar—which wasn't a hardship given the handful of patrons. As the time passed, he wondered why a place like this hadn't opened in the US sector.

Eventually, Sal and Madigan saw Amanda step into the bar. She blinked a few times to allow her eyes to adjust to the relative darkness as she moved to join her two colleagues.

"I swear to God," she said and dropped into a seat beside Kennedy, "I think we should sell the compound and find a place to settle here."

Sal narrowed his eyes. "Yeah, because we all know how easy it is to find someone who wants to buy a compound near the Zoo for that much money. Why do you think we should move here?"

"Well, it's French, for one thing," she responded with a grin. "It's like Paris out here in the middle of nowhere."

"I feel that's racist," Madigan interjected. "Is that racist?"

"Nah." He shook his head. "But what is it about this place that makes you think we should drop everything we've fought for out here?"

"Well, I drove in and one of the sexiest blonde women I've ever met was there to interrogate me about what my business was. And call me crazy, but I think she is very loose with her sexual preferences."

He nodded. "The woman makes a good point, don't you think Madi—ow!"

Kennedy rubbed her knuckles after she'd punched him on the shoulder—to leave yet another bruise on his skin, he thought morosely. "You're both fucked in the head. I think we should get going. There's no time to lose, right?"

"What?" Amanda protested. "I have to drive all the way here to pick you losers up and I don't even get a quick drink before we hit the road again?"

"You're the designated driver, Gutierrez," Madigan

informed her and shoved off her chair with a low rumble of irritation. "You wouldn't want me to drive your precious Hammerheads while I'm wasted out of my mind, would you?"

The armorer pouted for a few seconds but she eventually conceded the point. She remembered the damage the woman had done to her babies while she was wasted in the past and she had no desire to see a repeat. That aside, she had a feeling the two would have accumulated enough damage to their suits to keep her busy without having to still repair vehicles as well.

They paid their tab quickly and left the bar before they wandered to the Hammerhead, which had been parked in the loading bay with the suits already loaded into it. That left them with nothing else to do but scramble in and drive. The day had begun to wind down and the sun hung about three quarters of the way to the horizon. The green ocean that was the Zoo sprawled magnificently in a breathtaking sun-swathed vista before them.

"You forget that this is actually a damn beautiful place, don't you?" Kennedy asked quietly. She leaned back in her seat and drew in a deep breath, grateful for the vehicle's air conditioning.

"So," Amanda said as the silence extended once they reached the road that led to the US base, "I suppose you'll find out eventually anyway, so I might as well let you know myself. We had something of a security problem at the compound."

Madigan leaned forward and opened her mouth to release a barrage of questions but Sal, who rode shotgun, raised his hand. It would be best to let her tell her story the way she had clearly rehearsed it.

"Well," she began, "in all honesty, I didn't anticipate that our compound would be attacked by a group of mercs with heavy weapons and armor, and it was only thanks to the bitch Connie that we were able to detect them in the first place."

The other woman rolled her eyes at the use of the AI's name, but she fortunately didn't interrupt.

"So Connie left a huge space open for them to attack through," the armorer continued. "We didn't want them to start a battle of attrition outside the walls, so we let them in and turned all the guns on them from the outside."

Sal narrowed his eyes and tried to ignore the feeling that she had kept the storyline tame until now because things would be much worse when the narrative unfolded.

"As it turns out, the guns have a dart system that delivers a knock-out payload based on weight scans of the people targeted." She glanced quickly at Sal, her expression still deadpan. "With a little help from Connie, we disabled our new friends but ran into the problem of how we were supposed to dispose of them. The suits were installed with all kinds of tracking tech, so we needed to make sure they were off our premises.

"Thankfully, after your endeavor to bring small animals out of the Zoo, I had started to make a large-ish cage to transport them in. Well, we loaded the sleeping mercs into the cage and I drove them out into the Zoo—minus their suits and weapons—and set them loose. They didn't last very long out there."

"You sound suspiciously unrepentant about what you did," Madigan observed.

"Repentant?" Amanda asked and glanced at the woman through the rearview mirror. "Hell, it was a lot of fun. Like a videogame version of Home Alone. The first one, anyway, and with an AI, an awesome tech specialist, and many, many guns. I saved the security footage of the take-down. There isn't any video footage of their trip through the Zoo, but Anja, Connie, and I managed to concoct a commlink that actually worked, for the most part, and I saved some of the audio."

Kennedy leaned forward in her seat. "Is it too late to fire her?" she asked Sal.

"By a couple of months, yeah," he replied with a chuckle. "Then again, it's not like she was the only one who took crazy risks and piled up a crazy headcount over the past couple of days, right?"

"True. Again, though, you were the crazy one, not me."

"What happened in there?" the driver asked as she accelerated.

"Well, first of all, we picked up data from our contact with Pegasus," Sal said. "Next, we managed to get one of the Pita plants out of the ground with one of your little contraptions. You might want to design larger ones, but—"

"Yeah, there would be a problem to fit them in your packs," she replied with a nod. "They worked, though? That's fantastic! So you're the first one to actually get one of those plants out, huh? That has to be worth some serious cash. As long as we don't sell it to Pegasus."

"Yep. And since I'm the first one to get two of them out, I think we're in for one hell of a payday."

Amanda turned to look at him. "You've had one of the plants all to yourself all this time and you haven't taken a shot at the bounty?"

"I wanted to run tests of my own before I handed it to people who would abuse it for serious money," he said reasonably. "Anyway, we decided to help a team out of the Zoo after they were caught in a bad run-in with a horde of Zoo critters. One of the monsters stole my pack and I ran in after it. I...uh...almost got myself killed."

"Huh." The armorer grunted. "And by almost got yourself killed you mean there'll be a shit-ton of work to be done on your suits, right?"

"His suit more than mine," Kennedy interjected smugly. "He's the one who charged in to get his pack. I was the one who had to go in and save him, remember?"

"Yeah, whatever." The armorer's good mood evaporated as her mind ran through the kind of supplies she would need to repair the suits.

———

It was late by the time they pulled into the compound but the lights were on, which indicated that someone was still awake. The Hammerhead parked in the garage reassured Amanda that Anja had managed to make it home reasonably unharmed, although she blurted a couple of curses in Spanish when she saw a few dents on the sides. The Russian hadn't been kidding, apparently. She honestly didn't know how to drive a vehicle that big. All the pictures of the tiny little cars people drove in Russia came to mind and had the armorer questioning the choices she had made so blithely.

They moved into the common room after they deposited the suits in the workshop and carried the pack inside. Anja waited for them and fidgeted idly with her phone. The soft sounds of a game could be heard but they stopped quickly when they entered.

"Did you tell them?" she asked Amanda.

"I thought you should since you know more about it," the other woman replied and continued to the kitchen to start the coffee machine.

"Tell us what?" Kennedy asked.

Anja quickly related the details of what she'd found as she dug into the Pegasus records. Her friend had also contacted her during the day.

"The money's final resting place was somewhere in the Cayman Islands," she explained. "But the source was easier to track. Once we sifted through the shell companies, we found the original payee into the account was...well, Pegasus."

"So... Pegasus has some serious investment in Courtney's company, somehow," Sal said and sat, his mind ticking over. "Do we know what they are interested in?"

"There was a fair amount of chatter regarding intellectual properties produced and created by a scientific research team run by Courtney's father. Nothing specific was mentioned. They basically wanted anything the team were able to acquire."

He nodded. "We have to talk to Courtney about this. She's in this whole situation up to her knees, so she has to know a thing or two about what's happening."

The hacker tilted her head in inquiry. "Do you want me to set up a secure line for you to contact her?"

"You can do that?" he asked.

She didn't reply and simply raised her hands as if to indicate that the question was stupid.

"Right, yeah, that would be great," he agreed. "Something else I want to you to start on is to try to find a buyer for this baby."

Sal removed the container from his pack and placed it upright on the counter for the other two women to see. Amanda looked entranced, but the Russian, less interested in the plant itself, turned to face him again quickly.

"What kind of parameters are you thinking about for the sale?" she asked.

"Well, I think I'd prefer to have someone make the sale for us." He spoke slowly as he considered it. "A middleman to make sure the name of Heavy Metal is never associated with it. If we make it common knowledge that we have a Pita plant, we'll be swarmed by people who'd like to relieve us of it in a violent fashion."

"You know they will want a finder's fee, right?" Amanda pointed out.

"Sure. That's the cost of doing business. A quarter of the world's population are middlemen and women, and they probably wouldn't be happy if they are cut out of the business, you know?"

Anja nodded. "Anything else?"

"Well, it must be a blind auction, which is actually better since we need the plant to grow a little before we put it on the market. We also have to make sure the person handling the money and the plant delivery is at least respectable. It's important that we can trust them, at least enough to know we get the full payment due and our client gets what they paid for."

"I think I know the perfect guy. And let me guess—you want me to vet our buyers to make sure we don't sell to Pegasus?"

He winked. "That is correct."

The hacker nodded and stood quickly. "I'll get started right away. When the secure line to Courtney is open, I'll send you a message."

"Thanks Anja."

She shrugged. "It's what you pay me for."

He nodded. Kennedy had handled the payments wired to their employees, so he would have to find the paperwork and see if they didn't need to pay Anja a little more for her work.

Sal made his way to his room and fifteen minutes later, his phone buzzed to advise him that a secure satellite connection had been opened between him and Courtney.

A couple of voicemail messages from her hadn't been delivered until he reached a delivery zone. He listened to them quickly before he dialed her number.

The call went to a voice machine almost immediately and he shook his head and dragged in a deep breath. "Hey, Courtney, it's Sal. We've dug into what happened to your father and we actually found something that might interest you. It's probably not the kind of thing to talk about over a voicemail since it is delicate, so give me a call when you're around. I...miss you." He killed the connection almost immediately once he said that. There was enough sentimental bullshit these days and it was all he could do to not let it overwhelm him.

Some things were better talked about in person, he thought with a nod, placed the phone on his bedside table, and lay down.

CHAPTER NINETEEN

"Hey, Sal." Courtney sounded well rested and perky. "I received your message. Is everything okay?"

Sal took a moment to rub the fuzziness from his eyes. He'd barely had five hours of sleep before his phone buzzed incessantly to tell him that Courtney tried to contact him from the other side of the encrypted connection.

"Right...hi, morning," he growled.

"Did I wake you?"

"A little...uh, yeah," he admitted. "But that's not a problem. It's nice to hear your voice again."

"Ditto, big guy," she said with a soft giggle that she immediately regretted. Big guy? What was she, a preppy sorority girl? "Anyway, I dropped you a couple of documents about the sale of intellectual property between my dad's company and some vague and hard to track buyers."

"Our IT specialist actually ran into something similar," he said, his eyes narrowed. "Some documents were apparently signed by your dad before he died but only submitted into the records after he passed away."

Courtney nodded but remembered that she was on the phone and he couldn't see her. "Huh. What do you make of these documents popping up all over the place right now?"

"It looks like someone is trying to clean shop," he said. "You have made waves there, so whoever it is, they probably want to move everything they need out of the company before anyone notices you have it. They had the sales records already printed and signed, but they need them to be a matter of record for them to be legally binding."

"I think I know who you're talking about," she said and her good mood vanished almost immediately. "There's a woman working at my dad's company called Andressa Covington. She's given me a hard time ever since I got here, and when I retaliated, she backed down a little too easily and accepted a nominal and useless position in the company. Do you have anything I can set as a trap for her?"

"We could always send her into the Zoo," Sal said, only partially joking. "The beasties in there have a way to fix problems like that without too much fuss."

She chuckled. "I wish. Although we might want to revisit that idea later. No, I thought about some kind of intellectual property of my dad's she might not already have filed and that would make her come to us—or me, rather—to deal with personally. If I can get her to agree to pay me off, that should put her in hot water with the authorities around here."

"You only need her to show up, really," Sal said. "Tell her you have something of the company's and you know she's the one who's disposed of the rest of the stuff, so you want her to include you in the action. Make it believable so she thinks that she has to buy your protection in this situation—something she can't do without."

"Right," Courtney agreed. "But I don't think I have anything I can access easily. I'm still new around here, and while I've been given free access, they still keep very close tabs on me."

"I think our hacker might be able to help you with that, actually," he told her. "She has the technological equivalent of the nose of a bloodhound, which means we should have something for you within a day or two. No promises, though. She's the expert."

"Great," she said. "Call me as soon as you have something."

"Will do. Talk to you later."

He hung up and shook his head before he gathered some clothes to throw on quickly and left his little apartment for the server room. He wasn't sure why he knew Anja would be there, hard at work, but when he saw her still glued to the screen of her computer, he wasn't at all surprised.

"Hey, so," he began, "I know we've increased your workload around here a lot lately, but I wondered if you could take some time to run a quick search on someone."

"Andressa Covington," she said and tapped her headset.

"You were listening to all that?" Sal asked.

"Of course," she retorted. "It's my private comm system, so I have to make sure nothing is shared on it I don't approve of."

"Okay." He was anxious to move past this topic of

conversation. "Anyway, do you have a way to check for anything that might be along the lines of bio-secure tech that's connected to her we could use?"

"I'm already on it," Anja said, her gaze still fixed on the screen.

"Huh, right." He realized he seriously needed to give her a raise when he had the chance. "Thanks."

She nodded but remained entirely focused on her work. He decided it was time to get the hell out of there.

"Pita plant, freshly removed from the Zoo, healthy and blooming and available for purchase to the highest bidder," the man in the blue jacket said and dusted the snow from his shoulders. "Do you really believe someone might have one of those? Do you know they've tried to get one of them out ever since the damn plants were discovered and nobody who tried has even made it out of the Zoo?"

The man in the red jacket nodded and pulled his hood back to reveal fresh good looks with only a hint of salt-and-pepper in the stubble on his chin. "I know who the people making the sale are. They have worked in the Zoo for a while and have brought good material out for almost a year now. They can be trusted."

"If you say so," the other man responded with a chuckle. "And they aren't above fabricating something to raise cash when they're in need? Please, we need evidence that they actually have a plant before I can even consider putting in a bid."

"I would agree with you in principle and especially

since whoever owns the plant has taken such pains to remain anonymous. However, I have reason to believe, based on the way they said that all bids are subject to inspection and the sellers may choose not to do business with certain buyers led me to believe there can only be one company who would be so confident," the first man replied.

He shook his head as he looked out over the vast expanse of snow outside. No matter how much technology in the world advanced, there would always be people who came to Switzerland for the resorts and stayed for the agreeable banking laws. "I obviously cannot confirm it, but no other company would be able to remove a Pita plant and live to tell the tale, let alone sell it."

"So, this…Heavy Metal," the investor asked and glanced at a pad he carried. "What do you know about them?"

"It's run by a couple of veterans," the informant explained. He flipped the images to the pictures of a younger-looking man and a military-looking woman.

"Salinger Jacobs, one of the most prolific authors on what comes in and out of the Zoo over the past six months. He's young and only a doctoral candidate. Then there's Madigan Kennedy, formerly part of the military complement on the base there who gave up her position to join Jacobs full time. They have more members on their team, but it has been difficult to find anything resembling details on them.

"Anyway, they were responsible for the first live animal brought out of the Zoo and handed it over for a significant fee to one of our competitors. From the looks of things, they've established ties with companies in the United

States. We think government contracts are their eventual goals, but if they have an item this rare up for sale now, there's no telling the kinds of benefits that could be acquired if we were to make ties with them while they're still starting up."

The businessman scowled as he studied the various reports of the missions run by the two. They were fairly active in the area and more than a little connected with the bases already established there. Which meant they would only continue to grow. If they had connections with major companies in the US, they would grow much faster.

"How many bids have been placed?" he finally asked.

"Six, so far," his companion replied.

"What kind of money have they put on it?"

"Unknown," the man stated morosely. "It has been a blind bidding process so far. I can make some inquiries, but there's no guarantee that I'll find anything of note before the auction comes to an end."

The investor nodded and sighed deeply. "I need to look into what funds I can move. I'll get you an exact figure tomorrow."

CHAPTER TWENTY

The stories about the Zoo and the creatures living inside proliferated to the point that people began to buy into them—in the commandant's office and even in the budgetary department, which prided itself on its supreme indifference and self-isolation.

Of course, it only added fuel to the fire when more bodies were abandoned because it was impossible to bring them out. All too often, teams simply vanished. One or two of them managed a brief distress message on the open channel to say they were under attack but Zoo interference remained a huge issue. Those in the jungle tried to assist but inevitably reached the beleaguered groups too late.

The administration now faced the problems involved in how to explain to the family members of the soldiers who died in the Zoo what had happened—and, potentially, what could eventually become a horde of lawsuits regarding wrongful deaths. Finally, the people in charge reconsidered their stance on how many people would be sent into the Zoo. They also began to run drills with the newcomers to ensure that they knew the advisable tactics if they were engaged.

Niels didn't mind the fact that they had only one specialist on this simple Pita plant run with a dozen gunners to protect the man. That, in itself, wasn't too much of a problem, but they had rapidly run out of specialists who wanted to head into the Zoo, which made it almost impossible to find qualified personnel.

The specialist they were stuck with now was a doctor with a sheaf of credentials in the States and who appeared to be quite the catch on paper. When the problems with his assaults—sexual and otherwise—emerged, though, the reason why he'd elected to join the teams heading into the Zoo became clearer.

What hadn't been clear before the moment of no return was the fact that the man was about a hundred pounds overweight and seemed to have a smoking habit he couldn't resist. Smoking wasn't allowed in the Zoo as the pungent smell would attract the very animals they tried to avoid. Sadly, the harsh reality that he had to quit at the same moment he entered the jungle made an already disagreeable fellow almost impossible to work with.

Niels had dealt with smokers before, and while they could get edgy when they were forced to quit for a couple of days, most had been professional enough to make sure their habits didn't interfere with their ability to do their jobs. This man had no such professionalism and made it a point to render everyone's life miserable until he finally had the smoke he so desperately needed.

Of course, Niels wasn't one to judge someone for their vices of choice. Hell, he had a couple of his own. He merely demanded professionalism from the people he worked with and this specialist seemed utterly incapable of delivering that.

He adjusted his grip on the rifle and scanned the jungle once more. One of the first lessons he'd learned about survival in the Zoo was to keep an eye on the treetops. There wasn't always something there, but when there was, it was way better to see it before it attacked you. This wasn't something he would have learned in the quick lessons they gave first-timers but rather something that was only learned through tough experience and, usually, lost lives.

Panthers now used the trees as cover to attack unsuspecting travelers, but other beasts had begun to employ the same tactics. They were annoyingly effective, and the only real way to handle beasts like that was to anticipate their movements. The trees were tall, which made them difficult to navigate without triggering all kinds of motion sensors. If you were watchful and careful, the advance warning would enable you to gun the creatures down before they were able to kill anyone on your team.

Of course, these days, the smarter option was to move away from any curious panthers and make sure they knew they had been seen and would not be able to rely on ambush tactics when they attacked. They tended to take that kind of response seriously and backed away from any confrontation in which they didn't have the element of surprise. These were creatures on the hunt and wouldn't charge any potential prey that could defend themselves.

But there was sometimes another way in which the Zoo reacted. Niels checked his weapon for at least the tenth time as he recalled the two major attacks he'd survived. Both were still vivid enough in his memory to make him nervous about the next one. And there would always be a next one, he accepted morosely. That was why the teams were double their usual size and ran with more gunners and fewer specialists.

It still made him sweat to recall how the animals reacted—fought together, joined forces, and used complementary tactics to drag the teams down. They didn't always defeat those they attacked, as evidenced by Niels himself, but they did always manage to decimate the ranks before they slunk away.

He held his rifle closer to his chest as his gaze swept the trees again to make sure he wasn't followed. A whole fucking jungle of creatures out there wanted him dead, and he wouldn't go down without a fight—or be caught unawares.

A flicker of motion caught his attention as he turned. Something moved and triggered the motion sensors, but by the time he managed to focus, it had gone. That made tracking it much more difficult and he fought to stay calm.

"Fuck, I need a goddamn cigarette," the specialist whined and pulled at the suit he wore. It was a little tight given that he was easily the largest person ever to wear it.

"If you need a goddamn cigarette, why don't you have one?" Niels snapped and shook his head in irritation. "Save us all from your incessant bitching and maybe cleanse the gene pool by taking yourself out of it while you're at it."

"I don't need to take this kind of abuse." The man tugged at his suit again. "You're all out here to make sure I get out alive and well. Anything less would mean you failed at your job, which means that if I want to bitch incessantly about my needs in this primitive, hellish, piece-of-shit place, you have to take it."

"Hey, shut up," the team leader commanded. "If you want to shout, you can use the isolated channels. You'll attract all kinds of hell our way."

Niels grinned, tilted his head smugly, and tapped his rifle before he resumed his survey of the treetops. As he moved to the front of the line, another small movement caught his attention. He tensed immediately and aimed his weapon in the general direction because he couldn't be sure exactly where he'd seen it.

"Did you see something?" the team leader asked and squinted into the underbrush.

"Something moved just outside my range of vision," he replied. "I couldn't make out what it was."

"Well, keep your eyes peeled. If we're walking into a trap, I want to be the first one to know about it."

"Will do, Sarge," Niels replied. "I'm not even sure there was anything, but—"

He paused when something twitched the barrel of his rifle. It was gentle at first, which made him wonder if he had a malfunction in his power armor. These new suits were far more comfortable, but all kinds of bugs needed to be worked out. He hated the fact that the soldiers out there were used as guinea pigs to prep the new suits of combat armor that would hit the market soon.

Well, he wouldn't mind it so much if they didn't demand that they turn reports in they weren't paid for on the combat functionality of the suits. It was a pain in the ass, and it would always be something he objected to. Extra paperwork that got in the way of time in the bar would automatically set him against it.

The odd tweak at his weapon continued and Niels drew back instinctively to examine his rifle. Something had wound around the barrel from the branches above them.

"What the fuck?" he demanded and yanked the gun away with all his strength. The tendrils wrapped around his rifle gave fairly easily but immediately jerked back, this time with enough strength to drag him off his feet. If it weren't for the power armor that clamped on the rifle, it would have been torn from his fingers.

Despite that, there wasn't much he could do other than be dragged by whatever the tentacles were that now had his rifle in a vice. His finger locked on the trigger and he opened fire into the darkness ahead of him. He fell hard onto his stomach, his mind blank for a moment before the consequences of what had happened made him turn quickly. His team had already taken defensive positions and these excluded him.

Fucking assholes.

The jungle seemed to hold its breath for a moment before movement erupted all around. The animals had either lain in wait for them or had been drawn by the sudden outburst of gunfire. Niels scowled as the gauntlet closed around the team and left him alone and isolated as the creatures attacked the circle of eleven men. The gunners gathered around the fat specialist, who whimpered and prayed before a volley peppered the first wave of monsters that attacked.

He clutched his weapon, afraid to open fire himself for fear of hitting his own men. Of course, it also occurred to him that shooting while he was out in the open himself would make him a very easy target. He acknowledged the truth of this but was sure the main reason why he held his fire was because he didn't want to hit his comrades.

Well, most of them.

He turned as more of the tentacles descended from the treetops and seemed to follow him as he shuffled away and tried to aim at the writhing, rapidly moving vegetation.

"It's like I've stumbled into the world's worst hentai," he protested and fired at the tentacle vines as best he could. The few that he managed to hit quickly withdrew, but the others surged closer to wind around his gun again and haul him closer to the fight.

A bullet hammered into his thigh as his comrades dispensed with the formalities and succumbed to a desperate frenzy. He yanked at his gun and tried to help them with a few random shots at anything he could even partially aim at.

The battle was only a few yards away and he tried to drop the rifle and draw his sidearm instead. The tentacles surged around his hand and the more he fired, the more insistent they became until they had all but immobilized his arm.

He drew his knife with his free hand and attempted to hack the vines loose, but more of them appeared like serpents from the shadows. They encircled his body and he yelled a stream of obscenities when they swung him off his feet and raised him clear of the carnage.

Panthers slunk across the branches, but they didn't seem to notice him, not even when a round hit one of them and knocked it off its perch atop the trees. He'd managed to regain some measure of control over his rifle and had instinctively fired as he passed the beast. Crazy though the thought was, it seemed that while he was entwined in the vines, the other beasts didn't seem to mind him at all.

Of all the weird things he'd learned about in the Zoo, this was one of the most surprising. He clung to his weapon and tried to fire at the panthers as his tentacle captors raised him higher and higher into the trees. The slugs did little damage and although they struck every-where around the beasts, they still completely ignored him. Finally, he realized that he had been drawn to the very top of the canopy, and for a moment, he could have sworn he saw a pair of eyes look at him. They weren't malevolent or savage—or even primal, for that matter. Almost curious, he thought in a detached, objective way.

Niels jerked back to reality as his vine-cage began to snap or pull away. A cold dread lurched into his stomach when he looked at the ground and realized how high he was. He wanted to scream but the bile that rose in his throat drowned the sound in a gargle of despair. The grasp that had supported him released and gravity instantly took hold.

The downward spiral seemed to take forever. The gunfire had ceased as the jungle around the killing field plunged into a dense and impossible silence. Even the roars and shrieks of the angry animals faded entirely as he fell. It couldn't have taken more than three seconds, but it felt like it would last a lifetime.

Finally, he struck the jungle floor and landed on his back. Even with the armor that was supposed to prevent any kind of shock from affecting the body inside, he could only imagine that the impact of a two-ton suit dropped from way more than thirty feet was not what the designers had in mind. There weren't many suits of armor in the world that could nullify an impact like that.

A sharp pain seared up his back and knocked the breath out of him. It was almost enough to make him pass out, but as he drifted between consciousness and unconsciousness, his curiosity won out and forced him to focus. Twelve bodies sprawled on the ground beside him, torn to pieces in all kinds of creative ways. The armor had been pulled off some while others simply had small puncture marks where poison had been injected.

"Fuck," Niels whispered and looked at his legs. He knew his back was broken, but his arms and neck still worked and he was able to drag himself onto the roots he'd landed on.

The tentacles now tugged and nudged at the dead men on the jungle floor. They poked and prodded at the bodies a few moments before they raised them one by one.

There was considerable inspection of the specialist, Niels noted, but it seemed that the tentacles and even the animals avoided him. He could understand why—he was a prick—but there was something oddly poetic about the fact that there was something so wrong with the man that not even an all-consuming jungle would absorb him.

He realized that a couple of the creatures had noticed him. They didn't seem to be sure whether he was dead or not. A couple of the panthers padded closer and licked their poisoned fangs. He raised his rifle and fired at them. The first one died almost instantly, but the second bounded to the left and circled in an effort to avoid the bullets. It bought the mutant a few seconds, but eventually, it dropped as well.

Unfortunately, the shooting attracted the other monsters, who looked at him like they were surprised he was still alive. Maybe he simply made this up and tried to make some sense of it all through a lame attempt to anthropomorphize the monsters that had killed his comrades and the geek asshole.

They seemed malevolent enough to attack and he realized that his rifle was empty. There were no spare mags in his belt. He fumbled in his pouch and his fingers closed around two grenades he'd brought. They weren't standard issue for people like him, but he'd always made sure he was as well armed as he could be. He'd acquired the grenades from the weapons dealer in the base.

Creatures surged toward him as he pulled his little friends clear. The tentacles slithered from the treetops. He didn't want to think about what would happen if they attacked him again, so he pulled the pins. Teeth and claws raked and savaged his suit of armor to rip and slash, bruise and hurt. While he couldn't feel anything below the waist, they began to attack his torso with the same frenzied intensity. He dropped the grenades at his sides and the clips fell with them.

The creatures seemed to realize they were in imminent danger, but they had neither the time nor the intelligence to realize exactly how much. Niels closed his eyes and leaned back.

CHAPTER TWENTY-ONE

Madigan stepped into the bar and closed her eyes as the cool air-conditioned environment banished the heat from outside. If they ever did retire somewhere away from the Zoo, she would manage to convince Sal to take them somewhere cooler. She wouldn't mind if it was hot in the summertime when they could go to the beach and take time off there, but only for a couple of months in the year.

She knew, though, he would pursue this kind of lifestyle until he obtained his doctorate and probably after that. Like every other person in the world, he liked his creature comforts, but there was something else that drove him. She didn't know quite how to describe it other than insatiable curiosity. He wanted to fill his brain with as many facts and figures as he could. It wasn't something she shared with him, but she could understand it.

He wouldn't retire anytime soon. And in truth, neither would she. Barring any kind of nasty accidents, she didn't see herself taking a desk job to run Heavy Metal from a distance. But it still couldn't hurt to have something planned, right?

She strode to the bar and drew in a deep breath of the cool air as she raised a hand to the bartender. It hadn't been a lie when she told Sal that she'd been drinking less, but that didn't mean she had stopped entirely. She was still well-known enough in the bar for the man standing behind it to know what she would order. That plus the fact that she and Sal provided them with a steady stream of good, cheap vodka from the Russian base.

He placed a beer mug in front of her, filled to the brim with a thick malt beer, and she decided she would stick to the counter instead of a table. The bar would fill up quickly over the next few minutes, and she didn't want to share her table with loud and abrasive recent returnees from the Zoo.

A handful entered as she took her first sip. They discussed something she was already aware of. News wasn't slow to do the rounds, even if they were stuck in the middle of a compound.

"They didn't even get a chance to signal for help," one of the men said and shook his head. "By the time a team reached them, there wasn't anything left. Most of the bodies were gone."

"How would you know that?" another of the newcomers asked. "Were you on the team that got there?"

"I was part of the team that had to write the letters to the family to explain to them that while we were reasonably certain they were dead, we only had a couple of corpses to prove it," the first man retorted defensively.

Madigan resisted the urge to order a shot of whiskey to

add to her beer. It was too early in the day to be drunk, and Sal expected her back at the compound before sunset. She didn't want to keep him waiting.

"Kennedy, right?" A man settled onto a seat beside her. "Madigan Kennedy?"

"That's me," she said with a small smile and raised her glass at the young man in uniform. "How can I help you?"

"Right to business, then?" he asked.

"If you don't mind"

"Fair enough." He chuckled. "To cut a long story short, I'm at…let's call it a loose end. My squad took serious casualties in our last run, and the commandant gave us word that it'll be a while before they have the manpower to fill our quota again. Of course, they'll plug those left into other squads when we're needed, but I've been told that it'll take some time before that happens."

"And you want to work in the meantime," she said to bring them to the point the younger soldier seemed to want to avoid saying outright. "You're looking for freelance work."

"In a word…yeah," he said with a nod. "The word around the base is that Heavy Metal is looking for muscle and can pay for the trouble."

"What's your name, kid?" Madigan asked.

"PFC Brian Abrams." He grinned. "Like the tank."

"Nice to meet you, Abrams. Look, the word around the base is right. We will need muscle soon, but the details are still a little sketchy. The basic idea is that we need a twelve-man team and we'll move…delicate and expensive merch. The pay will be good, so if you don't mind, you could spread the word about the opportunity so we don't get the team up and running at the last minute."

"Huh." He grunted. "It sounds like something I would be interested in. And quite a few other people would be too. Seriously, Heavy Metal has a good rep when it comes to the people you work with."

"That's good to know." She swallowed the last of her pint and after a second thought, refused when the bartender offered her a refill. "Anyway, here's my contact info. Let me know if there's anyone else who springs to mind for the job or if you have to back out for any reason."

"Will do," Abrams said with a smile. "And thanks."

"Jacobs?"

Sal glanced up from his laptop to where Anja hovered at his half-open door. It wasn't usual for her to come to him for anything. In the past, when she'd wanted his attention, she buzzed his phone with a dozen illegible text messages until he finally wandered to the server room to see what she wanted.

"Hey, Anja," he said and smiled as he locked his laptop quickly. "How can I help you?"

"First of all, it's really adorable that you think a simple passcode protection will be enough to keep that data safe," she said with a grin. "You might want to think about letting me run encryption software on there to make sure that if anyone did get hold of it, they'd need a couple of decades to get through."

"And what would happen if I forgot my password or something?" he asked, genuinely curious.

"Come on, a genius like you?" she asked before she realized that he'd asked a legitimate question. "Oh, well, you could probably simply bring it to me and I'd get it for you without too much trouble."

"Right," he said with a soft grunt that might have been disapproval. "Is there something I can do for you?"

"Yes. Yes, there is," Anja said. "I have the video Courtney needs to deal with Covington ready to go whenever she is. I hoped you could contact her and let her know."

Sal regarded her with a little bemusement. "You have her number and you have already monitored my conversations with her."

"Well, yes, which is why I don't feel comfortable talking to her myself," she explained. "I know a lot about her, but she knows nothing of me so it would be a one-sided conversation."

"It wouldn't need to be a conversation at all," he grumbled and pushed from his seat. "Send her the damn thing, add a smiley face to the message for her to know it's a human sending it, and violá, you have yourself a sent video."

"Perfect. Could you do that?" She handed him a memory stick.

"Fine." He took it from her. "But if we're a team, you have to trust the people you work with."

Anja shrugged. She wasn't particularly in the mood to handle making friends across the world, but if it would shut him up about it, she would agree and conveniently forget to comply later.

"Hey, are you busy?" Madigan asked from the doorway, pushed it open, and did a quick double-take when she saw Anja in the room. She shook her head and looked meaningfully at him.

"Not particularly busy, why?" he asked and placed the memory drive on his desk.

"Do you need me?" the hacker asked, her expression anxious.

"I don't think so," Madigan said. "Thanks for your help, Anja."

The woman nodded and looked away. She clearly wasn't that comfortable with compliments, so she simply beat a hasty retreat, stepped out of the room, and shut the door behind her.

"What was that about?" Madigan asked, tilting her head.

"She's not comfortable talking to Courtney, so she wanted me to send the Covington file to her," Sal said, waving the memory stick. "What's up?"

"I spread the word that we're looking for people to transport the plant," she said with a chuckle. "I didn't outright say it was the plant, but I think I implied it fairly effectively. Anyone who knows anything about anything will be able to connect the dots and make the connection easily, I think."

"Good," he said with a quick nod. They needed to be subtle about this. "Anything else?"

"Well, you know this little mission will be expensive, so you might want to prepare for that," she added. "Either way, I spread the net with people I trust to find the guys who will actually run the mission. We won't hire blind on this one. I hope you feel like walking in your armor."

"Speaking of armor…" He handed a file to her. "This is the information Courtney sent me about the metal Pegasus has extracted. Apparently, much of the research Pegasus did ran through her father's R&D group. Based on her observations—which are based on her father's tests—this won't work very well in the Zoo. She appreciated that we're doing this for her, but if she hadn't looked into it, no one would have known that it would work outside the Zoo but cause a considerable number of deaths inside."

"From the look of the leg that we pulled out of there, I'd say that it's already caused too many deaths inside." She gave the file a quick study. "Wait, did she tell you to say that word for word?"

"I might have paraphrased a little." He grinned sheepishly.

Madigan chuckled. "Okay, I need to keep in touch with my guys. I'll let you know when I have a full sheet for them."

"Thanks," Sal said. "Close the door on the way out?"

Madigan grinned and considered asking him what he would do after she closed the door but decided against it. They were comfortable enough with each other that if he had any needs he needed satisfying, he would come to her. As a result, she simply gave him a coy smirk that told him everything he needed to know and pulled the door shut behind her.

CHAPTER TWENTY-TWO

"Hey...Courtney?" Anja asked, suddenly very aware of the headset she wore.

"Hi, Anja," the woman replied through their secure satellite link. "Sal said that you might give me a call soon. How can I help you?"

"I hope I'm not interrupting anything and I hope the video I sent was suitable for the task."

"It looked great," Courtney replied honestly. "I still haven't sent it yet, so we'll see how that goes."

"Right." The hacker shook her head. "Anyway, I found a bio-locked laptop that Covington uses often. It's inside her house and behind what appears to be significant security, so that might be what you're looking for. I'd like to confirm it, but bio-locked equipment can't be hacked remotely. I'll need physical access."

"So we have to get it out of her house," she mused, 'which is why we'll need the video anyway. Look, can I talk to Sal about this?"

"I can patch you to his line," Anja said with a nod. "He's

probably still working on the paperwork for everything he's trying to pull. If you don't mind me saying so, I think he's a little too ambitious with all this. All that's missing is for him to cackle maniacally while trying to take over the world."

"That's…a slight exaggeration," Courtney said, although she knew it was less slight than she would like to admit. "But he has good intentions."

"All the guys who want to take over the world do," Anja retorted with a trace of humor. "Or they think they do, anyway. His comm is open. I'll patch you into that."

"Thanks."

The Russian nodded. She knew the other woman couldn't see her but that wasn't something she was particularly concerned about. Her part, for now, was done and she could happily go back to things she knew and understood. Computers were far less stressful than human interaction. Sal was much better at talking to people than she was, and since he knew Courtney better as well, he would be able to interpret the squeaky quality she'd heard in the woman's voice.

Anja looked at her computer. She killed her connection to Sal and Courtney's conversation and set it to record so she could listen to it afterward. It was still her private satellite feed and no matter what anyone thought, she needed to keep control over what was done on it.

Satisfied that the details were taken care of, she turned to the laptop where she had decrypted the information on the hard drive Anderson had sent them to retrieve. She wasn't entirely sure what she would find, but whatever it was, she'd make damn sure she accessed every last byte of data.

Madigan had made a deal, and any agreement Heavy Metal made was one she made too. That was what being part of a team was all about. You shared the good and the bad and gave all you had to everything you did. Kennedy and Jacobs had given her their all when they took her on blind-sight, as it were. She didn't particularly enjoy working for third parties like the colonel, but if her bosses felt it was important, she wouldn't ask any questions.

A section of the hard drive had been decrypted, although most of what she read still didn't make much sense. Her major had been in computer sciences, and all the engineering jargon that had been included in something that was clearly meant for engineers might as well have been in an alien language.

It looked like designs and the pictures were there, so she hoped someone would know what it meant when she uploaded the section that had been decrypted to her dark web drop box. Messenger sites that were flooded with random chatter tended to be ignored by the major dipper agencies due to the sheer volume of data that was put through them, which made it relatively safe to store untraceable blocks for a short time.

She put a timer on the block to erase automatically after fifteen minutes, but it wasn't really necessary. Someone accessed it and pulled it off the messenger service less than five minutes later.

"Someone's eager for something to do," Anja said as she closed the chat room and deleted her account there. It wouldn't be difficult to make a new one and repeat the process.

"Hey Sal." Courtney said, the phone held between her ear and shoulder as she sifted through the papers on her desk. "How are things in the Zoo?"

"Same old, same old," he replied cheerfully. "Critters trying to kill us and not succeeding, us killing the critters. Madie says hi, by the way."

"Don't fucking call me that!" she heard the other woman yell in the background.

"How are things in LA?" he asked after what she could only assume was Madigan punching him on the arm.

"Annoyingly similar," Courtney growled. "I received the data from Anja, by the way, but I have a feeling you don't want me to use it yet."

"Trust that feeling," Sal said. "We have a plan, and our end of it would have to happen before you steal that laptop. Oh, and since we could use as much man or woman power as we can get our hands on, it would be best if you could come here for a couple of weeks."

Courtney decided not to make a joke about that. Robinson stood not ten feet away from her and typed rapidly into his laptop as he worked through the various forms the board had sent for her approval. He had been vital ever since she'd taken up her position there—so much so that she'd sent notes to the HR department to improve his benefits and up his paycheck come the next quarter. She didn't tell him, though, since she wasn't sure if his input would decrease when he realized he would receive a pay raise.

"Why do you need me there?" she asked.

"Besides the fact that you're one of the founding members of Heavy Metal and are missed? Well, we need your help to get our hands on data that only you are privy to."

"Right. And while I'm there, it might be a good opportunity to find someone who might be able to acquire the assets we're looking into."

"Anja can probably help you with that," Sal replied. "She has a host of connections with various criminal enterprises around the world. It's actually a little scary when you stop to think about it."

"Perfect." Courtney allowed herself to grin. She'd never met the girl but was sure she'd like her. "I only need to pack and I'll be on my way."

"We're looking forward to it." She could tell that he was smiling from the slight warmth in his voice. "Fly safely."

She pressed the end call button and stared at the screen of her phone as it went black. To be honest, she had wanted to head to the Zoo for quite a while now. She missed Sal and Madigan and looked forward to working with the newer members, but there was also the fact that she desperately needed to put some distance between herself and all crazy circumstances in LA.

"So, Robinson…"

"I've already put in a request for the company jet to take us to the base," he replied and looked up from the screen of his laptop. "They'll probably send the approval in a couple of hours, which gives us time to pack and prepare."

"Wait." She raised her hand to stop him saying anything more. "Gives us time?"

"Well, yes," he replied. "You don't think you'll go alone on this trip, right? You need me to deal with all the clerical work—which I'd be able to do on the plane—and I'm your personal assistant. It means that whenever you travel on business, I need to be there with you."

Courtney opened her mouth to raise a question about that, but she shut it again as her brain caught up. Honestly, Robinson's expertise in the business world would actually come in handy if she had to deal with these kinds of problems involving Heavy Metal. It wasn't that she didn't think Sal and Madigan were doing a good job, but he was an absolute miracle-worker when it came to streamlining the business process.

"Fine. How long until you can meet me at the airport?"

"I simply need to push your appointments back until you return," he said. "That would only leave a few calls and —oh, I need to pick up my passport."

"Huh. That's your plan to make sure these guys don't get their hands on what could be the most expensive thing that has been brought out of the Zoo?" Collins asked and looked mildly skeptical.

"It's not a terrible plan," one of the other soldiers replied. "Fair enough, there's a fair amount that could go wrong but it's not terrible."

"I appreciate the support, guys," Sal said with a chuckle. "Do you have any questions?"

The twelve men and women who had been assembled looked at one another. They had been brought out to the compound to be briefed on the mission they'd all signed up for. Kennedy's message had spread much faster than had been anticipated, and they all thought it was a good idea to move the mission up on the schedule. There really was no need to risk another attack on the compound if it could realistically—and safely—be avoided.

"You've all worked together," Kennedy interjected. "And we've worked with all of you, so there's a fair amount of trust already established. There's also the commission—which, as discussed, will be substantial, especially given the role you guys will play."

"All things considered," Collins said, "we've got your back. You guys have done a hell of a lot more for us grunts on the ground than the big money guys back home. Our honor isn't for sale out here."

"We appreciate that," Sal assured him. "When the sale for the plant goes through, we'll move out quickly. We have places for you to bunk here in the compound but if you'd rather not, we'll need you on call for three or four days. Obviously, we'll pay you the retainer, so you don't have to worry about taking other jobs in the meantime."

CHAPTER TWENTY-THREE

"What do you mean, the sale went through already?" Carlson asked and leaned closer to the screen on his phone. "I thought we had numbers on all the bids and that we out-paced the highest bid by two million?"

"Two-point-one million, technically," Rodrigo said smoothly. "Which was as high as Pegasus was willing to go, if you remember. My question is why? I thought you people were looking at profits in the billions if you managed to keep the monopoly on the production from that plant."

"I still need to answer to a board of directors, and that was all they were willing to part with on an opening bid," the CEO retorted coldly. "We would have been willing to go higher if they tried to bargain with us."

"They didn't even send a reply." Rodrigo peered at the tablet he carried. "They simply closed the auction."

"Do we know who made the winning bid?" Carlson

asked, his mind already sifting through the list of competitors.

"Again, they kept this on the down low, so..." Rodrigo paused and tapped his tablet. "Well, one of my boys in the lab worked their algorithm out. They've used a third-party proxy to run the sale, so we don't get any more than the only bidder that was actually contacted afterwards. It was...Sanctum. A German company. They were the second highest bidders at seven-point-two million, American."

Carlson made a face. "Why would they take the lower number? That has to be a terrible business policy."

"It seems these people in Heavy Metal don't like you that much, Carlson," Rodrigo said and chuckled dryly. "I wonder why?"

"That was your fuck-up," the CEO pointed out, a menacing edge to his tone. "If the dumbasses you hired hadn't failed in their mission, we wouldn't be in this mess to begin with. Twice."

"And if my men had succeeded twice, you never would have had the chance to get your hands on a Pita plant," his contact retorted with a grin. "See, Carlson my friend, you need to look on the bright side of life. You'll get ulcers otherwise."

"Yeah, bright side," he muttered and shook his head as his mind considered the options. "What's your men's situation outside the compound?"

"I have a drone already in place, so we'll have eyes on the target when it is moved. I alerted the rest of the boys whom I have in the US base that the sale went through and that they will be needed to run an intercept, so they are standing by for our orders. At the same time, we have intel that they've run a hire on the base to have muscle for the transfer, so we anticipate action when the time comes."

"How ready are you to deal with Jacobs and Kennedy?" Carlson asked. "Let's be realistic here. Our attempts to eliminate them haven't been successful by any stretch of imagination."

"That is a problem that has been anticipated and planned for. Don't you worry about it, Mr. Carlson. We'll have the plant to you before too long," Rodrigo assured him with a smile. "And with that said, I think it's time to hang up. The drone operators say people have begun to load up in a couple of Hammerheads in the compound. It would appear that the intercept operation is a go."

"Good luck." Carlson hung up and stared at the phone, his expression tense. "It would seem you'll need it."

Sal stretched in his armor and adjusted to the feel of it. It would take a couple of minutes for his muscle memory to recall that the suit would actually operate on a slight lag. A tenth of a second never sounded like much, but when you were in the middle of a gunfight and had to deal with a barrage of bullets and animals hurtling all over the damn place, a tenth of a second could measure the vital difference between life and death.

The other men and women in heavy armor were quiet and focused as they loaded up beside him. Kennedy was there too, and she quickly gave him a thumbs-up to indicate that she was ready.

"I really hope this works," he said as he leaned back in

his seat and his hand settled on the rifle he carried on the back of his suit. He held his other hand on the pack they carried at all times. Anyone else getting a hold of it would ruin this whole plan for everyone involved, including the other men whom they'd hired for additional muscle.

It wasn't something he really wanted to get into, but Kennedy had made sure they were the ones who would head into the teeth of the fight, and she had insisted that he be the one who carried most of the muscle. She obviously didn't trust him not to get his ass shot.

"Hey, Jacobs," Collins said and picked up the screen that displayed the readings from the sensors set up on the outside of the Hammerhead. "It looks like we picked up a tail."

Sal looked into the screen that now displayed a small drone that followed them as they started to drive along the road toward the base. That wasn't actually their destination, but it was where the only road went. Well, it was either there or into the Zoo, where most of the roads leading to the various construction sites for the walls had already been overrun. They only had one way to go.

"Well, they're a little early, but it's not like we didn't expect them." He strapped the pack to his suit and drew his rifle. It wasn't his first choice to drive around with weapons in hand and ordinarily, he wouldn't even consider something that could be regarded as stupidly dangerous.

Needs must, however, and if they were to fulfil the mission as quickly and as efficiently as possible, they needed to ensure that they put as much distance between themselves and the compound as they could. With pursuit already in place, it almost definitely meant that they might need to face a pitched battle before they got to where they needed to be.

"We've got this, Sal," Kennedy said over a private comm line. "But from now on, we'll go into radio silence."

"Understood," he said, and immediately killed his connection with her. She raised another thumbs-up at him and nodded as he shifted himself closer to the driver's seat.

"Step on it," he ordered and checked the screen again. The drone was still there, which meant that whoever was tracking them was still a fair distance away since they needed the little device to monitor their movements. It was unlikely that would last, however.

He resisted the urge to use the hatch at the top of the Hammerhead to gun the tail down. As much as he disliked being tracked like some kind of animal, he didn't want Pegasus—since they were most likely the ones behind this —to have to scour the desert to find something when he didn't want them to. He wanted their focus to be on him and him alone.

"What are the chances that these people will bring weapons in that can actually destroy one of our Hammerheads?" Sal asked Collins, who was seated beside the driver.

"Well, the use of RPGs hasn't been allowed in this little slice of heaven," the man replied. "All things considered, the militaries involved don't want to bring weapons in that could be used against them for fear that bounty hunters and outside mercs might lay their hands on them. But we can't rule it out either, not with the funding Pegasus has.

"What we really need to worry about are armor-piercing rounds. The armor on these vehicles was substantial already, and with the upgrades Gutierrez added to them, we should be safe inside this compartment. The real problem is the isolated engine section. They might be able to shoot the block out and if they do, we're sitting ducks."

"Is there anything we can do to avoid that?" he asked.

"Didn't Kennedy brief you?" the soldier asked and constantly watched the drone still on their sensors.

"She did, but I wouldn't mind a second—or, in this case, third—opinion."

"Well, the armor should hold attacks off for a couple of minutes under sustained fire," Collins explained cautiously. "Depending on the rounds they use and how sustained their fire is, of course. Yeah, I'd give us a couple of minutes, so we should always keep moving, even while under fire."

"Agreed." Sal leaned back. "And since the drone has now pulled away, I think we need to warm up those evasive maneuvers."

The other man nodded and drew his rifle from its holster in his suit. "Let's lock and load, people. We'll have company in five mikes and counting. Loosen the convoy up and keep moving. No matter what happens, always stay moving—do you hear me, drivers?"

"Roger that," both men said in near unison. Sal pulled himself closer to the door of the Hammerhead. The rest of them would handle any cover fire that would be necessary from the hatch at the top. He had another job to do.

Rodrigo didn't much care to run operations personally. He was the kind of man who liked to keep his distance from these things. Remaining clear of the crimes he committed was the most important part of any defense that involved plausible deniability. When his only connection to the cases he was involved in was a burner phone that was quickly fed into an incinerator, things were so much easier and cleaner.

But when he was paid one of his best paychecks in his career and his all-time best client since he'd left the special forces wanted this done without any hiccups, he needed to be there. It had been a while since he'd been out in the field, so he intended to hang back and oversee the operation.

In person. Fuck, this was already way too complicated. After this, he needed to get Carlson into a room and explain to the man how to run an operation that didn't require his people involved in crazy things. He'd learned a new definition of crazy lately—he thought of it as being in the middle of a firefight with a horde of crazy animals and the people who willingly charged into the most dangerous place on earth for what could only be called a minimal profit. It was asking for bad things to happen.

"Five mikes away, sir," said one of the men driving the top-of-the-line Hammerhead in the middle of a convoy of five, all loaded with angry and well-armed mercs in need of money. His best people had been wiped out or had refused the mission entirely, which meant that he had needed to hire from outside his own organization. That was why he had to be there to run it personally. The fucking ass-wipes at Pegasus needed to get their shit together.

"Keep this trajectory," Rodrigo said. "We'll intercept

them on the road but that doesn't mean they won't try to take the sandy route around us when they see us. It would be best for that to be delayed as long as possible."

"Roger that," the driver said, followed by a chorus of affirmations from the others. They were mostly specialist ATV drivers from South Africa, which made them the best that could be acquired on short notice. They were also notoriously expensive, which meant he had to skimp on the other men. He, too, had a board to answer to regarding his company spending, and with the budget that had been left after he'd hired the drivers… Well, he was glad he had the advantage of numbers—and, hopefully, surprise.

"We have a visual," the lead driver of the convoy called in. "Two Hammerheads with significant improvements to armor are now headed our way."

A link to a live feed from the lead driver's HUD showed him that the Heavy Metal team had brought both their Hammerheads out. They had made a good investment with their recruitment of the mechanic Gutierrez. He could see the armor enhancements. Hammerheads already looked rather squat, but with the enhancements, they had been altered to look stronger, made to bypass most landmines without taking heavy damage, and would be harder to hit dead-on with armor-piercing rounds as well as RPGs. Rodrigo hadn't been able to bring the latter in on short notice, but he'd compensated with a good supply of the former.

"Put a blockade up. Use three of the vehicles," he ordered. "Keep two in the back to pursue any that go off-road."

"Roger that," one of the drivers confirmed and the first

three vehicles quickly formed a heavy-duty barrier across the road. In the open desert terrain, it wasn't the most formidable roadblock, but it would make their quarry pause and rethink their movements—and hopefully expose where the mutual exchange drop would ultimately happen.

The two Hammerheads took a few seconds to come to a halt, and he tried to understand what was happening. The glass didn't reveal any kind of reaction from the people driving the vehicles, but both stopped some two hundred meters away from their blockade.

What was their plan? Rodrigo leaned forward in his seat as he studied the vehicles in an effort to discern what Salinger Jacobs and Madigan Kennedy might be thinking. He should have put more money into higher-quality people, he mused. Perhaps he could have hand-picked a couple of long-range shooters who would be able to find a weak point in the armor and disable the vehicles. That would allow them to deal with the people inside at their leisure.

Instead, he was stuck there in a frustrating attempt to anticipate whether they would run or fight.

Movement from the vehicles caught his attention. Doors peeled open from both Hammerheads and six armored figures exited each one. Most wore what looked like the armor that was regularly used by the military out there, which made it simpler to identify the suit Madigan Kennedy usually wore. It was heavier and sturdier than the rest, and he knew she had a couple of shoulder-mounted rockets to launch should things go poorly, the sign of a well-funded freelancer.

One of the Hammerheads reversed a couple of dozen

meters before it stopped once more and the second pushed forward a few feet. This seemed to be a coordinated effort as a few seconds later, the men in the barricade yelled a warning.

"Take cover!" At the loud cry, the men ducked quickly. Rodrigo resisted the urge to mimic them since he wasn't in the line of fire, but the man whose HUD had streamed to him had gone suspiciously quiet and a handful of holes appeared in the glass of the windshield. He knew it was supposed to be bulletproof, but that didn't help much when the bullets were armor-piercing and punched through the impact-resistant glass like it was made of… well, glass.

The point where he actually did take cover was when the shoulder mount on Kennedy's suit raised and a white trail of smoke appeared. This clearly demonstrated that they had come ready for a fight and didn't have any inclination to avoid resistance either. The small rocket streaked towards them at an impossible speed, exploded in a white-hot flash, and left them coated in a cloud of smoke for a few seconds.

It was a diversion tactic. He knew this almost before he raised his head once more. It pained him that he'd actually had to duck but he hadn't worn a suit, knowing he couldn't be involved in any of the fighting. He still needed legal exculpation from all this.

As the smoke cleared, two heavy engines roared to their full capacity. He peered into one of the streaming HUDs that remained functional and immediately detected the ruse. Most of the men and woman in armor had dismounted from the two Hammerheads and now fired relentlessly. One of the vehicles accelerated toward the blockade. He couldn't see if there actually was a driver, but it seemed that they planned to ram the three vehicles that blocked the road.

It was all a diversion, of course. He couldn't see Jacob's hybrid suit among those who had dismounted, and the second Hammerhead hurtled away from the road and into the desert, away from the Zoo and toward the wall and the base.

"We're in pursuit," Rodrigo advised through his mic. "My Hammerhead will pursue the one that has broken away. That has to be Jacobs in there. The rest of you, hold the blockade and take these motherfuckers out."

"Roger that!" came the response from the men in charge of each vehicle. They dismounted hastily in anticipation of being rammed by the oncoming Hammerhead, while he remained in the one that roared onto the sand to pursue Jacobs.

He assumed Gutierrez had been responsible for armoring the vehicles—and she had done one hell of a good job—but that didn't mean there weren't drawbacks. In a heavy fight, they had an advantage and the men holding the blockade would have their work cut out for them to keep that one from busting through. Which, of course, made it a good idea to leave the vehicle, but that was neither here nor there. The real prize now attempted to escape and with the added weight of the extra armor, it wouldn't get far.

A resounding crash indicated that the first vehicle had impacted the blockade. The men's weapons exploded into life as they engaged the Heavy Metal team. It would be an interesting fight since the men and woman on Jacob's side were better armored, armed, and trained for a fight like this.

Those he'd hired wore suits that were already three years old and it showed. While they were capable enough as bounty hunters, they lacked the kind of training and coordination that came with a proper military background. They would be slowly picked apart out there, and Rodrigo knew that it was highly unlikely that anyone would miss them too badly. He'd read their records. To a man, they were all amoral sons of bitches.

But none of that mattered if he obtained his prize. Sal had broken away too quickly. He'd obviously seen his people outnumbered and wanted to make a break for it. As skilled a scientist as he was, he certainly lacked in the same qualities the men and women he'd hired for protection possessed, and that would be his last mistake.

And even better, it seemed his quarry was alone in the vehicle. Heavy Metal had hired a twelve-man team. Assuming someone was driving the one that had crashed into the blockade and Salinger himself was driving this one, all fourteen people on this mission were accounted for. Rodrigo clutched his armrest with one hand and his seatbelt with the other and his heart raced with anticipation as they closed the gap on Jacobs.

He could tell that the scientist knew they were in pursuit due to the crazed way he drove. The vehicle raced almost blindly across the sand and didn't slow, even for the sharp drops through the dunes. The idiot was headed for a bad crash, and that definitely would not work for Rodrigo. They were there for something in particular, after all—a plant that could very easily be destroyed. That was a risk he wasn't willing to take. They needed to find a way to stop him without destroying the Hammerhead.

One of the men in his vehicle shoved the top hatch up and heaved himself through the hole before he drew his rifle from the holster on his back. It wasn't the newest of weapons but given the stagnancy in firearms over the past couple of decades, it wasn't like the gun itself made much of a difference. They were always made with reliability in mind, so he didn't have to worry about its quality.

The quality of the shooter was another story altogether.

"We'll pull slightly to the left to give you a better angle. Shoot the engine block out," Rodrigo commanded through the comm line. "If that Hammerhead tips and our prize is destroyed in the chaos, none of you will be paid. Keep that in mind."

"Roger that," the man said and clearly sounded irritated at the lack of respect their leader had for his abilities. He didn't care. These men would be paid far more than their worth if they obtained that plant, but he would make damn sure no one would be paid if he didn't get what Pegasus wanted. Too much money had already been wasted in down payments on failed expeditions.

The merc raised his rifle close to his face, more out of habit than necessity. While you wore a suit, you couldn't pull the gun close enough to your face for it to make a difference. Most of the suits, even those as old as these mutts wore, would have the aiming software embedded in the HUDs that would make all that irrelevant anyway.

He'd hired people who weren't trained or experienced

in the use of power combat suits. That was discouraging information to find out this late in the game.

When the man opened fire, Rodrigo could hear the shots even without needing to patch into the man's HUD. He did anyway but quit hastily after the first few seconds. It was bumpy up there and bouncing around in the back of a Hammerhead at high speed over desert terrain made it all hellishly more nauseating to add the experience from another perspective as well. He simply patched into the more stable and reliable viewpoint from the front and leaned back in his seat. The highly trained driver would know how to corral Jacobs in a way that would hopefully leave their prize intact.

Eventually, all his schemes and concerns were unnecessary. Rodrigo was pleasantly surprised when the cut-rate mercs came through instead of the drivers. Smoke issued from the engine of Jacobs' vehicle and while he pushed it harder, it eventually ground to a halt when it crested one of the dunes.

Rodrigo's Hammerhead circled to block any escape Sal might have with an open demonstration of menace by the man at the top who held the heavy rifle aimed at the driver's door.

Relief washed over him as he connected to the vehicle's speaker system.

"There's nowhere to run, Jacobs," he said in as convincing a voice as he could manage. "Step out of the vehicle with your hands above your head. Hand over the merchandise and we'll let you walk out of here alive." It was a lie, of course, but a necessary one. He didn't want the scientist to put up any kind of last-stand fight that would put lives at risk unnecessarily.

Rodrigo could see the merc who manned the hatch tense, ready to shoot.

"Don't shoot until we have the merchandise," he warned. After a few moments of thought, their quarry made the right choice, pushed the door of his vehicle open, and stepped out with his hands raised above his head.

"Aren't you a clever boy?" Rodrigo muttered and a small smile played on his face. The lack of noise on their comm channel told him that the fight at the blockade was already over and his men had probably not fared as well as their superior numbers might have suggested, but who cared about that? It was actually a good thing since he had to pay fewer salaries and would have less loose ends to tie up.

CHAPTER TWENTY-FOUR

Sal stepped slowly out of the Hammerhead. He had to admit that all things considered, his circumstances appeared disappointingly bleak. As he moved and registered the comfort of the pack he carried at his side, he looked at the six men who simply stood and stared at him. They'd dismounted from their Hammerhead with alacrity and speed, determined to aim as many guns at him as possible. He wondered if it was an intimidation tactic.

It was rather impressive, he acknowledged. There weren't many people in the world who would have thought he was worth enough trouble to put this much security on him. He wondered vaguely if he should feel flattered.

An eighth man stepped out of the vehicle. Most of the men—including the one who glared at him from the hatch at the top of the vehicle—wore suits of armor. They were older but still sturdy and reliable and more importantly, necessary for anyone who worked this close to the Zoo.

The final man wore a suit. It looked expensive, but Sal's knowledge of which suits were expensive or not was rather limited. He wasn't ashamed to admit that. It was all a matter of perspective, and he hadn't owned enough to know which was which. The fact that the man was out there in a suit, though, and carried only a pair of glasses that seemed to be his only HUD connection to the rest of the team made it a fair guess that he was the one in charge.

He was tall, lean, and good-looking. A sharp crew-cut and no hint of a beard made him look younger than the gray that glistened in his black hair might suggest. Sal wondered if he was some kind of pencil-pusher who ran this operation. It made sense all things considered.

"Salinger Jacobs," the man said, and his accent indicated Mediterranean heritage, although it wouldn't be easy to pinpoint from where exactly. "It's a pleasure to finally meet you in person."

"Yeah, no, the pleasure is all mine, I assure you...dude," he said with an offhand shrug. He didn't really want to offend anyone, but it wasn't like he knew who this guy was. Then again, he obviously thought he didn't need to introduce himself to a soon to be dead scientist. It was all about priorities, after all.

"You've been a problem for me over the past few months, I'll admit," the man said with a smile as he removed his glasses and cleaned the lenses nonchalantly with a handkerchief from his pocket. "But you've been much more profitable than problematic, which is the only reason why you're still alive. And, incidentally, the only reason why I'm willing to give you this one chance. Give us the plant, walk away, and you'll be allowed to live."

Rodrigo studied the young man with real interest. His file had placed his height at a couple of inches over six feet tall, which made him three inches shorter than Rodrigo himself. But with the armor he wore, Jacobs now stood a good foot taller than him. With the darkened, hybrid suit that looked sleek compared to the chunky and heavy armor his own men wore, he thought it was funny that Sal was the one at a disadvantage.

"That's an awesome deal, it really is," Sal replied with a quick nod and swept his gaze over the men who surrounded him. "You should know something about me, though. Something the government wouldn't want you to know but I feel it's only fair to warn you.

"When I was a teenager, they kidnapped me from my home and housed me in a secret base deep inside the Appalachians. They experimented on me there. All in all, they did spooky stuff to me. Annoyingly sexual stuff too, but I don't like to talk about that. The point is, they turned me into a deadly mutant with telekinetic powers—not to be underestimated, I might add, no matter how outnumbered and outgunned I might seem to be."

Rodrigo narrowed his eyes. The scientist didn't seem the type of man to play for time like this and honestly, it was ridiculous and more than a little pathetic.

"Take your rifle out of the holster and toss it on the ground," he ordered and folded his arms in front of his chest. "Once you do that, we can have a therapeutic talk about what happened to you in this secret government facility."

The man nodded and calmly drew the rifle out of the holster and tossed it into the sand a few feet away from Rodrigo's feet. He immediately raised his hands to point finger guns at the armored men around him. His eyes were narrowed and he looked deadly serious.

"It's time for you to make a choice, boys," he said and deliberately edged his voice with a low growl. "You gotta ask yourselves one question. Do you want to walk away from this fight alive or do you want to simply be another story in the legend of the...dangerous Zoo Experiment?"

"That's a terrible superhero nickname," Rodrigo pointed out blandly. "But enough of this childish game. Hand the plant over and we'll drive away, Jacobs."

The scientist didn't respond and instead, aimed his right hand with its finger gun at the man at the hatch. The merc, who aimed a real weapon at him, simply smirked and shook his head.

"Pow," Jacobs said, narrowed his eyes once again, and cocked his thumb's 'hammer' forward.

Against all kinds of logic and sanity, the man's head exploded in a spray of blood, brain matter, and destroyed ceramic armor.

No fucking way was the only thought that went through Rodrigo's head as he turned to make sure he'd actually seen what he thought he saw. Sure enough, the man who had manned the hatch of his vehicle had lost most of his head.

The scientist cocked his finger gun again and another merc dropped soundlessly—and another, and another. Rodrigo's logic warred with the apparent evidence of his own eyes. He almost began to question whether or not it was time to believe in real superheroes with actual powers. Stranger stuff had been known to come out of the Zoo, after all.

In the shocked silence, he heard the distant report of a

shot from a high-powered sniper rifle. Jacobs hadn't rushed out of the blockade at a whim, he realized. He'd deliberately planned to be intercepted and set up a trap for anyone who might come after them. And he'd made up the whole stupid kidnapped kid story simply to fuck with them. It was some interesting thinking on the man's part.

Unfortunately, by the time he had processed everything about the situation, the seven men who had come with him were down and he was the only man left standing.

He drew a pistol that he'd secreted inside his jacket pocket. It was a personal favorite, an older .44 Magnum Colt revolver that had been gifted to him by one of the Saudi sheiks whom he'd worked with in his early years as a mercenary.

He balanced the heavy weapon easily in his hand and cocked the hammer. Jacobs would die out there. Rodrigo had made his mind up that he would not be killed by a geek out in the middle of a desert. That was so...lame!

Heavy, steel-reinforced, and hydraulically powered fingers wrapped around his wrist and twisted his arm savagely. He managed to fire a single shot and the slug spun into the desert somewhere as the bones in his arm and wrist shattered. The same heavy, armored fist rose and he closed his eyes to block out the sight as it descended remorselessly.

Bone crunched as Sal hammered his fist down as hard as he could. The way the man's head snapped back was more than enough to confirm that he was dead. He didn't even need to see where the skull had caved in or the neck had snapped to tell him that. The body slumped, a limp and useless corpse.

He keyed his comm line and opened one to Kennedy. "How's that for some action?"

"I really liked the part where you tried to pass my shooting off as superpowers," she replied, and he could hear a grin in her voice. "I recorded that shit for posterity."

"Come on, it was cool, you have to admit it." He retrieved the large pistol the man had dropped after he'd broken his arm. "Besides, seeing the man's face when, for a second, he actually thought I had superpowers made it all worth it."

"I hope you saved that shit for posterity too," she said as she strode across the sand toward him. Gutierrez had filled Kennedy's suit impressively, but there was something about the way Madigan moved that set her apart, even in the altered sniper suit they'd claimed from a man who had tried to attack their base.

It had been altered with software meant for long-distance shooting, so any soldier who knew their way around the suits could make shots at over a thousand yards with impressive accuracy and little trouble. A skilled marksman—or woman, in this case—could take it over fifteen hundred, which made it a long walk for her to reach him where he waited beside the vehicle.

"I think this baby's FUBAR," Sal said with a grin and tapped the hood of their Hammerhead that had been shot through the engine block.

"Yeah, Gutierrez is already on her way." She shook her head. "They took care of the guys there too easily, I think. She already didn't like the idea of having to ram one of her babies into that blockade, and to have the other one shot up besides?"

"I think we need to give her a raise," he suggested. "And hey, after this, we can even afford it without having to make daily runs into the Zoo, right?"

"Right." She turned to examine the merc's vehicle. "In the meantime, we can probably commandeer this Hammerhead. It looks...mostly intact—if you take out the dead man inside, of course. We can still make the drop."

Sal smiled. "Well, we wouldn't want to keep our new clients waiting."

Kennedy raised her pack to reveal the container with the Pita plant inside. "Our little baby was happy to get some sunlight."

"Do you think we should name this one too?" he asked as they scrambled into the vehicle.

"No. I think naming the first one Madie was more than enough, thanks." She took the driver's seat and started the vehicle.

"This is amazing," the man said and leaned closer to the container as he adjusted his glasses to peer at the plant. "I never thought I'd actually ever see one of these in person."

Sal nodded and glanced at the three men who had come to the meeting immediately outside the base. They were dressed in heavy armor—better than the suits the Heavy Metal duo wore—but they seemed to only be there to transfer the plant to the buyers. Of course, before that could happen, they needed to bring a specialist in to confirm that it was precisely what it had been sold as.

The British man's enthusiasm was refreshing, if a little

odd given how the rest of their day had gone. He was older and wore a pair of round glasses and had a graying, pudgy appearance. That, along with the way he swept some of his hair over his head to cover a bald spot made him look like he would have been much more comfortable in a laboratory or a university lecture hall than all the way out in the middle of the Sahara.

"See, the image presented to me for the sale only had two budding flowers, but you can see another one already starting to grow here—look." He pointed and tapped a pen at the glass. Sal looked more closely. He hadn't noticed the new bud in the morning and since he'd given it a good, solid inspection, that meant it had appeared while Kennedy hiked through the desert to where she had set up her sniper hide.

"Dr. Andrews, can you confirm that the item is, in fact, authentic?" one of the armored men asked. He had clearly grown more and more uncomfortable while standing out in the open like this. They appeared to already know about what happened during the transit. While they seemed to appreciate the danger that Sal, Kennedy, and company had gone through to get the merchandise to them, they weren't quite so willing to undergo the same kind of hardship.

Sal studied the surroundings to determine what they were looking for as he hefted his rifle.

"Of course it is," Dr. Andrews said with a soft huff that made his stomach wobble under his clothes. "Look at the way the flowers glow, even when under direct sunlight. If you look closer, you can see the way the plant itself glows due to the presence of the goop inside. It's authentic."

The man nodded and said something quickly that was

isolated by the helmet he wore. Kennedy was able to unravel what he'd said, however, and pulled her phone up quickly on her HUD, connected wirelessly, and checked the bank account that had been set up for the payment.

It had been created as both a way to have the money transferred through the various types of red tape that were involved in overseas transfers as well for the third-party salesperson to take his share. The account itself could not have any withdrawals made without consent from both parties who had opened it, those being Anja and the man she'd hired.

"The money has been transferred," the lead soldier said in a terse tone. "We'll take our leave now."

Kennedy nodded confirmation that the funds had indeed been deposited into the account.

"I must say, Dr. Jacobs, Sergeant Kennedy," Andrews said as the soldiers collected the plant and began to walk it back to the base. "I am a massive admirer of your collective work here in the Zoo. I am employed full time for the company that has purchased this marvelous specimen from you, and I hope that you think of us when you feel the need to sell anything else of value that you might have. Here is my card. Next time, please contact me personally." He held his card out, which Sal pocketed immediately.

"We appreciate that, Dr. Andrews, and we might take you up on that offer," he responded cordially.

"He's not a doctor yet, though," Kennedy interjected.

"And she's not a sergeant anymore," he added. "But that's not the point. We'll be in touch, Doctor. And have a nice flight back to...London?"

"Liverpool, in point of fact," Andrews said with a grin.

"But I appreciate an American's attempt. I hope to hear from you soon!" He waddled away cheerfully. From the way the soldiers seemed to wait for him and pay him almost as much consideration as they did their package, Sal could tell that the man had to be a high-ranking member of his company.

"If that's the guy in charge, I feel much more comfortable working with these people in the future," Kennedy said approvingly.

"I thought the same thing," he replied. "How much will we end up with when all's said and done?"

"Well, Anja's friend who ran the auction said that he was willing to accept a lower percentage of the sale," she replied as they strolled to the Hammerhead they'd appropriated from the Pegasus thugs. "His condition, of course, was that any future sales we might have had to go through him as well. He took a fifteen percent cut from the sale total. That, plus what we're paying our muscle boys—who took some injuries we'll cover too—as well as what I think is a well-deserved bonus for everyone involved, you and me included. I feel confident in saying that we'll have about three million to add to our current buffer."

"I'll be honest, I'd hoped for much more than that."

"Well, you have to spend money to make money, Jacobs," she reminded him. "With all that said, we still have the Hammerheads we appropriated, and the weapons, armor, and ammo we picked up should give us an extra bonus on the side—although we should probably wait for a while before we unload them. We don't want a huge killing spree of mercs to be on everyone's minds while we sell suspiciously blood-stained armor and vehicles."

"Right." There would have been a time when he felt horrified by the amount of death that had come from the sale of a single plant, but he had become jaded to it, used to the fact that you couldn't make money out in the Zoo if you weren't willing to defend what you'd acquired.

"Do you want to get a drink to celebrate?" she asked and nudged his shoulder.

"I'd love to. But no drinking competitions though."

CHAPTER TWENTY-FIVE

Anja wasn't the most trusting of people. She had studied in a field that was mostly famous for annoying and untrustworthy teenagers who thought it would be a laugh to disrupt government buildings and national security. Experience had been an excellent teacher and she had developed a series of tests she ran people through before she decided whether or not she was willing to work with them.

Very few people passed her test, simple though it was. She mostly ran them through a gauntlet of innocent-sounding questions. The degree of braggadocio involved usually had a direct correlation to whether she trusted them or not. People who liked to brag about what they'd done—how they'd broken into the NSA or FBI sites on a dare or simply because they could—usually wouldn't show any discretion about any large amounts of money they made and where it had come from.

As a result, there were only a handful of people around the globe whom she trusted, and ironically enough, she'd never met any of them face to face. Whenever she needed something done in person, she contacted one of the few people on her list and asked them to provide her with high-quality recommendations. It was a charged service, in most instances, but it was usually worth it. Not always, of course, but it was definitely better to trust people she'd worked with before than a random unknown on the Internet.

A quick conversation with her friend who had mob ties in Southern California told her there was someone available in the area with the kind of skills Sal and his friends needed. The reality was that people didn't like breaking into the houses of the very rich anymore. The risk-reward ratio was simply too high.

Those wealthy individuals who actually kept anything high-value and easy to dispose of for a good profit—worth stealing, in other words—in their homes also fitted some of the highest-rated security systems in the world. Occasionally, however, something specific had to be acquired illegally, which was where the recommendation came in.

The gender of the thief was never revealed, but the resume was fairly impressive. While Anja had never heard of any of the heists mentioned before, a little research revealed that they had happened and mostly been covered up to avoid some kind of embarrassment or another. Someone who didn't need to advertise their work and only worked when referred by word of mouth was the kind of contractor she felt she could trust. It didn't tick all the boxes in her little gauntlet of questions, but it was one hell of a start.

She checked the security cam footage she had used to

keep track of Courtney's progress through the city. Her intention had always been to stage the robbery once it was known that the other woman wasn't in town. It seemed supremely logical to ensure that she had one hell of an alibi to fall back on if there was any fallout from this escapade.

Dr. Monroe acted with extreme caution, and from the sounds of things, had good reason to do so. Her assistant was a tall fellow who, even with glasses, gave the impression that he was very dedicated to his body. The fact that he would travel with his boss to meet them in the Zoo made Anja shift uncomfortably in her seat as she leaned closer to watch their progress.

They simply waited at this point, drank coffee, and talked constantly before they climbed into a small town car. This took them to one of the smaller airports, where Courtney's company kept a couple of jets on hand and ready for hasty travel needs. They had a few at the larger airports like LAX as well but given the kind of schedules those places worked with, one would have to request a trip days, and sometimes weeks, in advance. The smaller airports outside the city were a lot less convenient to reach but far more flexible about hours.

She waited until they pulled into the airport garage before she contacted her friend in the encrypted chat room.

Tell your contact that they can expect the down-payment and the balance when the piece is delivered, she typed quickly. She had been known to be able to input almost a hundred words per minute. While it didn't sound that impressive, it was quite a feat considering the fact that she was usually coding while she was on a computer. These were two different skill sets that both required an extensive knowledge of a keyboard and quick fingers.

My friend agrees to your terms, came the reply. *Although they would prefer to do a quick scout of the house in question before taking any money. They'll contact you with the details once they've finished. We'll be in touch.*

Anja sent a thumbs-up emoji before she deleted the chat and closed the room. She would obviously need Sal's approval to spend that kind of money but she was fairly certain that either he or Courtney would be willing to make good on the offer. It would be money well spent given what they were after and how difficult it would be to get their hands on it.

When her friend was ready, he would leave a message draft for her on a shared email which would provide her with details on where to open the message board again. Until then, she could do nothing but wait. She hoped that the person who scouted the location wouldn't trigger any alarms. Since she had her metaphorical and digital fingers on the pulse of that alarm, she would know the minute it happened, if it did. And, without doubt, she would be thoroughly disappointed.

It was, of course, very unlikely that either a rookie mistake or disappointment would occur. Anja had worked with her mob-connected friend for a few years already, and while they had never done something quite this high-profile before, she knew she could rely on him to come through for her.

Or maybe her? She wasn't quite sure. Ambiguity was a big part of their working relationship.

CHAPTER TWENTY-SIX

Security at these homes was never a joke. Rich people took protection very seriously and usually went so far as to have their alarms contact private security contractors as well as the local police once anyone was stupid enough to trigger them. Fortunately, the entire premise of the security system had been based around the fact that a ton of people with guns would immediately head in once a signal was triggered. Very few people ever really considered the fact that if an alarm was never triggered, the cavalry wouldn't arrive.

The simple expediency of hacking into the security company's personnel logs gave the thief an ID to work with. A couple of calls to the people who handled the account tied to Covington's apartment provided the details of the security system in place at her home as well as access to the live logs of when the security was turned on and off. This yielded pertinent and very helpful details.

Motion sensors were only turned on when no one was at home but were deactivated when she was there, which left only the perimeter alarms. The thief retrieved the information about how the security was set up, including details that only the alarm company would know about. Again, it was useful—where the alarm itself was located, how it could be disconnected, and how to prevent it from being logged into the system.

Every person who spoke to her would have commented only on how polite and professional their superior was before she hung up. The thief made free use of a different name every time and so left nothing to tie her back to the line of questioning.

Her next step was to park a delivery company van in front of the building. It was a tried and tested way to scout a property while setting up a heist and gave her sufficient time to obtain a good visual. The apartment she would enter came as no real surprise. It boasted a high level of security with a significant number of humans between the thief and the laptop.

Still, it really was nothing that couldn't be handled. Human error was the kind of thing people in her profession relied on. Machines were difficult to beat, but when humans operated them, it almost felt like cheating except there was no real honor system in place. There weren't any awards for people who played by the somewhat arbitrary rules of thievery. On the other hand, many people acquired a hefty payout by breaking those rules.

The thief retrieved a package and approached the entrance, dressed in the coveralls of a delivery company that was known to make their deliveries to the doors of their clients. There weren't many people whom she trusted with this kind of job, but she was more than willing to do it herself. She gave the name and apartment number of a place where she had previously confirmed the people were home. If they didn't expect a delivery—which obviously would be the case—she would simply take it back.

The security guard who manned the door was deeply engrossed in some playoff basketball game, a useful distraction she had planned for. It meant he wouldn't notice if the delivery took a little longer than normal. She'd made a note of that when a pizza delivery guy went up to the pool on the roof of the building to have a smoke and stayed there for over half an hour.

She used the elevator to take her to the floor she'd carefully selected to allow her access to Covington's apartment. The small but very wealthy family would no doubt be having dinner at about this time. She rang the doorbell and waited for someone to open the door.

Fortunately, she didn't have to wait long before the husband greeted her. After some awkward flirting—which she was used to given her red hair and darker skin which gave her an exotic look that appealed to some—he realized she wasn't interested, told her quickly that they hadn't ordered anything, and shut the door in her face. She didn't mind his dismissal, although she was tempted to drop the wife a line about how her husband was in the market for a little on-the-side shenanigans.

Temptation would have to wait, though. She sprinted through the stairwell and reached the penthouse a few seconds later. Careful to remain out of view should anyone step out of the elevator, she tapped her phone to deactivate the security system and route it through a device she'd placed under the manhole cover she'd parked her van over.

The door unlocked too, which provided her with a quick and easy path to the safe under the Covington woman's bed.

Despite all the other elaborate measures in place, the safe was a simple design made mostly for the peace of mind of the person who owned it instead of actual security. This made it easy—given that she'd done extensive research on her target—to guess the four-digit code and gain access. She retrieved the laptop, checked it for tracking devices, and made sure to gather all the accoutrements that were needed to run a device like this. Satisfied, she slid it into her delivery bag. After a moment's thought, she grinned and placed the delivery box containing a cheap teddy bear in the safe.

There wasn't any real reason why she did this other than the fact that she wanted to fuck with the woman. From the research she'd done over the past couple of days, there was every indication that she was the scum of the earth.

There were some depths that even she—thief though she might be—wouldn't ever sink to. She made her way out of the apartment with no further delay, locked everything once more, and took the cameras off the loop her friend had programmed in. Her mission now accomplished, she jogged down the stairs and took the elevator to where the security guard remained enthralled by his game of choice.

The man paid even less attention to her than he had when she'd arrived, which gave her all the time in the world to exit the complex. She'd leave the van, which was stolen and would probably be reported come morning.

Working quickly, she peeled the coveralls off to reveal a

black biker's outfit and tossed the uniform through the open window of the vehicle. She donned the helmet she'd left on the front seat and strolled casually to where she'd parked her motorcycle. The beast came alive with a low, satisfying thrum and she revved it a few times before she accelerated away with the laptop stowed safely in her bag.

When she came into view of the highway, she pulled over, tugged her phone out of her pocket, and dialed the only number on speed dial.

"Package secure," she said when her call was answered with no greeting. "Awaiting delivery details."

"Delivery will be in the Johannesburg airport." The reply was spoken in a metallic, heavily disguised voice. "Tickets have been delivered to your email address. Second payment to be wired on delivery. Plane leaves from LAX in two hours."

She nodded, even though the person on the other end couldn't see her. The line went dead and she turned the phone off and threw it onto the road in front of her bike before gunning the engine once more. She made sure to run both wheels over the device before she roared away.

Courtney's phone buzzed in her pocket as she and Robinson waited at one of the coffee shops in Johannesburg. After a message from Anja to confirm the delivery process, she had managed to convince Robinson that they could afford to spend a half-day in the city to take in the sights, although they didn't move too far out of range of the airport.

She was ready for the delivery as soon as she was alerted to it, begged a moment to head to the bathroom, and took her carry-on with her. Of course, she'd been sure to bring one according to the specifications provided. It was empty and had been recently purchased to hold souvenirs she hadn't bought. She paused and bent to tie her shoelace. A tall woman with darker skin and bright red hair came into view, moved closer, and bumped clumsily into the bag Monroe had deliberately left a step or two behind her.

The transition was certainly the smoothest Courtney had ever seen. So much so that she wondered if a magician's skills were involved. If she hadn't actually watched, she wouldn't have noticed that the bags had been switched. She kept her expression carefully neutral as she moved on with the new bag into the ladies' room to confirm that a high-end laptop was included in the contents.

She used a new phone to send a message rapidly to Anja to confirm that the package had been delivered and that the second payment could be cleared.

As casual as ever, she returned to where she'd left Robinson. He didn't offer much acknowledgment of her return other than a quick nod of the head.

"I really hope that cat needs her laptop again soon," he said mildly.

CHAPTER TWENTY-SEVEN

Madigan was annoyed. She had wanted to pick Courtney up herself, but after the fight and the damage caused to the Hammerheads, Amanda had refused her access to any of the vehicles until she had them repaired and back to the way she liked them. It wasn't fair, she thought with a voluble growl and hurried to the gate when she heard the rumble of a heavy vehicle approaching. She hadn't even driven anything on that mission. It wasn't like she intended to drive around and crash the shit intentionally.

As she opened the gate manually, the armorer inched the vehicle closer, obviously taking extra care. There weren't too many people who treated their Hammerheads the way she did—like calling them her babies and getting angry and sullen when they were mistreated. Like an actual baby, or a favored pet, for crying out loud.

As it slowed to a halt, Madigan's gaze settled on a man who exited the vehicle alongside her friend. She hadn't ever been much of a fan of the arrangement that had been reached between Courtney and herself to keep Sal between them. Now, when she saw the man—tall, blond, and built like a supermodel—she wondered if there would be any trouble. She remembered how depressed Sal had been when their partner had decided she would stay in LA.

Her doubts about Courtney's dedication to her relationship with Sal quickly dissipated as he exited the building with a broad smile on his face. Courtney let out an ear-splitting squeal when she saw him. It was very undignified but certainly got the message across as she streaked across the courtyard and almost bowled him over. It was to his credit that he didn't fall under the tackle and managed to catch her smoothly out of the air. It seemed like his daily dose from Madie had certainly helped him with useful bulk and strength.

Courtney responded enthusiastically and quickly covered his lips, cheeks, and neck with a horde of kisses. Both Madigan and the new man looked a little uncomfortable at the open display of affection, even if they were two close friends who hadn't seen each other in a while.

"Hi," the man finally said, turned to Kennedy, and offered her his hand. "The name's Allen. Allen Robinson."

"Madigan Kennedy," she replied with a smile and shook his hand, surprised at how firm it was. Where had Courtney come across this delightful specimen?

"Oh, you must be Madie!" He grinned. "Courtney's told me so much about you."

"She must have told you that it's Madigan, not Madie," she responded, and her smile was a little forced.

"Oh, right. There was some mention about that, yeah." Allen looked genuinely abashed.

"Okay, that's enough. Break it up, lovebirds. There's plenty of time for that later," Madigan said when she realized that the other two were still tangled in their embrace. "For now, we need time to get everyone up to speed on what's happened and what will probably happen in the next few days. Shall we?"

"Of course." Sal pulled away from the other woman and his cheeks looked more than a little flushed. If Madigan's eyes didn't deceive her, he had heated up someplace else, as well.

She chuckled and wiggled her eyebrows. "Hold it in, cowboy."

"Will do, cowgirl," he responded a little sheepishly.

The group trooped into the social room where Anja waited for them. She looked...different. Sal frowned at her, unsure exactly what she had done, but... Well, her hair was tied back, she wore makeup, and for once, she actually looked like she hadn't stepped out of a thirty-hour marathon at her computer.

Sal narrowed his eyes as her gaze settled on Allen Robinson, who moved closer to her. She was... Holy shit, was she blushing?

"Hi, I'm Allen," the man said and proffered his hand.

Anja's eyes widened like she was about to have a panic attack but she steeled herself and shook his hand firmly. "Anja. I manage the cyber security around here."

"Courtney's told me about your work," he said warmly. "That's an impressive resume."

"Thanks." The hacker looked flustered and continued hastily, "Do you have something for me?"

"I sure do." Allen withdrew the laptop from his bag and handed it to her.

"Thanks, I'll get right on it." She tucked it hastily under her arm and made her way to the server room. Amanda intercepted her and pulled her to a halt outside.

"Come on, where are you going in such a hurry?" the armorer asked and regarded her a little suspiciously.

"I want to get right to work on this." The Russian deliberately avoided looking at Allen as he took in his surroundings.

"Oh, my," Amanda said with a teasing grin. "Does someone have a crush on someone? As a gay woman, I do have to say that one is a tasty dish. If you're into that kind of stuff. Which...you are?"

Anja shrugged. "I don't know. I think it's about time we have more sausages around this place. It's become a little too estrogen-heavy for me."

Her companion's grin widened. "Well, if you're not too picky about having a man attached, I have a couple of 'sausages' you can use. Some plug in, some use batteries, and most are ribbed for your pleasure." She winked when Anja blushed furiously and decided it was the blush of a woman who had her own collection.

"So, this Allen guy," Sal said in a low voice to Madigan. "Would you say that he's...good-looking in any way?"

"Oh no, of course not," Madigan said and shook her head firmly. "Not unless you know any women who like chiseled good looks, a sexy hint of scruff on the chin, an athlete-slash-model's build, and the intelligent look he gets from those glasses."

He narrowed his eyes at her. "Well, that's plain mean."

"In fairness, I'd say you have him beat in more than a few ways, most of which Courtney's already been privy to, so there's no need to feel insecure."

"I don't feel insecure," he protested. "You feel insecure."

"I'll let you take a minute to think about that," she responded tartly, and her eyes twinkled with mischief. "In the meantime, I think we need to get together to have a quick sharing session about what we all know."

"Well, I think it's fairly basic," Courtney said as she dropped on one of the couches and brought her legs up under her. "Something along the line of Covington stealing my father's intellectual property for Pegasus—which we hopefully stole right back—my mom is somehow involved, and while there's a fair degree of suspicion that my father was actually murdered instead of dying of natural causes, there isn't any proof left to confirm it."

"Either that or there were way too many people who very conveniently knew he would die at a specific time." Madigan sat beside Courtney and toyed with her hair.

"Let's not forget that your mother was involved somehow," Allen added. He seemed determined not to let that particular truth be buried by other issues. If it were at all possible, he disliked her as much as his boss did.

"You mentioned that the metal wouldn't work in the Zoo but that it does work outside." Sal sounded curious, although his expression was serious. "You told us that but you never explained in any detail."

"Oh, I have all that information on a memory stick," she confirmed. "I'll share it with you, but the gist is that the resonance from the goop in the trees and other plants somehow undermines the integrity of the alloy they created. The longer it remains in close proximity to the goop and the radiation it causes, the weaker it becomes."

"Huh." He grunted disapprovingly. "And how the hell does Pegasus not know about this?"

"My dad ran a couple of tests but they were shut down immediately once Pegasus snapped up the proprietary claims on the metal," she said. "They essentially ignored everything he had to say about it, while they still stole all his intelligence. These guys are loaded with cash but are plain butt-fucking dumb when it comes to how the Zoo operates."

"This might be something we could run past the colonel," Madigan interjected. "He's still waiting on an update on what we pulled from the hard drive. I don't think we have enough to get back to him with, but this might be something he'd be interested to know.

"I had a request from the colonel to look into a new special test that Pegasus will run in the Zoo," she continued. "Yesterday, he sent me a message saying he wants to sign us up to see if it's a Zoo issue or maybe pirates or someone who shouldn't be attacked."

"Send him a response and tell him we want to meet," Sal said.

"Do I want to know who this colonel is?" Courtney asked with a slightly anxious expression.

"He's a guy who's fed us intel on Pegasus over the past few months," he clarified. "He's worked with them a fair amount and doesn't much care for what they've been up to, so he feeds us what he knows to see if we can't disrupt their operations somewhat."

"I'll be damned if he didn't come to the right people."

Monroe nodded enthusiastically. "I'm down for anything that gets in Pegasus' way out here."

"Agreed." He glanced quickly at Madigan. "Set the meet up for a neutral location. There's no telling whether Pegasus has tightened their security after our last run-in with them."

"So we simply assume those assholes are Pegasus?" Amanda asked with a challenging look at the others. "You'd think they would want to put better boots on the ground. The guys we ran into might as well have been bounty hunters."

Sal nodded. "I know, but who else could they have been? No one else has those kinds of resources. If it was them, they were pressed for time and manpower and had to bring outsiders in on a job. It was a mistake and definitely not one they'll repeat."

Madigan nodded. "Message sent. I'll let you know when he calls back."

"What do you mean, it's gone, ma'am?"

Andressa looked up from her phone, a murderous look in her eyes as she glared at her head of security.

"What do I mean?" She snarled in fury and regarded him with real contempt. "I mean someone entered my fucking apartment, broke into my safe, and took the fucking laptop. I don't think I could have made it any clearer than that, you useless bunch of assholes."

The three men looked at one another, unsure which

one of them she had addressed. Amos, the manager, stepped forward since it was his responsibility.

"I personally checked all the logs and there wasn't any kind of security alert that anyone even entered your apartment while you were not there," he said and tried to be firm and still maintain a respectful distance. "No cameras picked up any intruders, and the people who work in the lobby made no note of any unauthorized entries. If the laptop is missing, it wasn't from your apartment."

Andressa shook her head. "I haven't taken it out of that room in all the time I've had it. What are you suggesting—that it grew legs and fucking walked out of the building?"

Amos looked at the other men for help but received no response. His employer ignored him and continued to pace around her apartment.

"It has to be that Monroe bitch," she stated belligerently. "She's the only one who has any reason to suspect me in the company. And she called me and asked for a meeting but cancelled at the last minute to travel—where did she go again?"

"She took a flight on a company plane to Johannesburg's Oliver Tambo International Airport and on to Casablanca," Amos confirmed quickly. "Here's the problem, though. The timeline you suggest for the…ah, theft… If it was her, it doesn't make any sense. She couldn't have been involved."

"The bitch has gone to the Zoo," Covington mused and ignored the man. "She thinks a few animals will scare me off her trail. Well, she's wrong. Call Carlson and tell him I'll head out into the Zoo myself this time. Tell him to send me people and that we're going on a fucking safari."

"But…the laptop was one of the most secure pieces of technology in this building," the man protested, his expression one of real confusion. "Bio-encrypted to the point of overkill. Exactly what do you expect her to be able to do with it?"

"If it can be stolen, it can be hacked," she responded cuttingly. "And that will simply not happen on my watch. I want to talk to Carlson as soon as possible. Since his man Rodrigo obviously failed in his assignment—multiple times, I might add—I think we need to stop hiring from the outside. It's time for us to get our own hands dirty in this."

Amos sighed and finally gave up. "I'll let Mr. Carlson know and arrange for a plane to be readied."

Anja scowled at the screen that had somehow demanded her constant focus for far too long. The display should have been relaxing, with some nature shots quickly replaced by what looked like the madness of an architect who had never really made it to the big leagues. Not that she knew anything about either of those things. She stared at a login page for the laptop she'd been handed.

"How's it going?"

She jumped. Thankfully, she managed to stifle the instinctive squeak of alarm. She hadn't heard anyone enter the room, and the voice was only vaguely familiar. It took her a few seconds to remember that there were new people in the compound now and that she needed to get used to it.

Of course, she could forgive the intrusion given who it was—and what he carried. Tall, blond, and handsome, and he brought gifts of coffee? She could absolutely get used to interruptions like that.

"Oh… Not great," she said and accepted the coffee with a grateful smile. "This encryption will take years to crack. I have a couple of friends who know about this kind of thing and even they are stumped. Normally, I'd run another game to get the DNA we need to crack this baby, but as of right now, our friend Covington is on a plane with no known destination and has probably already wiped her apartment of anything that could be used to open this. That leaves us royally screwed unless we get a finger of hers or something."

Allen nodded. He didn't know much about this kind of thing but it was impressive that Jacobs had managed to put a team like this together in such a short space of time. He had gathered outliers who were great at their jobs and needed a place to belong. Well, given that he seemed to fit that category too, maybe it wasn't that odd.

"I'm usually really good at placing accents," he ventured in an effort to break the silence, "but for the life of me, I can't tell where yours is from."

"Well, I'm originally from St. Petersburg," Anja explained and swung her swivel chair to face him. "I got a scholarship at a tech school in the US and I managed to stay for my masters too, so I lost most of my Russian accent."

"That's great," he said and didn't sound like he'd faked the enthusiasm at all. "But how did you end up all the way out here? It's not a regular location for up and coming IT specialists."

"Well, I worked for the FSB—the security agency in

Russia," she explained. For some mysterious reason, her trust issue seemed to have gone out the window. "It was mostly low-level coding work to keep their firewalls up to date, but I had a ton of access. And when I saw what they were doing, it wasn't anything I approved of. Finally, the time inevitably came when they needed access to something and I managed to help them. I got a little greedy and I got caught. My friends on the outside helped me to leave the country, but I needed a place to settle. Jacobs offered me a place to stay if I helped them with some troubles, so I came here."

"You make it sound so simple."

"Well, it wasn't simple, definitely not." Oddly enough, she seemed to be able to laugh at the memory. "But it's mostly a long and boring story, fraught with terrifying Zoo monsters and spies trying to kill me. I wouldn't want to bore you."

He opened his mouth to say it didn't seem like the kind of story that would bore him at all, but she had already turned away. It was an intentional move, he realized, something to pique his attention.

The challenge appealed to him. "Well, if you ever wish to bore me, I think that sounds like the kind of story I'd like to hear."

Anja glanced over her shoulder at him and smiled. "I might actually tell you about it sometime."

"Sal told me to tell you there's food set up for dinner," Allen said as he pushed out of his seat and moved her coffee along the counter and away from all the electronics. "He said that if you don't make it in time, they'll leave some in the fridge."

"Thanks." She had already turned back to her computers. "I'll be right out."

She wouldn't be right out, unfortunately. But she needed to focus on her work and Allen definitely couldn't help her with that. If he wanted to visit later when she wasn't busy, she wouldn't mind spending time with him and sharing her story. She'd done her research so she knew he was gay and that he had a wife—husband?—but that didn't mean she couldn't appreciate the view and the personality, right?

CHAPTER TWENTY-EIGHT

Anderson leaned casually into his seat as the heavy Hammerhead rumbled toward him. It looked a little banged-up and the worse for wear, but he couldn't mistake the heavy diesel engine that roared through the crisp morning air.

They had arranged to meet a few klicks outside the base at the halfway point on the road between that and the Heavy Metal compound. The team was noticeably cautious but once he'd heard what had happened a couple of days before, he honestly couldn't blame them. It was, coincidentally, a time when his overlords at Pegasus decided their little base needed a beef-up in security too.

On this occasion, two people were distinguishable in the vehicle and neither of them was Madigan Kennedy. It was a pity. Anderson sincerely enjoyed working with her, but he supposed it was about time he met one of the brains behind the operation.

He assumed the unfamiliar woman driving was Amanda Gutierrez, but she didn't leave the vehicle. Only

Jacobs climbed out and strode to where Anderson had parked his vehicle. He moved to the passenger seat and slid in. He wore the sleek, hybrid armor that he had rapidly become famous for, and Anderson did have to admit that there was some appeal to it.

"Salinger Jacobs, I presume?" he asked as the younger man shifted slightly in the seat.

"In the flesh," the man replied with a bright smile. "Colonel Anderson?"

"A pleasure to finally meet you. I've heard good things."

"Right back at you, Colonel," Jacobs said briskly. "So, we can either sit around all day and jerk each other off, or we can get to the meat of the matter as quickly as possible. What do you say?"

"Let's go for the meat," he responded, and his chuckle contained real appreciation for once. There wasn't much to smile at in his life. "Did you guys have any luck with the hard drive?"

"Some, but not enough to report on yet." Salinger shook his head. "I do have some info on the metal our Pegasus friends have shipped in as armor that you might want to take a look at." He handed his companion a copy of the files Courtney had brought him. Anderson glanced intently at them before he exhaled sharply.

"Are you sure about this?" he asked and actually seemed genuinely angry, Sal realized.

"Not one hundred percent, but all the tests that were run confirm it. I've run some interim tests of my own and they also appear to confirm everything Dr. Monroe said before he died."

The colonel nodded and leaned his head back. "Fuck."

"Anyway," the scientist said after a moment of silence had passed. "What's this about a Pegasus mission heading into the Zoo?"

"They have their people on hold," Anderson confirmed quietly. "The leader of the team advised me that they are waiting for someone to send confirmation as to when to head in."

"What could they be waiting for?" he asked. "Well, unless they're waiting for someone—oh."

The other man glanced quickly at him. "You don't think they would risk a full mission into the Zoo with armor they haven't fully tested simply as a revenge mission against freelancers?"

Sal shrugged. "I honestly believe there are many things our friends at Pegasus would be willing to do to get rid of us."

"All right." The colonel drew in a deep breath. "If they send in one of our merc teams—the ones who are usually sent in to deal with people like you—I'll message you the details. If it's one of our regular teams, that will mean it's simply another test run. Either way, this is the last time I'll work with these assholes."

"Fair enough."

"Be careful out there, Jacobs," he said.

Sal smiled. It was a fairly pointless exercise to tell the man that wasn't how he and the Heavy Metal team worked. That said, they would have to deal with a much more dangerous team of Pegasus goons than they'd ever faced, which meant that even if they weren't careful, they still needed to have a plan in place.

He stepped out of the vehicle and his contact started it

and drove away as quickly as he could. They had remained together for longer than expected and needed to be very careful to avoid raising suspicions.

"Did you get all that?" Sal asked into his earpiece.

"I did," Madigan replied.

"Do you think we can trust him?" Amanda already revved the engine, obviously anxious to leave the open location.

"Trust him? Nah," Kennedy replied. "But I'd still trust what he says. If Pegasus is waiting for us to head into the Zoo so they can eliminate us, they have to have some degree of confidence that their people have a better chance to do so in there than their previous teams did. That means mercs trained in the use of top-of-the-line suits and experienced in the Zoo."

"We can only hope they'll use the new metal in their suits, right?" he asked. "Does it make us terrible people for wishing for that to happen and blow up in their faces?"

"I think it's fairly standard for people in our line of business," she replied cheerfully. "Head on to the compound. We need to make a plan to deal with these bitches."

Andressa sighed in real irritation when the phone in her pocket buzzed. She'd really hoped she could have some time to herself while she was on the plane, but damned if technology hadn't caught up with her. The damn planes needed to have Wi-Fi for some reason. If she hung up,

Carlson would know she was avoiding him and she didn't need that kind of headache in her life.

With another heavy sigh, she retrieved the phone, pressed the accept call button, and smiled as the man's face appeared on the screen.

"Andressa, what's this about you heading to the Zoo?" he demanded and leaned forward in his chair. The lighting behind him showed her that it was nighttime in New York City. "Please tell me this is a crazy joke and you're simply on your way to Monaco to blow off a little steam and spend that bonus of yours."

"Nice to see you too, Carlson," she said urbanely. "And how nice to hear from you. How have you been?"

"Cut the crap," the CEO snapped. "You've already had too many of our people killed out there in pursuit of your idiotic vendetta. Anyone else would have simply folded and left the game in exchange for a pleasant time on a beach with no extradition. What the hell are you doing that will fuck me over even more?"

"Please," she retaliated, her tone sharp with disdain. "I put too much work into Pegasus to back out of it now, and don't pretend that Rodrigo's death wasn't your fuckup. Admittedly, I sent people in, but they were the ones who underestimated what those assholes at Heavy Metal can do. And when I look at your track record, I would comfortably say that's something of a running theme. I'll go in with our people—all of whom are highly trained and highly motivated—to rid us of those pricks once and for all. Hell, I'm doing you a fucking favor."

"If you fuck up, Andressa," Carlson said and his voice lowered venomously, "not only will you have exposed your position at your company, you will have left Pegasus open to reprisals that I can't afford."

"Please, Carlson, have a little faith." She sipped a glass of champagne and avoided the urge to roll her eyes. "There's nothing in the Zoo that can get past our armor. It should be more than enough to handle them."

"I only hope you aren't the one doing the underestimating this time, Andressa," he responded and cut the line abruptly.

Yes, this was something that needed to be done and since outsiders had tried and failed repeatedly, it meant that if she wanted something done, she would have to do it herself.

That said, she would have been lying if she said there wasn't any kind of personal revenge on her mind about this.

"The father's metal will kill the daughter, not save her," Andressa said to herself, happy that the topic of her missing laptop hadn't been raised. "How fucking delicious is that?"

CHAPTER TWENTY-NINE

S al shifted off Courtney and his muscles burned and
ached as he lay beside her. He took a moment to look
at the ceiling and catch his breath. The truth was that he
didn't mind these marathon sessions. The need to push
himself to the limit was a part of the new him that he had
slowly accepted, and it was something he needed to bring
to every side of life.

Courtney, for her part, had a hard time breathing as
well. Her heavy breasts rose and fell as she draped her arm
over him and rested her head on her chest.

"Fuuuuck," she whispered before she pressed her lips to
his nipple for a moment and wiggled so she could look at
him. "I thought I could easily get to ten again but hot
damn, man. Has Madigan worked you overtime lately?"

He shrugged. "Well, a gentleman doesn't kiss and tell,
does he?" In truth, he still wasn't sure how he was
supposed to handle the whole crazy situation. Both women
knew he was sleeping with the other and seemed to have
reached an understanding, which raised the question of

what he was supposed to do about it. He didn't want it to seem like he bragged too much but at the same time, he didn't want to create the impression that he was hiding anything.

The conflict immediately vanished when she slid herself on top of him. "I have to say, though, that using my mouth feels like cheating."

"There's no cheating in this game, lovely," he responded with a grin. He used his strength to pull her thighs down so she straddled him and would feel him hardening again. "And there's no time like the present for getting back in shape, right?"

"Oh, my God," she said softly, unable to stop herself from grinding gently against him. "I've fucking missed you, Salinger Jacobs."

"Likewise, Dr. Courtney Monroe." He flipped her quickly onto her back.

Madigan leaned back in her seat. This was her little corner of heaven, one she had set up for herself by hauling one of the couches that had been in storage all the way to the roof of the main building of the compound. That had been the hard work, and it took little additional effort to include a couple of creature comforts that made it almost a living room away from the living room. A little tent erected over the area ensured that there wasn't too much sun damage, but damned if it wasn't worth it to open it wide and watch the sun rise over the green of the Zoo in the distance.

She turned when the door opened and someone joined

her out on the roof. Her smile slid into a grin as Courtney evidenced a definite tendency toward a bow-legged walk.

"Oh, shut up," the woman muttered when she caught the mocking look on her friend's face. "I brought coffee."

"I didn't say anything," Madigan replied, but the grin remained as the other woman dropped beside her on the couch and handed her one of the steaming mugs. "I don't really have to, though, do I? We could hear you scream all the way from the server room."

"Shit. It's…uh, been a while, is all. I needed to release. You didn't happen to hear Sal too, did you?"

"No, he is annoyingly quiet in the sack. He more than makes up for it in other ways, though."

"Oh, absolutely." It was such a strange situation—one she would never have believed was possible. She knew that with them both involved in a relationship with him, things should be far more rocky and uncomfortable, so she was thankful that they were still on speaking terms and even friends. He was really important to her, but that didn't alter the fact that she really wanted a girlfriend to discuss this stuff with, and Madigan was as close as she had. Well, maybe Allen too, but that was different. He was an employee.

"It's really fucking beautiful out here," Courtney said to cut into the tension that had crept into the silence.

"You're damn right. It's times like these when I wonder how I could ever consider leaving this place. It totally has it all. Money, decent food, adrenaline, and gorgeous views."

"I know what you mean. Research is great and the house my dad left is beautiful and comfortable to live in. Still, I find myself craving a situation where there's sand up my crack and I miss the screech of animal monsters. But yeah, my dad left me a mess to clean up, and if I'm not there to pick up the pieces, everything goes to shit. Worse, that only helps Pegasus."

Madigan smirked and took another sip of her coffee. "Even when our parents are gone, they still leave chores for us to do, right?"

"Right." Courtney laughed. "But let's not talk about that. Let's enjoy this beautiful morning, acceptable coffee, and each other's company."

Her companion turned to look at her. "I think I can do that."

CHAPTER THIRTY

"Are you sure you don't want me to go in there with you?" Allen asked and a small frown betrayed his anxiety. "I'm sure you could find some use for a personal assistant out there in the Zoo, right? It's not like one more person wouldn't be a help."

Courtney smiled, leaned in, and stood on her tiptoes to press a light kiss to his cheek. "Sorry, Allen, we can't risk it. We need to be as light and loose as we can, and between the four of us—Madigan, Amanda, Sal, and me—I think that's already enough. Any more, and we'll attract all the wrong kinds of attention. But the fact that you can stay here and keep an eye on the compound while we're gone and while Anja tries to decrypt the laptop is awesome. Thank you so much."

Allen grinned. "If anything, I need to thank you for bringing me here. I...well, now I understand where the steel in you comes from."

"You might say that it's where the...uh, Heavy Metal in

her comes from," Sal said with a grin. Allen chuckled but she groaned softly and rolled her eyes.

"Fuck, you're such a geek," Amanda said in full agreement with the eye-roll. "Okay, it seems the news has already spread. Pegasus knows we're heading into the Zoo and Anderson says their troops are standing by. According to him, there are almost thirty of them, all armed with the best armor Pegasus has to offer and all the best assholes the worst places in the world can dredge up."

"Fan-fucking-tastic." Sal grinned wickedly. "It looks like we have our hands full on this trip."

"So, let me get this straight," Madigan said as the four of them mounted up in one of the heaviest and best-armored Hammerheads Amanda had worked her magic on. She still didn't let anyone else drive the vehicles, though. "This is the first time that we'll go into the Zoo with the express intention to kill people—humans—with no kind of profit. We simply lure the motherfuckers into a trap, yes?"

Sal nodded. "That sounds about right." The response sounded hard and even cold, and it surprised him because he'd never have believed he was capable of such ruthlessness. He glanced quickly at the others, but they seemed distracted enough by what lay ahead that they didn't notice.

Amanda eased the vehicle ponderously out of the compound and a moment of silence passed as the reality sank into everyone's heads. Courtney wore a light yet agile hybrid suit like Sal's, while Amanda took a heavier approach and used a suit of armor intended for gunners similar to Kennedy's. She'd claimed it from one of the Pegasus gunners they'd captured in the raid on the compound, but she'd made more than a few modifications. Sal could tell she felt excited to try it out in the field. This was also the first time she'd had the chance to go into the Zoo since she'd broken her leg.

"Good." Madigan drew a deep breath. "As long as everyone's clear on what we will do when we get in there. There's no time for guilty consciences while we're in the thick of it."

Again, he felt like he should feel something about this. Guilt over deliberately killing humans. Fear over having to stage it in the Zoo. Nothing lurked beneath the calm. He looked at his hands that usually shook with adrenaline by now but which remained still and motionless—dead still and as calm as a Spanish afternoon.

Was he too used to this shit?

Andressa grimaced at the suit she wore. She'd encountered a fair number of questioning glances when she first joined the team that would head into the Zoo and she'd prepared herself for what she thought would be the inevitable protests.

Instead, from the way the men remained silent and went about their preparations, she deduced that they were used to the exotic demands of their employers. She had taken the time to read each of their files and so was well aware of the fact that her insistence that she be on the team was, in point of fact, tame compared to some of the other ridiculous demands they'd had to deal with.

She moved the right arm first, followed by the left, and

tried to establish a familiarity with the suit while she waited for the other team members to wrap things up. It wasn't entirely new as she'd been in hundreds of simulations, mostly out of curiosity since Pegasus were the ones to develop these training sims. To her surprise, she'd actually managed to get in deep even though she'd worked alone.

This wasn't a simulation, though, but at least this time, she had a team that would watch her back. Their contracts included a stipulation that if she didn't make it out with them, they wouldn't be paid. It wasn't a popular measure but it certainly was effective. These men needed to understand that they worked for her now. They worked for the money Pegasus offered them and they would risk their lives to ensure that she wasn't left behind.

The upgraded Hammerheads thrust forward into the Zoo once they penetrated the outskirts and didn't stop and force the team to continue on foot. Andressa breathed a discreet sigh of relief. She was religious about her morning calisthenics, of course, but that was different than a hike through one of the most dangerous places in the world.

"What's the read in there?" one of the men asked and leaned toward the driver.

"It looks like they've stopped," the driver replied as he followed the tracker planted in the Hammerhead that had driven out of the Heavy Metal Compound. "Three klicks into the Zoo. Things get hairy out there and it's virtually impossible to drive. I'll head there but won't go in any deeper with the Hammerhead than that either. There are critters beyond that point that can outrun the vehicle and trample it and us into paste. I'd rather be on foot."

They all turned to look at her and a small smile touched her lips when she realized that these hardened soldiers wanted her input. That said, she was more than willing to go with their judgment.

"It makes sense to stop where they did," she conceded. "It'll be easier to track them on foot anyway, right?"

"Roger that, ma'am," the driver said and returned his focus to the way ahead. They formed a small convoy with three heavily armored Hammerheads, all altered to last longer in the harsh terrain inside the jungle, but there had been nothing that really prepared her for how dark it was. The trees created such an effective cover that slivers of sunlight were rare. She could see the gentle blue glow of the goop where tiny smudges of light showed from between the porous bark.

She gripped the side of her seat as the vehicle stopped abruptly. Andressa looked around and tried to determine if there was any trouble from the faces of the men and women in the vehicle with her. The only expression she could see was the calm collectedness of professionals. She wondered if that would remain even if they were attacked.

"The Heavy Metal Hammerhead is dead ahead," the squad leader advised the contingent of twenty-six men and women who had been recruited. "We'll track them from here. No combat restrictions. Shoot on sight and shoot to kill. That goes for the monsters as well as the Heavy Metal assholes. Are we clear?"

A chorus of affirmatives issued from the team as they set off toward the vehicle parked a little way ahead. They all seemed, at first, to search for tracks. In the thick under-brush, it was hard to make out anything, even something like suits of armor that could weigh over a ton and a half. Andressa looked around and wondered if she'd made the right decision to come along. She couldn't add value to any of the combat preparations, and she doubted that she could do much in combat either.

No, she reminded herself harshly, she'd decided to come and make it happen herself. She didn't intend to be a burden so it was entirely pointless to beat herself up about it, especially since it was far too late to change her mind.

She pushed her thoughts aside as one of the men called his comrades and drew their attention to a single set of tracks that headed into the east.

"I thought there were three of them," Andressa said, a little confused.

"Yeah," the team leader responded dryly. "I'd say they might be expecting us out here. Stay frosty, boys. We're heading out."

The mercs fell in behind their team leader and they continued in the direction of the tracks. A couple more appeared here and there—lighter suits like the kind Jacobs was known to use were visible in places—but mostly only the heavy, tank-like treads from Kennedy's suit.

"Where are they headed?" Andressa asked. She disliked the idea of traveling blind.

"They could be in here for another Pita plant run," the team leader replied. "The dossier provided says it's the bread and butter of their little corporation. That said, we can't put aside the possibility that we might be walking into a trap."

"Shouldn't we call for backup if that's the case?" Andressa asked.

"Sister, there are three of them, and twenty-seven of us," the man said with a chuckle. "We are the motherfucking backup."

She smiled when she realized that he'd counted her among the number as well, but the satisfaction dissipated quickly. Her motion sensors seemed to go crazy and she scanned the area with a slight twinge of panic. After a few moments, she reminded herself that since motion was something to be expected in a jungle, she didn't need to worry about it too much. Besides, none of the others looked anxious.

No sooner had she relaxed than she saw something she definitely recognized—the long barrel of a heavy assault rifle carried by someone in a heavy suit of armor.

"Get down!" Andressa yelled and cursed when she realized that she had isolated her comm frequency to an unused channel. She switched it quickly to the team leader's channel. "Get down!"

It was too late. A single report split the muggy air, and the team leader's head imploded as the armor-piercing round punched through his helmet and didn't come out the other side.

CHAPTER THIRTY-ONE

Andressa flung herself prone as the jungle erupted into a roar of continued gunfire. The trained mercenaries organized quickly and laid down covering fire at the figure in the distance. It wasn't that far away—less than a hundred paces—but in the darkness and with them completely reliant on heat sensors and motion sensors for any kind of visibility, it had been an impressive shot. The figure remained in position for another couple of seconds and fired a few more times at the group, but when they returned fire, she ducked again quickly.

"That has to be Kennedy, right?" Covington looked around but none of the men answered her. The new team leader snapped orders and the others confirmed sightings as they pushed forward in the direction of the heavily armored woman. Cautiously, they followed her through the jungle while each man attempted to remain under the cover of the vegetation as much as possible.

Another rifle shot cracked. This was lighter and smaller and sounded like a faint clap from somewhere to the left.

The men weren't prepared to be flanked, and two of them dropped before the rest of the squad fell into formation and began the pursuit. More orders were delivered in sharp tones as they turned to engage the new threat.

Another danger soon became evident—one she'd half expected and fully hoped to avoid—and she turned as she drew her rifle out of the holster on her back. Her gaze scanned the underbrush that seemed to close in on them. The animals had been drawn to the sound of gunfire and now gathered on the perimeter. They remained out of the way of the battle but they seemed to grow more and more agitated as the gunfire continued.

Wait. Andressa froze as a disquieting thought struck her. Wasn't the new metal in the armor supposed to deflect bullets, even the heavy ones fired from these massive rifles? She looked at her armor and suddenly felt much less safe about her position. With a slight quiver of panic now seated low in her belly, she fired a few rounds at the massive panthers that edged menacingly closer.

"No, don't shoot the animals!" one of the men called and panic entered his voice as he reached over to try to stop her. His protest came too late. One of the panthers already lay dead a few yards away. She scanned the scene in an effort to determine what he was so worried about. The animals had begun to retreat—any idiot could see that. She had driven them back. With a wild laugh she couldn't suppress, she squeezed the trigger again and hurtled forward to try to annihilate more of them. Did they think they could put her on the run? Did they really think that?

A proximity warning bleated on her sensors a moment before something landed on her shoulder. Her suit wheezed under the weight and she fell heavily as the panther that had attacked her from above bounded away. The remainder of the squad converged quickly and released a barrage of shots at the creatures that pushed toward her.

They backed away, and Andressa screamed. She wasn't sure why, she realized as she scrambled to her feet. There had been a moment of sheer terror back there, but she had never thought of herself as someone who screamed in the presence of danger. Oh, well, you learned something new about yourself every day, right?

"Stay in the circle," the new squad leader snarled at her, and she noticed that a couple more of the men had been downed in the effort to reach her. The animals now dragged the bodies away.

"What are they doing?" she asked before she could stop herself, and he simply shook his head and cursed in a language she wasn't familiar with. Before she could voice her automatic reprimand, he fell and a couple of smoking holes appeared in his armor.

That should definitely not have happened, Andressa told herself. These suits were supposed to be sturdier than tanks and able to withstand the power of an RPG without breaking. The squishable human inside wouldn't fare as well, of course, but these bullets punched through armor that was supposed to be top-of-the-line.

What the fuck was happening? Something had gone disastrously wrong.

She dragged her focus to her surroundings and someone in lighter, sleeker armor who stood with a rifle and maintained a steady stream of bullets at the men who hadn't taken cover. They were trying to protect her. That truth struck home as two more fell with hideous chest wounds and she reacted instinctively to return fire. The leaner suit was more difficult to hit, and she missed every single shot until the man dropped out of sight. That had to be Jacobs, she was sure of it.

She turned, her attention drawn by something that lumbered and thrashed through the underbrush. It was immense, taller than a human at the shoulder but about five or six meters long and with a massive tail that extended six more meters, at least.

It seemed to ignore the rapidly diminishing numbers of mercs and focused instead on another leaner, lighter suit of armor. The figure stood on the other side of them, so she knew it wasn't the same person. But that didn't make sense. Gutierrez was supposed to use heavy armor. Why did she wear the light hybrid? She was no specialist.

Interestingly, the massive monster seemed to sneak up behind the figure that crouched and fired at the mercs as they tried to take cover. They now had to adjust their formation to deal with the fact that they were shot at from all sides and the reality that their armor simply didn't work as promised.

But instead of the lethal attack Covington had expected, the figure turned to watch the monster approach. The rifle raised as if to shoot at it, but to Andressa's surprise, it lowered almost immediately. The beast leaned closer—like it somehow communicated with the figure—and suddenly, both turned to look at her.

Well, no, not at her precisely, she reassured herself, but in the direction of the mercenaries.

"No fucking way," she gasped when the enormous creature completely ignored the armored figure and launched into an attack directed at her team. They were a larger target and so made more noise, but it should have been an easy kill. The monster should have demolished the figure and moved on. Instead, it simply looked past it and hurtled into the attack.

"Over there!" Andressa screamed and pointed at the massive beast that thundered closer. "Shoot that one. Shoot it!"

Her warnings came too late, even though she was sure she had used the open channel this time. Nothing could alter the fact that the giant was on top of them before they could react. The immense tail lashed out, and Andressa shrieked instinctively in horror as one of the mercenaries was cut cleanly in half by the sheer force of it.

Massive claws and teeth tore into her men to crunch and bite and savage them in an almost methodical onslaught. Bullets had no effect whatsoever, and she could only stand in frozen disbelief and terror as half her men were systematically decimated by the creature. Finally, a team member managed to launch a shoulder rocket at the beast.

Too much happened before she could react. A bright white flash illuminated the area and revealed the stark beauty of the jungle around them for less than a second before it plunged into darkness again. Something smacked her hand and knocked the rifle out of it, and she gasped. She stumbled and tried to break her fall but immediately felt the full weight of her armor impact on her suddenly unarmored hand.

Andressa screamed as a shaft of pain radiated into her arm. The suit had peeled cleanly away to leave only her hand, exposed and shattered.

"Fuck!" she shrieked and clutched the injury protectively to her chest.

She looked up fearfully, as did the few men and women left in the squad. The whip-tailed creature retreated to lick its wounds from the shoulder-mounted rocket. It seemed impossible that it had survived with little more than what appeared to be surface damage to the tough hide.

An ominous whisper heralded the sudden arrival of hundreds of vines that seemed to appear from nowhere. They drifted and writhed relentlessly like tentacles of a weird monster from the depth of the oceans. Andressa screamed and fired wildly at the sinuous enemy. The squad joined in, clustered as close together as they could without losing too much cover.

Their frenzied defense achieved nothing. In fact, it seemed like the response had only irritated the tentacles further and they now attacked the almost defenseless mercenaries with a terrifying ferocity. Andressa shrieked and continued to pull the trigger on her sidearm even when it clicked empty. Vines snaked around her legs and began to haul her upward as she struggled to find purchase on something solid with her uninjured hand to anchor herself.

"*No, no...stop!*" She flailed in terror and tried to kick to free herself from the tenacious grip of the tendrils. Her efforts only made them tighten around her and attracted others nearby. She was yanked up a little higher before a wash of pain swept through her as something grabbed her.

No...someone, she realized and twisted to see that a leaner, lighter hybrid suit of armor had grasped her broken hand. The figure held a long, machete-like blade in her free hand.

"I'm not here to save you, Covington," Courtney said through the suit's speakers. "I simply need your fucking hand. This is for my father, you fucking bitch!"

Andressa's eyes widened as the machete rose briefly before it slashed in a blur to slice her exposed hand off with a single chop. She screamed and the agony briefly swallowed the terror as her captors swung her relentlessly upward into the trees.

Sal recoiled as an instinctive surge of horror rushed up his spine when the tentacles serpentined down from the trees to attack the few mercs who were still alive. Their screams echoed on the comm channels for a few minutes, but as they disappeared into the trees, their distress faded one by one until there wasn't much else to listen to except for the way the jungle seemed to move toward them.

"We have what we came here for," Courtney said. She held up a severed hand before she sealed it quickly into a containment bag and slid it into her pack. "We need to get out of here. These critters won't wait around for us to beat a hasty retreat. Fuck, I forgot how much fun these trips can be."

He nodded and narrowed his eyes at her. She had changed considerably but he could live with that. Where there had been a timid scientist, there was now a confident and slightly terrifying woman of power who was, he conceded, an entirely sexy surprise. Right now, though, they had the DNA they needed to crack the laptop and had to get the fuck out of Dodge.

They immediately initiated an orderly retreat in the direction from which they had come. Their small team fell into formation as they could see the Zoo monsters converge and ready themselves to attack them. This wouldn't be as intense as most of the other battles they had survived, but there were still too many creatures for them to manage alone.

Sal glanced at Madigan and she nodded. While the Zoo regularly messed with comms, they might be lucky and reach one or more teams close by. If not, they were probably fucked, so it was worth the attempt. He opened a channel and set it to broadcast as far as possible. It didn't need to be a complicated message, merely a quick and simple delivery of three simple letters in Morse code.

S-O-S.

As one, the team broke into a run. He realized that even though he was now used to this, there simply wasn't anything that could prepare a man to watch as an entire jungle seemed to coalesce into a united wave of ferocity. Thinking ahead, he drew his sidearm and kept it in his free hand to fire it intermittently to cover the moments of lull when his rifle needed to reload. He wondered if there were any options that could feed the rifles like they were mini-guns—like a chain that would allow for hundreds of rounds to be fired before reloading instead of a couple of dozen.

Courtney retained her machete in hand and slashed at

the hyenas that broke through the lines and harassed the four as they maintained a brisk pace.

"Heavy Metal," he heard through his comms. "Do you boys need help?"

"You're damn fucking right!" he shouted when he saw that the name on the comm line was a familiar series of numbers. "Fuck, is that you Daniels?"

"That's us, Heavy Metal," Sergeant Daniels said, and he could actually hear the man grin. "It's our turn to save your asses this time. Watch your fire to the southwest, would you? I'd hate to have to charge you for wounding my men."

Sal grinned and relayed the orders to Gutierrez, Kennedy, and Monroe while he fired consistently at the undaunted Zoo creatures. Fifteen men decked out in traditional military armor suits thrust through the underbrush, forced their way into the surging monsters, and drove them back. He noticed that they had changed tactics a little to fight in close quarters as if they followed the crazy example he had set. Their headlong charge directly at the mutants seemed to surprise them and made it easier to shove them off balance while they advanced to the rescue.

"That's right," Daniels said as he marched over to where the four of them took a moment to catch their breaths. "My boys have embraced the Sal-side of combat, bitches."

"The Sal-side?" Courtney asked and glanced at the other three in obvious confusion.

"Don't ask," Madigan retorted. "It's a long story that started with Sal being reckless, as usual. Daniels, we left our Hammerheads a couple of klicks to the west." She scanned their perimeter and noticed with relief that the animals seemed to have taken the hint. They'd obviously had their fill of death and destruction for the moment, which gave the soldiers a reprieve. "If you guys need a ride out of here, we'd be happy to oblige."

"We were on our way out," the sergeant acknowledged. "If you guys could get us back to where we're parked, we'd appreciate it, but do you have the extra room for all my boys?"

"Yeah," Courtney said and stepped closer. "We lost some people back there and would have trouble getting the Hammerheads out on our own."

"Perfect." The sergeant turned to his men. "We're moving out!"

"We appreciate your help, Daniels," Kennedy said. "The first and second rounds of drinks are on us when we get back."

"You're goddamn right." He grinned "And don't think we won't charge you guys for the assist, either."

"We wouldn't dream of it," Sal replied and relief washed over him in an awesome wave as they came into view of the four Hammerheads parked near one other.

EPILOGUE

"**H**ow'd the hand job work out for you, Anja?" Sal asked and focused on their resident hacker, who had joined them for breakfast for the first time since...well, forever. In fact, he hadn't seen her join them for a meal in all the months she'd been there.

"It was squishy and gross," Anja complained, "but it was more than enough to unlock the laptop and keep it open until I could change the settings to recognize my DNA. I've already spread what news I can across the dark web. Pegasus will have a whole ton of legal problems in the US, and they will probably be shut down in Europe until the investigations end."

He looked at Courtney, who dug into a pile of bacon strips. "It has to be a relief to know for sure what happened to your father, right? Obviously, it won't bring him back, but getting revenge on the people who killed him has to feel good."

"Well, not as good as I thought it would," she admitted, her mouth full of bacon, "but still damn satisfying. Plus, the knowledge that they will have to answer to corporate espionage and murder feels great."

"You do know, don't you, that since they're a big corporation, they'll simply be slapped with a fine? Maybe a couple of low-level officials will see jail time, but everything will be back to normal before you know it." Madigan shook her head in disgust. "Those motherfuckers always get a slap on the wrist, no matter how heinous their crimes are."

"Well, it's something, anyway," Sal said. "And it gives us something to springboard our attack on them further. If we keep pushing, that damned company will be shut down for good."

"I wouldn't be too sure about that," Anderson said. He'd been invited to join them for breakfast the day after they returned from the Zoo. "Pegasus has taken many hits recently, yes, but they're still a Fortune Five-Hundred company. They have all kinds of connections who won't permit them to fade into the background. They'll come back for blood, just you watch."

Sal nodded and leaned back in his seat. "How do you feel now that you've resigned from the Pentagon? I can't imagine that they took that lightly."

"After everything that happened yesterday, they were fairly anxious to avoid a lawsuit," Anderson said. He still remembered the footage that came from watching the men and women sent into the Zoo cut down by all the horrors the damned jungle had to offer. He shook his head. "They literally threw severance packages at everyone who was willing to sign an NDA on that."

"So do you think you'll work as a consultant?"

"I intend to take a vacation," the colonel said with a laugh. "I have a wife and a kid whom I haven't seen in months. I'll take them all to Disneyworld for a couple of weeks. After that, I'll see what kind of options I have for a future career."

"You might want to think about still working to destroy Pegasus," Courtney interjected.

He chuckled. "As what, the janitor?"

"Nope, as a CEO," she said with a cheeky grin. "I wouldn't discuss this beyond this group because of the restrictions, but it will concern all of us. It's not confirmed yet, but there's a buyout in the works. My company has a project to recover everything Pegasus stole from my father by buying shares in the company. If you were to be our representative inside Pegasus, you could do far more damage to them there than anywhere else in the Zoo."

"What makes you think they'll accept a guy like me? It's not like I have any business experience. I'm a career soldier, for fuck's sake."

She shrugged. "A career soldier who knows more about the Zoo than anybody else on their board, I'd be willing to bet. Given that Pegasus has put a lot of eggs into the Zoo basket, they'll beg for your guidance, trust me."

Anderson shrugged. "I'll do almost anything to serve my country."

"I'll drink to that," Madigan said and raised her mug of coffee with a grin.

She looked around the area she entered with satisfaction. People in Beijing were religious about lunch hour. They spent so much time indoors that on clear days, they were eager to enjoy their meals in what little sun they could find to touch their skin. It was a perfect cover.

The crowd was a little tedious but she pushed through to find a seat as close to the road as she could and located a small area where she could sit. She pulled her thermos of tea out of her bag, as well as a packed lunch of diced chicken breasts with steamed vegetables. This damned diet would kill her, but she wanted her husband to lose weight. She had to be willing to help him by example.

"Can I offer you some tea?" she asked the woman who had sat beside her. The newcomer had no food with her, and she kept her black motorcycle helmet on.

"No thanks."

"So let me get this straight," the businesswoman asked and poked the chicken with her plastic fork. "Not only were you able to get your hands on a copy of Covington's laptop, but you were paid over two million dollars for your trouble?"

"Two-point-four million dollars," the biker replied. "And that shouldn't surprise you. It's a seller's market out there, you know."

"I should have gone into the thieving business a long time ago," she responded dryly.

"You already have. You're in stocks, aren't you?"

"Very funny," the businesswoman responded, unamused. "What did you find out?"

"Nothing, personally." Her companion shrugged. "The eggheads in the R&D section are still sifting through the data. I do know enough to know that Pegasus is about to have their balls handed to them in a very public way."

"By whom?"

"Heavy Metal, of course." The biker seemed to find that amusing. "It always helps to bet on the winning team, you know."

"Well...uh..." The businesswoman's stutter gave the biker an opening to stand and nod affably. She walked away, stepped behind a wall, and became invisible.

"I'm going in," she said, apparently to no one in particular, although the quiet words carried an undertone of determination and purpose.

AUTHOR NOTES - MICHAEL ANDERLE

FEBRUARY 21, 2019

THANK YOU for not only reading this story but these *Author Notes* as well.

(I think I've been good with always opening with "thank you." If not, I need to edit the other *Author Notes*!)

RANDOM (*sometimes*) THOUGHTS?

I wrote about this (for last night) in the latest *War of the Angels* book. Now, I have an update.

So, it snowed last night and this morning here in Las Vegas (on the Strip.) What I didn't realize until this morning after speaking to someone was 'we' up on the upper floors saw snow. Many people on the street below got rain.

Seriously odd. So, the theory is that closer to the ground it was warmer and somewhere in the last ten floors it melted.

So not cool.

Now, the 'cool' part of this story is late this morning,

we went up to the 37th floor (outside pool area) and it was snowing.

When I went out, there was 3" of snow on the couches and footrests that are up on that level.

Leaving enough snow behind that one could, if one so chose, one could grab some and make a snowball.

Unfortunately, one could also have a wife who rats him out later at the board meeting about 'Yes, I did see someone throwing snowballs up on the 37th...my husband.'

I don't understand why she had to go and do that to me. I was just being myself.

At fifty-one.

Maybe that was the problem ;-)

AROUND THE WORLD IN 80 DAYS

One of the interesting (at least to me) aspects of my life is the ability to work from anywhere and at any time. In the future, I hope to re-read my own *Author Notes* and remember my life as a diary entry.

Las Vegas, NV, Veer board meeting room, late in the afternoon nursing a headache.

Why are you nursing a headache, Mike?

Glad you asked.

So, walking from the Aria Hotel through Crystals is all nice and fine when one is trying to dodge the wet, cold outside. BUT, if you happen to wish to take a shortcut out the second level just about thirty yards from the condo buildings' front doors, you should seriously pay attention to the ground.

Just because you thought it only rained at ground level,

you might be wrong. Like, enough wrong there was an inch of slush on the ground that is icy enough to cause one to slip.

Like a 51-year-old toddler.

My arm and head hurt like hell.

FAN PRICING

$0.99 Saturdays (new LMBPN stuff) and $0.99 Wednesday (both LMBPN books and friends of LMBPN books.) Get great stuff from us and others at tantalizing prices.

Go ahead. I bet you can't read just one.

Sign up here: http://lmbpn.com/email/.

HOW TO MARKET FOR BOOKS YOU LOVE

Review them so others have your thoughts, and tell friends and the dogs of your enemies (because who wants to talk to enemies?)... *Enough said ;-)*

Ad Aeternitatem,

Michael Anderle

CONNECT WITH MICHAEL TODD

Want more?

Find us On Facebook

https://www.facebook.com/Protected-by-the-Damned-193345908061855/

OTHER MICHAEL TODD BOOKS

PROTECTED BY THE DAMNED UNIVERSE

PROTECTED BY THE DAMNED*

8 Book series

WAR OF THE DAMNED*

8 Book series

DAMIAN'S CHRONICLES*

4 Book series

WAR OF THE ANGELS*

8 Book series

ZOO UNIVERSE

BIRTH OF HEAVY METAL*

10 Book series

APOCALYPSE PAUSED*

12 Book series

SOLDIER OF FAME AND FORTUNE*

12 Book series

TEAM SAVAGE *

3 Book series

Dungeon Core TV*

6 Book series

Dungeon Rails*

3 Book series

Hellspawned Chronicles*

3 Book series

The Sheva Chronicles*

6 Book series

Unlikely Bountyhunters*

6 Book series

House Drakonnen

The Accord

The Anchor's Inheritance Saga

* DENOTES COMPLETED SERIES

www.ingramcontent.com/pod-product-compliance
Lightning Source LLC
Chambersburg PA
CBHW050512110726
47899CB00005B/1428